HER FINAL SECRET

PAUL J. TEAGUE

Storm
PUBLISHING

Ebook ISBN: 978-1-80508-498-3
Paperback ISBN: 978-1-80508-500-3

Cover design: Sara Simpson
Cover images: Shutterstock

Published by Storm Publishing.
For further information, visit:
www.stormpublishing.co

ALSO BY PAUL J. TEAGUE

PROLOGUE
HULL FAIR, OCTOBER 1999

Moira was anxious and on edge, but she went to the fairground anyway. She was determined to enjoy some time with her university mates. Everything was going to change after that night. Her life would never be the same again after they gave the cassette tape to the newspaper journalist.

The incessant pounding of the pop music and the glare from a thousand multi-coloured, flashing lights quickly distracted her and she was soon in the heat of the moment, screaming with joy, loving every minute of it.

Her friend crushed against her side in the Twister's carriage as Moira's favourite song – Ricky Martin's 'Livin' la Vida Loca' – blared through the speakers. She wished she could freeze time and savour this moment forever. It was a far cry from her child-hood in care.

As the ride spun around, gradually slowing now, Moira tried to take in the vastness of the fairground. It was an assault on the senses, a wall of noise and light, with screams of delight and thrilled shouts filling the chilly, October night. The smoky scent of barbecued food and the sweet aroma of a nearby doughnut stand wafted through the air. Sprawling across the huge Walton Street car park, the rides and amusements went on as far as the eye could see. The night sky was illuminated by its bright, luminous hue.

'I need a rest from all that spinning,' Moira shouted over the music as she and her friend stepped out onto the metal plat-form. It shook as they walked towards the small gate which the ride attendant was holding open. The queue for the next ride had formed already, and her legs felt a little unsteady from the constant turning.

'How about we try something a bit safer?' she suggested, pointing at the Hook-a-Duck stall directly in front of them.

In the distance a gleaming Ferris wheel lit up the sky, and laughter echoed from the Fun House; all around she heard the jingling of coins in pockets as fairground attendees considered which ride they'd go on next.

Still laughing, both girls handed over their loose change, took a hooked stick from the stall holder and did their best to catch one of the plastic ducks which circled the interior of the stand in a shallow pool of water.

'I reckon this is a fix,' she whispered. 'I'll bet it's impossible to win a prize—' Before she'd finished her sentence, the duck was hooked, and the stall holder held it up to show the girls that it was a winner. They released a whoop of joy, and Moira pointed to a large, yellow, stuffed monkey.

'I'd like that one, please.' She smiled at the attendant. 'I'm going to christen him Kong.' She laughed.

As Moira stretched out her arms to grab the toy, something caught her eye. An ice-cold shiver ran through her body, and her hands shook as they clasped the monkey. She began to trem-ble, her stomach knotted so tight that she thought she might pass out with the fright of it. She could hear her friend laughing and joking at her side, the whirring gears of the ride to the other side of them and the calliope music from a nearby merry-go-round, but none of it was sinking in. She'd recognise his bright red hair and eyebrow piercing anywhere. And those tattooed hands... the very thought of them touching her made her convulse with fear and shame. She'd once smelled his cigarette-reeking breath up close to her face; it had made her want to vomit.

'Moira! Are you all right?' came her friend's concerned voice.

A new pop song began to play out of one of the nearby speakers, another one she liked from the charts, and for one moment it was as if the fairground was trying to keep her from danger. She could let him walk off, into the heart of the fairground, well away from her and her new life. She was safe from him now, and after what Moira had planned, she'd finally wipe that evil damn smirk off his cocky face.

Her jaw tensed and her ears pounded as the rage began to rise inside her. Moira knew what happened on this night, when they visited the fair. After all, they'd done it to her before.

'I've got to go—' she said, her mind now fixed on stopping them. She couldn't let them get away with it this time, too.

'But we said we were going on the Galaxy ride next,' her friend interrupted, a confused look on her face.

'I'm sorry, I have to go,' Moira snapped back, her eyes transfixed on the man, anxious not to lose him in the crowd. 'I'll see you in the lecture tomorrow...' Her words trailed off. She wasn't so certain about that.

Moira didn't turn back, though. She had him fixed with her eyes, and the bastard was going to slip away into the crowds if she didn't hurry. Light-headedness threatened to overwhelm her, but she pushed through it, her anger driving her forwards.

Still clutching the stuffed toy, Moira set off through the dense, milling crowd.

'Are you all right? Moira—' her friend called after her, but her words were immediately absorbed by the raucous sounds all around them.

Moira barely registered as she followed the man in the

direction of the dodgems. She'd taken an innocent ride with him once, three years ago. She could still recall the flashing sparks in the wire meshing above them and the distinctive, oily odour of the metal flooring. They'd laughed and joked; he'd been pushed up close against her in the car and, stupidly, she'd thought nothing of it back then. Not until she'd seen how fast his eyes could turn to evil.

The pungent smell of vinegar splashed on hot fish and chips caught her nose and, momentarily, she was brought back to the here and now. She could still walk away from this; she had a choice. Her friend was just behind her – it would be as simple as anything to rejoin her and enjoy the thrill of the Galaxy ride and stick to the original plan.

It was tempting and she hesitated, doubting herself and wondering if she'd brought all this upon herself. After all, she had liked him once, thinking him cool and unlike the other carers. He was fun and great company – until he wasn't.

He hadn't spotted her yet. They'd be in here somewhere, all of them, pretending they were there for the benefit of the youngsters and hell-bent on giving them the night of their lives at the city's annual fair.

It became dark, suddenly; he'd stepped beyond the stalls, away from the glaring lights and thumping music and among the lorries and caravans which were grouped apart from the attractions. She'd been foolish to isolate herself. She was alone and had lost sight of him.

Moira's chest tightened as panic clawed its way up her throat. Her breaths came in ragged gasps. She glanced back at the safety of the lights, now a distant glow.

A voice came from behind her, much clearer in the crisp, night air away from the rides. She flinched, wishing she'd turned back.

'Hello, Moira. I've been watching you.' His voice was cold and sneering.

A chill ran through her and a sourness formed in her mouth.

His hand touched her shoulder, and her skin crawled. In an instant, she was that terrified teenager once again, powerless to do anything to protect herself. There was a sudden movement to her side, and she caught a glimpse of the mallet which struck her hard. It happened so fast that she could barely believe it, surprise quickly turning to terror.

Her legs weakened and her head pounded with a numbing pain.

Moira was on the ground before she had figured out what was going on. He dragged her by her ponytail across the grass and into the complete darkness between two caravans. She tried to find words to call out, but she was paralysed, gripped by a dark, deep fear.

He grabbed at her hair when she fought to get away, and she felt her hair shake loose as he pulled off her scrunchie in the struggle. Across in the clearing, there was enough light to see the stuffed toy she'd won, lying on the ground in the mud. It was splashed with blood: her blood.

Moira moved her hand to her head. It was wet and her hair was matted. Her head throbbed; her body was limp and weak.

There was movement at her side as the mallet was readied to deliver a final blow. Moira tried to cry out, but her voice would not come, her mind fogged by the power of the first strike. She closed her eyes, focusing her mind as best she could. She opened them again, staring directly at her assailant. She'd been so close to exposing these monsters, but she'd messed it up now. If this was where it all ended, she would show her absolute defiance. They had to know that they would never break her.

Her attacker looked to the side, distracted by something: a voice.

'Moira! It's me. Where are you? I'll walk you home—'

'Who is that?' he seethed in a whispered, contemptuous voice.

'Don't hurt her, please,' Moira begged. 'It's just my uni friend, Hollie. She's not involved in this. Please don't harm her, she can't hurt you—'

Her friend had come for her. Of course she had, that's what good friends did. But she was in terrible danger, and Moira had to warn her. Sensing what she was about to do, the man's hand came down across her mouth and nose. She gasped to catch a breath, but her airways were completely cut off. Her attacker was panicking – she could feel the doubt and fear in his grip. Moira was struggling now, her stomach heaving up and down in a fight for survival, her lungs craving air, her head pounding and her eyes bulging.

As Moira felt herself drifting away, her body relaxed. She'd only ever seen the gloating confidence of power and control from this man, but his panic in her final moments was a victory, however small the win.

She was almost gone now, but she forced her desperate glare towards her attacker, so she'd be looking directly at him when she died. She hoped her scornful, despising contempt would haunt his dreams.

As Moira faded out of consciousness, the last voice she heard was the anguished cry of her best friend Hollie.

ONE

PRESENT DAY, 06:48

It was misty and the fairground loomed up out of the haze. The usual brightly coloured stalls and rides were muted by the grey, damp gloom, and the entire site was quiet and still as if it had been closed for the winter season. They had a maximum of ten hours in which to secure and scour the area and gather what evidence was available to them, before they'd come under intense pressure to reduce the size of the cordon in order to allow some of the rides and stalls to open. Movement on the site was completely restricted at that time, but experience told her that luxury would not be afforded to them for long. They were on the clock.

She pulled her car up on a kerb at the side of the Walton Street entrance and switched off the engine. Hollie's eye twitched and she tried to settle the fluttery feeling in her stomach. The last time she'd been here she'd been a student and life had been a lot simpler. She'd been so excited about that night as they made their way to the sprawling fair; it had seemed like the entire city was there, it was so busy. A feeling of despair and emptiness engulfed her as she wondered what Moira would be like now as a middle-aged woman. Would they have kept in touch and still been friends? They'd never found out what happened to Moira that night, and a part of Hollie had always wondered if her friend was still out there somewhere.

She stepped out of the car and walked onto the fairground site, seeking directions from a nearby PC who'd been assigned to keep the area secure. Within a couple of minutes, she'd made her way through the boarded-up stalls and stationary rides to locate the crime scene. It was an ant's nest of activity, with suited scenes of crime officers meticulously working over the cordoned-off area, an operations tent already assembled and her own team of detectives interviewing fairground workers and getting the measure of the situation.

The secured perimeter circled a ghost train ride, which appeared even more ghoulish as it loomed out of the fog. She observed the spectral figures of the scenes of crime officers combing the fairground; it was a potential nightmare of misleading and contaminated evidence.

The exterior of the ride was adorned with artificial cobwebs, a creaking sign moved ominously in the gentle breeze and numerous ghoulish figures were painted across its front.

The carriages were all lined up in the centre of the structure, sitting on a narrow, metal track as if temporarily discharged from duty and taking a break before the crowds descended once again.

DS Ben Anderson joined her on the far side of the police tape.

'Morning, Ben. What have we got?' Hollie asked grimly.

'It's like an episode of *Scooby-Doo*,' Anderson began. 'I'm half expecting some henchman to walk out of that ghost train and blame those pesky kids—'

'Yeah, the press will have a field day with their headlines.'

'The murder is anything but *Scooby-Doo*, boss. It's a white male, in his sixties—'

'Amber thought potentially early fifties when she rang it through to me.'

'We've updated that now. He was aged sixty-eight. We have an ID already. He's retired police superintendent Gordon Carrick, boss—'

'Oh, a police officer?' She heard the pitch of her voice rising slightly.

'Retired, boss. He left the force at age forty-eight, he'd got his thirty years in by then.'

'Did you know him?'

'Not really. I was a DC back then; I heard the name but didn't have anything to do with him.'

'What do we know about him?' She stared at her colleague, intent and alert.

'Not much.' Anderson shrugged. 'He took his police pension and ran. He's a do-gooder; he was involved in the community and the like.'

Hollie bit her lip; murder scenes always required a steady mind.

'What are you thinking, Ben?' she asked, eager to get a grasp on the case.

'Our initial thoughts are a possible revenge attack from a historical policing case,' Anderson answered, his brow furrowed, 'but it could be any number of things, of course – he's been away from the force for so long now. God only knows who he's pissed off in his past.'

Hollie gave a small nod.

'Is Amber Patel checking for recent prisoner releases and his prior cases?'

Anderson's face gave her the impression he was waiting for that question.

'Yep, she's on it already, boss,' he confirmed. 'She'll call in the moment she finds something.'

Hollie surveyed the ghost train once again. There was a grim reaper model at the entrance holding a sign which read:

YOUR TURN TO DIE?

'Please tell me our killer didn't put that there?' She shuddered.

'No, boss, but you've got to admit, it's pretty spooky,' Anderson replied as he glanced over at the macabre figure.

'Where's the body?' Hollie tilted her head slightly as she surveyed the cordoned-off area. 'I don't see any activity around the trucks.'

Ben took a deep breath.

'I'm sorry to tell you the crime scene is within the ride. One of the trucks was pushed deep inside the structure, and the body was sitting in it when it was discovered.'

Hollie shook her head.

'This killer is having a joke, surely? This isn't some set-up, is it?'

'Sorry, boss, it's for real,' Anderson answered, his face completely straight. 'We've just released a photofit picture of the man we're looking for – he's made from sewn-together body parts, and he has two bolts coming out of his neck.'

He broke into a small smile, but Hollie wasn't in the mood for it. Not here, of all places.

'Well, whoever it is must have some strength,' she remarked, half to herself. 'Those wagons will take some pushing.'

Her attention was caught by a suited and masked police officer emerging from one side of the ghost train as if exiting the gates of Hell. She soon saw it was DC Harry Gordon and he was heading their way.

'Good morning, Harry, what's it like in there?' Hollie greeted him, her voice shriller than she'd anticipated. She was on edge. She'd need to play it cool for now but, at some point, she'd have to declare her connection with this place. It would be gathering dust somewhere in the non-computerised police records.

'Morning, boss.' Harry removed his face mask, revealing a faint morning shadow across his chin. 'It's a bit of a mess, to be honest.'

'I'll bet it is,' Hollie replied, thinking she'd better get herself suited up, too. A police tent had been erected to the side of the ride for that very purpose.

Harry's body tensed as he drew his phone out of his pocket.

'We just found something in the truck where the body's located—'

He used his fingers to enlarge an image on the phone screen, then held it up for Hollie and Anderson to examine. It was a photograph of the front page of the *Hull Daily Mail* dated the third of May 2001. Hollie read the headline aloud.

'"Abuse claims at city children's home dismissed as 'public hysteria' – Ambrose House city cop exonerated."'

A jolt of adrenaline shot through her, and she fought to steady herself.

Her university friend, Moira Kennedy, had spent her teenage years in Ambrose House.

TWO

Hollie walked around to the front of the ghost train truck to get a proper look at the body. She was accustomed to crime scenes, but nothing could ever prepare her for that initial glimpse of the corpse. She stifled a gag as her eyes fell on the man's body and her stomach recoiled at the sight of him.

The pervasive smell of oil and metal was making her feel queasy. She was pleased the dark, difficult and poorly lit journey into the heart of the ghost train was over, but she was already bracing herself for the walk back.

Who could have done something like this? It was a brutal attack, more frenzied than she usually encountered. She thought back to the last night she'd been there, a quarter of a century ago. Many of the rides were bigger and faster now, but the dodgems and waltzers were still there, much as it had always been. Her mind flashed back to her and Moira laughing their heads off on the merry-go-round. She could still recall her friend's shrieks of joy.

'I knew Superintendent Carrick of old,' Doctor Ruane began. The sight of Ruane in his protective overalls and hair covering had become all too familiar to her already. 'I'm sad to see him end his days like this.'

'Oh, I'm so sorry,' Hollie said, shifting on her feet. She wondered how many of the older officers had worked with the victim. Emotions would be running high – it was always the same when one of their own was involved.

'I didn't know him well,' Doctor Ruane continued, his expression earnest beneath his face mask, 'but you tend to encounter a fair few officers in my line of work. Do you want me to walk you through it, DI Turner?'

'Yes, of course, go ahead.' Hollie looked at him with concern. 'I hope this isn't too difficult for you?'

'It's fine, honestly,' Ruane assured her, his voice professional and steady. 'As you can see from the nature of the wounds, this was a violent attack. I'd estimate he was struck at least four times with the murder weapon. I'll know more when I can examine the body on a table, since the light is so difficult to work with in here.'

Hollie shone her torch directly at the body, looking for the points of impact. She screwed up her face, still unsettled by the nature of the attack. Doctor Ruane continued to share his hypothesis.

'I've seen this before; this level of violence usually accompanies revenge attacks, most often with abusers or sexual predators.'

Hollie flinched. She pictured Moira's tearful face from her student days, her friend overcome with emotion but always keeping her secrets to herself.

Doctor Ruane clocked her reaction with a raised eyebrow, but he carried on anyway. He was an old hand at this game, and he could sense something was up with her.

'I'll need to take a proper look to give you chapter and verse on the extent and precise nature of the wounds, but this was clearly a frenzied attack—'

'Revenge, if you ask me,' Anderson ventured.

'But he's a former cop—' Hollie began, realising immediately that it gave any number of people reasonable cause to seek retribution against Carrick.

DS Anderson made a *huh* sound.

'Is something on your mind?' Hollie asked, agitated.

'No, boss,' Anderson replied, taken aback by the ferocity of her challenge. 'As I said, I never worked with him. He was in another part of the city, but our paths crossed in passing. He knew my old boss though, DI MacKenzie. They were drinking buddies, I think, even after the superintendent retired.'

'As in my predecessor, DI MacKenzie?' Hollie checked. As they stood in silence, she became aware of the analogue watch ticking on Ruane's wrist.

'The same DI MacKenzie who died in the line of duty?' she continued. 'There's no chance this is linked, is there?'

Both Doctor Ruane and DS Anderson replied at the same time.

'I think it unlikely—'

'I don't reckon so—'

Doctor Ruane picked up with an explanation, his voice resigned, as if he'd seen too much death in his lifetime.

'I'm afraid to say that I attended the scene when DI MacKenzie lost his life. It was a violent and gruesome affair, but it had all the hallmarks of a professional killing. This seems to me to be the work of an opportunistic amateur.'

'My thoughts precisely,' Anderson added, sure of himself.

Hollie gave a small nod. She agreed, but she also knew from years of experience that coincidences rarely occurred in investigations like this one.

'Okay, thanks for your input, that's useful to know,' she continued.

Hollie hadn't wasted much time thinking about MacKenzie since starting at Humberside, even though she was the deceased man's replacement. But there was something about the surname that was now echoing from her past in the city. She was unable to put her finger on it, but a distant memory felt like it was tapping on her shoulder, anxious to get her attention.

'Have we notified next of kin yet?' she checked, keen not to get drawn into the past. She kept seeing Moira's face in the darkness, a plaintive look on her face, as if willing Hollie to do something. 'We are sure it's him?'

'Next of kin should have been notified by now, boss,' Anderson answered assuredly. 'He's got a wife and two adult children. The FLO is heading over there, too.'

'Okay, thank you, Ben. Doctor Ruane, please let me know as soon as you've been able to examine the body properly. DS Anderson, I'd like you to set in motion interviews with the ride owner and the show people. I want to know if there are security cameras or guards on site overnight and how easy it is to get into this ride when the fair site is closed at night.'

She paused for a moment to consider what else should be done. Harry Gordon had hung back; he clearly had something on his mind. She'd catch up with him outside.

'Let's get the cordoned-off area enlarged as soon as possible and see what DC Gordon has come up with. The last thing we want is for social media to start on the horror images.'

As she spoke, Hollie walked past Anderson, taking care not to trip on the single metal track which guided the ghost train carriages through the structure.

'Check what access the public has to the fairground site, please. I suspect it counts as a public thoroughfare and we may need to ship in some proper barriers—'

The light from Hollie's mobile phone had caught something in the area behind her colleague that was unlit by the makeshift floodlights their SOCO had set up.

'Are you all right, boss?' Ben asked.

Anderson and Ruane were following her gaze now, straining to see what her torch beam had caught in the darkness.

Hollie steadied her flashlight as best she could.

'I need SOCO over here now!' she called. There was an instant silence as her urgency alerted the surrounding officers to their superior officer.

She was staring directly at what appeared to be the murder weapon, which had been discarded almost out of sight behind a ghoulish figure. It was a bloodied mallet. Hollie was overcome by a feeling of nausea as she cast her mind back to 1999. As well as a discarded hair scrunchie and a stuffed toy, the police had also found a bloody mallet after the disappearance of her friend Moira twenty-five years previously.

THREE

HULL, 1999

'We'll meet you at The Turnpike at eight o'clock,' Hollie shouted up the stairs to her two friends. She hoped they'd heard her over Fatboy Slim's 'Praise You', but she wasn't so sure. She waited a moment, thought she heard a *See you later* over the pounding of the music, and set off anyway.

Hollie closed the door behind her and stepped out into the night. The evenings were drawing in fast already and there was an autumnal chill in the air. She could hear the thud-thud-thud of the girls' music from the street, and she wondered if the neighbours might soon be banging at the door again, complaining that they were making too much noise.

As she turned back to survey the house, she saw that Jim's light was on. Jim was the mysterious mature student who had lived in the house for four years already. He kept himself to himself and they rarely saw him.

Moira lived in a top-floor flat on Hardy Street, and it was just a short diversion over to her place to pick her up on the way to the pub. The streets were still busy at that time of the evening as students from the two university campuses headed out in groups to see what fun the night might hold. She arrived at Moira's house and rang the bell.

She heard Moira's footsteps coming down the staircase and turned to face the door, ready to greet her friend. As soon as the door opened, she could see Moira had been crying. Her eyes were red, her cheeks streaked with tears.

'Oh, Moira, is everything all right?' Hollie asked, reaching forward to touch her friend's arm.

Moira sniffed and wiped her eyes; it seemed like she'd been caught out, perhaps thinking Hollie wouldn't notice.

'It's okay, honestly,' Moira replied, shaking her head and looking down at the floor. 'I thought I'd be all right by the time you got here. Just ignore me, I'm being silly.'

Hollie had never seen her friend like this. Her immediate instinct was concern, but Moira didn't look like she was ready to talk.

'Let's go upstairs and make a drink, that'll help,' Hollie urged, her voice gentle and soothing.

She took her friend's hand, closed the front door and led her up the staircase. The hallway was lined with magnolia-painted textured wallpaper, and there was a stack of flyers on a shelf which was also piled high with free newspapers and unclaimed post. The hallway carpet was gaudily patterned and badly worn in the entrance and at the bottom of the staircase.

Hollie squeezed Moira's hand, but noticed it wasn't reciprocated. There always seemed a tiny part of Moira that wasn't quite present.

The television was on in the downstairs flat, and it sounded like they were watching *EastEnders*; she'd recognise Dot Cotton's voice anywhere. The shared hallway smelled damp and mildew stained the ceiling.

Moira had left her flat door open, so they stepped inside, and Hollie ushered her friend over to the two-seat sofa that was pushed against the wall in the sparse living room. Hollie knew the layout from previous visits, so popped the kettle on and pulled out two tea-stained mugs from the kitchen cupboard. The taps started a clanking noise in the water pipes when they ran. It always made Hollie jump.

She walked back into the living area again and sat down next to her friend. On the small table where Moira ate her meals, Hollie spotted an envelope and a letter. The letter had been screwed up into a loose ball.

Moira adjusted the single cushion on the sofa, a troubled look on her tearstained face.

'I didn't mean to load you up with my problems,' Moira said at last, sniffing.

'I wish you would,' Hollie replied, moving in closer.

Moira looked down at her hands which were clasped firmly around her mug, the steam wafting up towards her face.

'Did you get some bad news in that letter?' Hollie ventured, her voice uncertain.

Moira stood up and walked over to the scrunched-up paper. She placed her cup on the table and picked it up.

'I should have thrown this away...' she began, her words trailing off.

'What is it, Moira?' Hollie spoke softly.

Her friend's eyes had reddened, and her hands were trembling.

A car door slammed outside on the street and it startled Hollie. The sound of it seemed to shake Moira from her reverie. She rejoined Hollie on the sofa, leaving her drink. As she sat down, Moira unfolded the letter, smoothing it out on her lap, giving a small, embarrassed laugh as she did so.

'Promise this will stay between you and me?' Moira's voice faltered, and she looked earnestly into Hollie's eyes.

Hollie studied her friend's face. Was this a breakthrough at last? Was she finally going to confide in her?

'Of course. It won't go any further,' she promised. Her heart was thumping in her chest. 'You can trust me, Moira. You should know that by now.'

Moira handed her the letter. She said nothing, as if she expected what was printed on the page to be explanation enough.

Hollie scanned it, trying to get a sense of why this had upset her friend so much.

It was printed on headed paper, the name of a local firm of solicitors embossed at the top. Her body stiffened as it slowly dawned on her what this was about.

Hollie let out a short gasp as she read the words. She didn't take it all in at first, but she got the gist of it fast enough. No wonder Moira was so upset.

She placed the letter to her side and wrapped her arms around Moira. They stayed like that for a couple of minutes, in silence, Hollie fighting back her tears.

'Oh, Moira,' Hollie said at last, pulling away slowly and looking at her friend. 'I didn't know you were dealing with stuff like this. Why didn't you say? Why have you been keeping it to yourself?'

Moira's head was bowed.

The dull pounding on the TV in the room downstairs punctuated their silences. Hollie could feel the ceiling vibrations in her feet.

'When did you get placed in care?' Hollie asked, her throat dry, struggling to choose her words carefully.

'It's difficult to talk about—' came Moira's choked reply.

Moira looked away, towards the window. The flimsy curtains were still not drawn. The well-spaced but inadequate curtain hooks meant that they were barely hanging onto the rail, but the pattern was pretty, if a little worn by the sunlight.

Hollie touched Moira's arm, willing her to turn around. After some time, Moira's shoulders relaxed, and she faced Hollie on the sofa.

'I've kept this in my own head for so long—' she began, touching her forehead, an intense look on her face.

Hollie squeezed her hand, the tears forming in her eyes. She had to be strong; Moira seemed so close to trusting her now.

'It was on my twelfth birthday,' Moira started again, her voice hesitant, her eyes still uncertain.

There was a distant rumble outside. Hollie hadn't thought it was going to rain, but it sounded like thunder.

'Mum had a meltdown, she just couldn't cope with the stress of the birthday party. We were playing pin the tail on the donkey, and I noticed she'd gone. I was only young, but, you know, kids always know when something's up.'

She paused a moment as if struggling to find the words.

'I found her in the bathroom—' Moira froze, and tears ran down her cheeks.

Hollie felt a cold chill run through her body. Tears began to form in her own eyes, but she had to remain strong.

'—she was sitting in a bath full of water, with her wrists cut—'

Hollie felt like she'd just been punched in the heart. She gasped as she pictured a young Moira walking in on her mother like that, a sense of desolation washing over her.

Heavy drops of rain began to strike the window outside; it seemed like the sky had grown darker, like a storm was coming.

'We never blew out my candles after that,' Moira added, almost to herself.

'I'm so sorry,' Hollie said, squeezing Moira's hand. Her grip was too firm, and she loosened it. Her hand was clammy now, and she'd begun to shake.

'You could have shared this, you know. You didn't have to go through all this alone.'

She was crying with Moira, a new bond forged in tragedy.

Hollie picked up the letter again, her eyes fixed on the type-written words.

'What happened after that?' Hollie spoke softly, as if teasing out the thread from a cotton reel, gently coaxing Moira to say more. She could see from the letter that Moira's mother had survived the attempt to take her own life.

'She went to De La Pole—' Moira replied, her brow furrowing at the memory of it.

'What's that?' Hollie interjected, a little keener than she would have wished.

'It's a mental health facility in Hull. They moved her to somewhere she hated when it closed. She didn't cope well with the upheaval.'

The rain was lashing against the window now, and Hollie thought she caught another rumble of thunder. It growled far away across the city, like something had roused its anger.

'Her second attempt at killing herself was successful—'

'What?' Hollie asked, clumsily, taken aback by Moira's sudden revelation. Her chest tightened like it had been thrust in a clamp. She'd never had to deal with something like this before. She half-looked at the letter, thinking she must have misread it. 'Your mum is dead?'

She stared at Moira, thinking of her own mum, wondering how her friend could have kept this to herself for so long. What must it be like to lose your mother at such a young age?

Moira was crying again, her eyes red and her cheeks wet with tears.

Hollie moved in close, and Moira rested her head on her shoulder.

'I wish you'd spoken to me about this,' Hollie offered, her voice gentle, but she knew it was too little; nothing she said could fill this void in Moira's life.

'It's not something I like to talk about,' Moira answered, her voice shaky. 'You all have your nice lives at uni... who wants to hear about all my shit?'

'Did you have a relationship with your mum after her first

suicide attempt?' Hollie asked gently. Now Moira was talking, she wanted to encourage her.

Moira raised her head from Hollie's shoulder and wiped her eyes on her sleeve, sniffing as she did so.

'No, I'd only seen her a handful of times since I was taken into care. She died over the summer vacation. This is just tidying things up—'

The grip of guilt shook Hollie firmly as she thought back to her fun summer in Lancashire. They'd waved goodbye to Moira at the end of the summer term, their first year at university over and done with, with not a clue about what she'd have to face on her own. Some friends they'd been.

'Oh Moira, you should have said. We could have supported you.'

'I'm so used to being alone, it's difficult to ask people...'

Moira's voice trailed off. Hollie took her hand, desperate to let her know how much she cared. It seemed so inadequate. She'd never realised until that moment quite how bare Moira's living space was. There were no pictures or posters on the walls, and only one or two ornaments, which almost seemed like an afterthought.

They sat like that for some time, until Hollie spoke again, anxious not to let it drift away.

'So, were you in care in Hull? While your mum was in hospital, I mean.'

Moira swallowed hard. It seemed like she might not answer.

'It's not something I like to talk about,' she replied again quietly.

'It might help to share it,' Hollie encouraged her.

Moira studied her face, like she was trying to work out if she could trust her. Hollie met her gaze, a plaintive expression on her face.

'It's just that when I started uni, it was a chance to forget all that,' Moira began, her words coming slow and deliberately. 'It let me be someone else. It felt like a fresh start.'

'Were you unhappy in care?' Hollie pushed. Moira's look grew distant, like she was in another place. She began to cry again.

Hollie felt a turn in her stomach, and a sensation of sudden nausea engulfed her, an instinctive warning from her subconscious.

'Did– did they hurt you while you were there?' She trembled, hardly daring to ask the question.

Without warning, Moira's eyes flashed with fire and fury. Hollie felt her friend's grip firm on her hand and her body tensed on the sofa.

'I hate that fucking place. I spent six years at Ambrose House and detested every single minute—'

'Were you all on your own? Did you have anybody to take care of you while your mum was ill?'

The thought of it horrified Hollie. She was shaking now, fearful for the harm done to her friend.

Moira was sobbing, but she pushed through, like she was forcing her way through a violent river current.

'Just an auntie who would pop in once a year.'

Her memories seemed to whisk her away momentarily to another time and place. 'I used to beg her to take me away with her, but she would brush me aside and tell me her life was too busy to take in stray children. Imagine being described as a stray child. That still stings me.'

'I can't imagine what it must have been like,' Hollie spoke softly, still holding Moira's hand like they were joined now by these terrible events. Moira's words were dripping with hatred and contempt. She'd never spoken like that before.

'It must have been so hard for you in the children's home.'

Hollie looked into Moira's eyes; they were hollow and haunted.

'It was horrible. I never want to think about that place again. If I could burn it down and level it to the ground, I would. And I'd let the entire bloody staff burn with it.'

As she spoke, Hollie felt her friend's whole body shaking with the memory of it. Her past had reached out and shaken her, its grasp firm and unrelenting.

'It's okay, Moira, everything's going to be okay now. You're well away from that place. You're safe now, they can't hurt you anymore. I won't let anybody hurt you.'

FOUR

DC HARRY GORDON

Harry Gordon breathed in the cold autumn air as he surveyed the scene surrounding the fairground ride. It had got a bit crowded in the ghost train ride, and he'd had to fight off a panic attack. As far as he could tell, nobody had noticed.

Harry had always anticipated moving through the detective ranks at a pace, but seeing the pressure DI Turner was under, he reckoned he might hang on as a detective constable for a bit longer. As he surveyed the area surrounding the crime scene, he considered how he'd manage the present situation if he was in charge.

They'd created a second cordon around the ghost train, and he could see officers systematically working the area, searching for evidence and clues. He wondered if they'd close the site. He'd been to the fair for as many years as he could remember, since being a toddler; in his lifetime it had only ever not gone ahead due to COVID. He reckoned the fair would most likely stay open, even in a restricted capacity, which meant scouring the area thoroughly before the fair reopened again to the public that evening.

He'd been working as a detective long enough to see that

this was going to be a huge challenge for evidence gathering. Most of the city attended the fair at some time during the week, every single person leaving footprints, fingerprints and DNA across the entire site. Hull Fair was located on the sprawling Walton Street car park, which meant that all the rides were on a concrete surface. That meant there was very little chance of finding easily discernible footprints or tracks.

Harry had something on his mind. That body was heavy, so either Gordon Carrick had been walked in there and then killed, or his dead body was transported in some way. If he'd been killed away from the ghost train, there would be signs somewhere of copious blood loss, given the nature of the wounds that he'd seen on the body. With DI Turner having located the bloody mallet, it seemed more likely that the murder had taken place where the body was found. So how had Carrick got there in the first place? Had he been unconscious, or sedated?

'Any sign of footprints or tracks?' he called over to one of the suited officers who'd been searching the immediate area.

The shrug gave him his answer.

'Not a chance, sorry,' came the reply from the female officer. 'So far, we've no blood traces outside the ride and there are a million fingerprints and footprints. I'm not hopeful, but we'll keep looking.'

Harry thanked her then walked around beyond the cordon, taking in the wider area. Adjacent to the show ground site was Walton Street, which was lined with fast food trucks, the caravans of fortune tellers and various stalls selling novelty toys and confectionery. This was beyond the cordon, a public thoroughfare, and lined by houses.

He looked around, wondering how a body might be transported in such a public area without anyone noticing. His eye was caught by a movement at the side of an industrial bin that had been pushed into the gap between two catering stalls, which were now locked up and secure. A seagull was chancing its luck in the hope of finding discarded food. The bin had wheels, which could be clamped. If he wanted to move a body unseen, he'd place it in one of these bins, or perhaps in a mobile catering stand or ice cream van.

Leaving his latex gloves on his hands, Harry started to check out the wider environs, examining bins and anything which might be moved across the fairground site without catching anybody's attention.

As well as the heavier industrial bins, more conventional and lighter weight black bins were also kept securely on site, their handles looped and locked by a security chain. Harry walked over to a man wearing a full fluorescent coat, using litter picking tongs to clear up the mess around a static bin. He was wearing a bobble hat to keep out the cold and his breath left a trail in the air as he moved along collecting discarded cups and wrappers.

'Good morning,' Harry began, showing his ID. Not that he needed to, his attire was enough to explain what he was doing. 'Are you part of the cleaning team?'

'Yes, Hull City Council, mate. There are twenty of us working the site, only it's a bit easier today because you guys need us to steer clear of whatever is going on over there. What is it, a murder or something?'

He was fishing, but Harry knew better; information had to be released in a specific order, so next of kin didn't hear it on social media first.

'We pick up sixty-eight tonnes of shit like this during the event,' the man moaned. 'Why can't people just clear up after themselves?'

'Are those just regular wheelie bins you're using?' Harry asked, scanning the container for anything distinctive. A wheelie bin would be a great way of moving a body unnoticed.

'Pretty much,' the man answered, picking up a food

wrapper in which half a burger was still lodged. 'They have these identification stickers on, though – that's how we know they're ours.'

He pointed, and Harry drew out his phone.

'May I?' he asked.

'Be my guest, mate,' the man replied.

Harry thanked him for his help and continued his walk around the site, surveying everything, desperate to figure out how Carrick's body got in the ghost train.

After twenty minutes, he'd drawn a blank, so figured he'd better get back to the ghost train ride before DI Turner emerged again; she'd have a list of tasks as long as her arm to communicate to the team.

Picking up his pace, his eye was caught by a darting movement at the side of a hoopla stall. He shuddered – it was a rat moving between the stalls, no doubt feasting on the discarded fast food that was strewn across the ground from the previous night. Harry peered into the gap between the stalls. An overturned wheelie bin with its lid partially opened had been thrown in there.

The bin was empty; it hadn't been used for rubbish. Without touching it he scanned for the Hull City Council ID label which the litter picker had shown him; there was none.

The light was still poor, so he activated the torch on his phone, shining it across the bin, looking for anything which might differentiate it from all the others.

Then he spotted it: blood, he was certain. It was dried now, and the colour more dulled than if fresh, but the way it was spattered seemed like blood.

Harry hesitated a moment, eager to alert his colleagues to the find. What if he made a bad call and he was making a complete fool of himself? He'd never hear the end of the jibes in the office if he got it wrong.

Then, he spotted something, resting just under the lid. It

wasn't rubbish, he could see that much. He dug into his pocket searching for his pen so that he wouldn't have to handle whatever it was.

He leaned over, taking great care not to damage any footprints which might have been left in the enclosed area. He gently lifted the item and saw what it was immediately. It was a faded Polaroid photograph of a teenage girl on which was written the name *Tori*.

FIVE

DS Patel and DC Langdon were busy at their desks when Hollie got back to the office, both of them on the phone and tapping away at their PCs. There was a buzz throughout the room, the calm, professional thoroughness of a team who knew exactly what to do.

'Briefing room in five, please, everybody,' she announced as Amber placed her phone in its cradle.

'Morning, boss,' Amber greeted her, looking up from her screen. 'Did you enjoy your early morning alarm call?' There was a cautious smile on her face; early morning wake-up calls seldom bore good news.

'Yes, thank you, DS Patel.' She smiled, mock shaking her fist in jest at her colleague. 'There's nothing quite like a six o'clock call out in the morning. Do you have anything new for me before I address the troops?'

'I do,' Amber answered, snapping straight back to business. 'Jane Carrick, the victim's wife, has been informed of her husband's death, and DC Hayes is at the house now as her Family Liaison Officer. They're expecting you round there later this morning.'

'Great work, thank you. What about the children's home?'

'It's still open, boss. It's called – wait for it – the Caring Guardian Children's Residential Home.'

Amber forced a smile, and Hollie screwed up her face.

'Jeez, you couldn't make this stuff up.' Hollie winced. 'Is it privately run or county operated?'

'Private, boss. It was county operated previously. I've already put in a request for a list of names of the children who were placed there during the nineties and early noughties. That's not the best of it, though—'

'Go on. What have you unearthed?' she asked, eyes widening. 'And well done on getting onto that list of names already, that was my next question.'

Amber looked over at Jenni Langdon, who'd just finished her call.

'What did he tell you, Jenni?'

'I've just been speaking to the reporter who wrote the story on that 2001 newspaper article that was found near the body, boss. The reporter lost his job over it, but he's still adamant the abuse was going on at the home.'

'Did he say as much?' Hollie asked.

'I can give you his precise words,' she replied, checking her notes. 'He said – and I quote – "there's no smoke without fire as far as that shithole is concerned".'

'Good morning, everybody,' Hollie announced, calling the room to order. It was a little emptier than usual, but that was to be expected with the crime scene still being raked over and the incident room and team being thrown together. They were on the clock; the fair reopened at five o'clock that evening and they had free rein until then to examine the whole of the site.

'We have a retired police superintendent, Gordon Carrick, violently murdered on the Hull Fair showground at Walton

Street. I'm aware that some of you may have worked with Mr Carrick, and I know you'll be as anxious as I am to bring his killer – or killers – to justice. So, what do we know?'

DCI Osmond was sitting among the assembled officers. He stirred in his seat and then began speaking.

'I knew Superintendent Carrick,' he began, his voice sounding scratchy. He took a swig from his coffee cup. It was still early and none of them had had time to get hot drinks down them yet.

'We'd come up through the force as young officers together. We didn't mix socially, but our paths crossed, as they tend to do in a force like Humberside. He started his career in Grimsby then came over to Hull to take up his first senior position. He was a good copper, from what I know.'

A couple of other older officers concurred with that opinion.

'Were there any cases which might have come back to haunt him?' Hollie wondered aloud. 'Who might he have bothered in his policing career?'

There was a general consensus around the room that most of them had a long list of local criminals who'd be only too keen to get even with them.

'I've done some checking, boss,' Amber volunteered, 'and there's nobody of any note recently released from prison who might bear him any more of a grudge than usual. We're checking them all out as a precaution, though.'

'Great, thank you, DS Patel. I want to speak to his wife, ASAP.'

Hollie paused before continuing.

'Let's not exclude other reasons why somebody might want Carrick dead. Was it a family member, perhaps? Maybe it was a random killing. I know the grudge angle is more compelling at the moment, but we need to keep open minds here.'

There were nods of agreement from around the briefing room.

'DC Langdon, when can we speak to the journalist?' Hollie resumed.

Jenni was sitting at the front, primed like she was raring to get started. Her hair was now fully regrown from where she'd almost lost her life while investigating a previous case. Hollie shuddered as she recalled her colleague's head crashing on the pavement as the motorcyclist drove directly at her, unflinching in his evil, as she urged Jenni to get out of his way. It was almost like it had never happened now, but Hollie had to remember it was still only six months ago. The physical scars were mainly hidden, but the emotional scars always ran deep.

'Whenever we want to, boss,' Jennie replied. 'He's semi-retired and freelance-only these days. I've got his address, and he says he's happy to speak to us.'

'Just brief everybody on why he's of interest please, DC Langdon.'

Jenni stood up and joined Hollie at the front of the briefing room. She caught a hint of perfume on her colleague.

'Ray McGregor worked for the *Hull Daily Mail* in the nineties,' Jenni began. 'An article written by him was found at the side of Gordon Carrick's body—'

She held up a printout of Harry's photograph of the newspaper cutting from the crime scene, and the officers studied their own copies which had been distributed among them. Harry Gordon wasn't in the room yet. Hollie glanced through the glass panelling of the briefing room and spotted him at his desk, furiously typing at his PC. Jenni carried on speaking, oblivious to Hollie's distraction.

'Ray McGregor alleged that there was a child abuse ring operating in Hull at the time, and he staked his career on a damning report claiming that the Caring Guardian Children's Residential Home was part of it. The home is still open but with new ownership, new staff and a complete rebrand. It's private now, too.'

Jenni continued speaking after a short pause, scanning the room beforehand to see if there were any questions or comments.

'McGregor's career ended because of that article. There was a formal inquiry, but the entire case was dismissed as public hysteria and one man's misplaced obsession. Ray McGregor lost his job and has eked out a living selling dull court reports and freelance writing for local and national publications.'

'Okay, I want to speak to him as soon as I've checked in with Carrick's wife,' Hollie said, determined.

Jenni nodded.

'There's a crucial piece of information which links Gordon Carrick to that newspaper article.' DCI Osmond stood up to speak. 'Carrick won libel damages as a result of accusations made about him in McGregor's article.'

Hollie stared at the DCI. This was a bombshell to start the day. Harry Gordon caught her eye; he was on the phone now. What was he up to that was so important it was keeping him out of the briefing?

'What were the accusations, sir?' Hollie asked.

'McGregor alleged that Carrick was involved in protecting several of the great and the good in the city at the time, but there was no evidence, and no witnesses came forward. Carrick pushed it to clear his name in court and won substantial damages.'

'Was he still a serving police officer at the time, sir?' Amber Patel asked.

'Not after he won the damages, no. He was awarded over two hundred thousand at the time, a substantial amount back then, as McGregor sold the story in a freelance capacity, and it was fed to all the nationals. If it had stayed in the local press, the fallout might have been less. The nationals picked up the legal bills as he was working for them at the time and that's how his journalistic career was ended.'

'So, it's not much of a leap to assume it could be connected with those events,' Hollie confirmed, her policing instincts kicking in hard now. They'd caught a strong scent already, which was unusual so early in a case.

'If it looks like shit and smells like shit, it probably is shit.'

Hollie hadn't seen Ben entering the room; her gaze had been transfixed on the DCI.

'I might have put it more delicately, DS Anderson, but I agree with you, this is our best lead so far. Is there anything else to report from the crime scene?'

Anderson shook his head. 'We've spoken to the ride operators, and nobody heard or saw anything. There's 24/7 security of the fairground site during the fair, so it was patrolled at night, but nobody had anything to tell us.'

'And CCTV in or around the show site?' Jenni asked.

'Nothing on the rides,' Anderson replied, 'but there are the usual local authority cameras in the immediate area. I've got DC Norton chasing the council's cameras. Uniform are checking for anything else that might be useful.'

Hollie rubbed her hands, the rush of adrenaline making her fidgety.

'Was the mallet we think was used to murder the victim taken from the fairground?' she checked. 'And do we know at which ride it was originally located?'

A bead of sweat formed on her brow as she recalled the bloodied toy that Moira had dropped on the showground, and her throat tightened as her mind returned to that dark spot behind the fairground rides, desperately calling out to Moira, praying that she hadn't lost her in the throng. They'd found a discarded and bloody mallet after her friend disappeared. An icy shiver ran through her.

She could still hear the melodic organ sounds of the nearby

merry-go-round and taste the sticky sweetness of candy floss in her mouth. As a student, Hull Fair was just something that was there, the chance for a bit of fun and a night out. As a police officer, she wanted to know every detail.

'That's confirmed, boss,' Anderson replied. 'One of the show people reported it to us as missing when they saw the furore at the ghost train. It had been used to pitch a nearby marquee and went missing overnight. The description given by the guy matches exactly with the item that was recovered from the ghost train.'

Hollie's pulse quickened, and she felt her heart pounding heavily in her chest. She pushed through it, her legs weakening the further her mind reached back to that terrible time.

'How did the killer access the ride?' DCI Osmond asked. It was a good question. 'Have we interviewed the operator?'

'There's nothing suspicious there, sir,' Anderson informed him. 'The rides are left as they are overnight, they're switched off obviously, but they rely on patrolling security guards mainly to make sure nobody damages them. It wouldn't have taken any great act of espionage to hide a body in there.'

'Was Carrick killed on the site or beforehand?' Amber asked, shaking Hollie out of her musings. 'Or don't we know that yet?'

Hollie searched the room, noticing that Harry Gordon finally seemed to be getting ready to join them; he was collecting something off the printer. She wanted him to talk them through his theory with the wheelie bin. She turned to Amber.

'Doctor Ruane should be able to help us with that. Our early guess is that he was killed where the body was found. Would you let me know as soon as the body is moved from the crime scene, and Doctor Ruane completes his examination?'

Amber nodded.

'What's the full history of abuse allegations at Caring

Guardian, DCI Osmond? Were any staff removed or prosecuted as a result of the inquiry?'

'Nothing that I know of,' DCI Osmond replied. 'There was a big fuss about it at the time, but Gordon Carrick was exonerated, as you know. To my knowledge, no heads rolled over it.'

There was silence. Hollie placed her right hand on the table at her side, aware that it had begun to shake. All she could see and hear were the far-off screams from the fairground rides and the luminous glow of the lights as she desperately looked for Moira in the darkness.

'When I was in uniform, I had to drive one of the teenagers back to the home once, ma'am,' DC Philpot volunteered. 'It was no big deal, just a bit of shoplifting, it wasn't prosecuted, and the kid was let off with a warning. It was nothing to get excited about.'

She turned to face Philpot.

'Was this a regular occurrence at the home? Did the kids often get into trouble?'

'It goes with the territory, I think, boss,' Philpot answered. 'There are some troubled teenagers there, but from my experience they don't cause anywhere near as much aggravation as some of the other kids in this city.'

'Thank you, DC Philpot. Does anybody else have anything to offer about the children's home, either now or in the past? Other than the scandal we've already discussed, that is?'

There were no replies.

DC Gordon entered the room, a clutch of printed papers in his hand and an urgent look on his face.

'I've got something, boss,' he began, still slightly out of breath from where he'd been rushing.

'This Polaroid image,' he began, holding up a colour printout of the photograph that he'd found at the side of the bin. 'Tori is such a distinctive name, I figured I might be able to narrow down who she is. I did some digging and found some articles about a Tori Bellingham who was involved with a local mental health charity in Hull in the early noughties—'

Hollie wasn't certain where he was heading with this.

'How's this linked?' she pushed him.

'Tori Bellingham took an overdose in 2002. The *Hull Daily Mail* ran a short obituary about her at the time, and they just scanned a copy over from the archive. And guess what?'

He'd just captured the attention of the entire room.

'Tori was brought up in the care system. The last home she was placed in was Ambrose House.'

SIX

HULL, 1999

'We'd better get over to The Turnpike, Judith and Lucy will be wondering what's happened to us.'

Hollie wasn't entirely up for a night out after Moira's recent revelations about her past life; she was still stunned by what her friend had shared with her.

'Please promise you won't discuss that with anybody else,' Moira urged.

'I promise,' Hollie assured her. 'And if you ever want to talk to me about it, just let me know. I can't believe you've been carrying this with you all the time I've known you.'

As they chatted about other things, Moira finished getting ready, adding the smallest touch of make-up to her face and exchanging her jeans and university sweatshirt for a skirt and top. She asked Hollie to fasten a small, heart-shaped Good Luck charm around her neck.

'I love this locket,' Hollie remarked. 'It looks so nice on you.'

'Thanks.' Moira beamed. 'My mum gave it to me before she got ill. I wear it every day.'

'May I open it?' Hollie ventured.

'Yes, of course,' Moira encouraged her.

Hollie flicked it open. Inside was a tiny photograph of a much younger Moira with a woman who she assumed was her mother. Her mum was smiling, but it was hollow, and even in that tiny image Hollie could see she was troubled.

'Happier days,' Moira sighed.

Hollie fastened the locket around Moira's neck. Moira checked in the mirror that it was hanging neatly.

'So they gave you this flat when you left the home, to give you a chance to stand on your own two feet?' Hollie asked, admiring Moira's natural ability to pull her wardrobe together so effortlessly. She was securing her hair with a purple scrunchie, and her friend looked great.

'Basically. I get an allowance and someone to support me. It's a bit like being released from prison, I guess. Because I don't have parents to do all this stuff, I get a dedicated social worker to ease me into the adult world.'

Hollie hadn't seen the privilege she'd experienced in her own life until she'd left home and come to university. She'd always thought her life was normal, but since arriving at the University of Humberside, she'd met people who'd been brought up by single mothers and fathers, students who'd been carers for their parents and some whose parents didn't have jobs, due to redundancy, injury, illness and any other number of problems in their lives. It made her feel guilty that things had mostly been plain sailing in her own life. She was pleased she'd left home, because even she could see it had broadened her limited outlook.

'Anyhow, enough of my nonsense,' Moira announced, 'let's go and have a night out with the girls.'

Moira shook Hollie out of her contemplation, and she looked up at her friend and smiled. The mood was lighter now – it would be good for Moira to get away from everything for a night.

'Knowing Judith and Lucy, they'll be half-bladdered already.' Hollie smiled. 'Judith is anybody's after half a cider.'

The two girls laughed; suddenly they were teenagers again.

They headed down the stairs from Moira's accommodation and out onto the street, returning to Cottingham Road. It seemed like half the university population was out that night. The road was busy with excited students all heading to one of the various pubs which lined the route. As they reached the junction with Beverley Road, Hollie looked over at the Jacksons store on the far side.

'Do you mind if I pop over the road and draw out some cash from the cash machine? I'm a bit short,' she asked.

They waited for the lights to go their way, then crossed over to the convenience store at the far corner of the crossroads. There was a banner hung on the metal railing outside the store and Hollie pointed it out to her friend.

'Hull Fair. What is it?'

'Nothing much,' Moira replied, dismissive.

'Really? They seem to make a big thing of it in the city.'

'I'm not really interested, to be honest,' Moira replied.

Hollie studied her friend's face, then decided to drop the subject. She was usually up for a night out and a bit of fun, but she seemed to have a downer on this suggestion.

A homeless person was sitting at the side of the ATM, and Hollie checked him out before joining the line to get her money. He was sitting on a flattened cardboard box, which looked like it had been retrieved from a nearby industrial waste bin. His head was bowed, and he'd placed a paper cup in front of him into which passersby had thrown a mixture of coins. Moira reached into her pocket and threw in a pound.

The man looked up, his eyes widening.

'Simon!' Moira exclaimed.

Hollie saw that the two of them knew each other and drifted away from the queue to see what was going on.

'Moira, it's good to see you—'

Moira's brow furrowed and a look of concern washed across her face. A car horn sounded after a near miss at the crossroads, but all three remained caught in the moment, undistracted by what was going on around them.

'What the hell are you doing out here?' came Moira's intense, shrill voice.

Simon looked intently into her eyes. He gestured vaguely.

'I couldn't stand it any longer. Not after what happened... I had to get away.'

Hollie shuffled her feet, unable to make out what was going on between the two of them. It seemed to be a friendly exchange, but it was intense, too. Moira winced and then began to move her lips, stopping abruptly as she appeared to remember they were not alone.

'This is Simon Rose,' she said, indicating her friend. Hollie gave him a brief smile but didn't know quite what to do with herself, shuffling her feet on the pavement.

'We're friends. We knew each other—' She looked around nervously, and then lowered her voice. 'We knew each other in the home—' Her voice faltered. She seemed wary and uncertain. 'I haven't seen Simon for a while.'

A loose page from a newspaper blew along the pavement, catching on Hollie's foot. She shook it off and let it continue its journey along the path, never shifting her gaze from the two acquaintances. She could almost touch the connection between them: it was like a sparking cable, such was its power.

This was out of Hollie's comfort zone. Usually, when she passed homeless people, she'd avert her eyes, not quite sure what to do. Her mother always complained that they were drawing benefits and scamming people on the streets, but since leaving the prevalent influence of her home environment, Hollie was beginning to view the world in a different way. She'd begun to think it was more complicated than that.

Hollie studied Moira's friend. He was wearing a washed-out Iron Maiden T-shirt under his threadbare coat; the T-shirt looked well-worn, the transfer faded and peeling on the front. It seemed like he hadn't shaved or washed for a couple of days.

'Are you eighteen yet?' Moira asked Simon, her voice softening and conspiratorial now. 'You can't be out on the streets like this at night, it's not safe.'

Simon's body tensed and his look turned hostile. Hollie jumped at the change in mood and wondered if their exchange was about to turn sour.

A couple walked past, sharing chips and curry sauce from a polystyrene tray. Hollie caught the fragrant aroma of the sauce as the man and woman passed by, oblivious to what was playing out on the pavement. She wanted to get moving, though she was gripped by this exchange.

'I don't have much choice, do I?' he replied, his face reddening and indignant now. 'And it's not like that place is any safer. You know how dangerous they are—'

Moira made a face at him, and he stopped dead, his expression softening and his gaze submissive.

Simon was calm again now, and he spoke softly.

'Besides, it's Hull Fair time. You know I can't be there—'

Moira cut him off again, as if she'd been shaken violently by a memory or harsh recollection. She spoke sternly to Hollie, as if she was dismissing her. She pointed as she spoke, indicating that the cash machine was now clear.

'Hollie, you'd best get that money sorted. Simon, come into Jacksons with me, let's get you a sandwich and a drink. You can't stay out here.'

She held out her hand to help Simon up from his seated position on the pavement. His threadbare blanket slipped off his knees onto the flattened cardboard box which he'd been using to protect himself from the cold, harsh surface on which he'd been sitting. His movements were slow and stiff. He levelled with Moira and smiled conspiratorially.

'I stole some money from you-know-who before I ran away. Serves the bastard right.'

Moira shook her head but gave a little smile. Whoever he'd stolen from, it seemed like the normal rules of right and wrong didn't apply here. A lot of water had passed under the bridge with these two, much of it turbulent as far as she could tell.

Hollie wasn't at all certain about this, but she let her friend go ahead into the shop and she drew out her cash from the machine. She waited outside on the corner for Moira to come out.

Something was bothering her about it; she didn't know what to make of Simon. The relationship seemed troubled, yet they appeared to share a strong and loyal bond.

At last, Moira returned with Simon, who was tucking into the sandwich like he hadn't eaten for days. Their body language was more relaxed now, and Hollie guessed being able to speak more freely had helped with that.

Moira had a resolved look on her face, as if she'd now figured things out.

'I'm going to duck out tonight,' she announced to Hollie. 'I want to get Simon back to my flat so he can shower and get warmed up.'

A jolt of panic shot through Hollie's body.

'Can we talk?' Hollie urged her. 'Alone?'

Moira crossed her arms, her face stern. She immediately uncrossed them, reassured Simon she'd only be a minute and moved to the side with Hollie. They ducked into a side alley where the industrial bins were kept. Hollie caught the pungent smell of discarded food coming from the heavy metal container.

'You can't take him home to your flat,' she whispered, her voice urgent and pleading.

'Why not?' Moira's reply was short and sharp; it looked like she was committed to this course of action.

'He's homeless. And you're on your own.'

Hollie despised herself for even saying the words, and she saw from Moira's hardened expression that she was having none of it.

'We've shared things that you could never understand. Things I could never tell you.' Her eyes moistened as she looked directly at Hollie. 'I'm doing this, I'm not leaving him out here.'

Hollie exhaled quietly; she wasn't going to win this. She spoke more forgivingly now, the tension fast evaporating from their exchange as they reasserted their friendship.

'Are you sure? Do you want me to come with you?'

Hollie watched her friend's shoulders relax, and Moira reached out to take her hand.

'Go and join the others. I'll be fine with Simon. Honestly, Hollie, we're friends. I'll be all right.'

Hollie felt in her pocket and took out a pound coin. At least she could support her friend, even if she was still desperately concerned about her.

'Here,' she said, handing it over to Simon, like she'd just made a concession to her own conscience. He took the money, and Moira walked over to him. Hollie could not shake her sense of unease.

'I'm sorry to cancel our night out,' Moira began, looking at Hollie. Her voice was steady and unapologetic now she'd got what she wanted and no longer had to plead her case.

'Maybe we can go to the fair,' Moira then proposed, catching the Hull Fair banner with her eye.

Simon shuddered and looked like a dark spirit had just passed through his body.

'You're not going there, are you?' he pleaded. 'After every-thing – after what they did—'

Moira cut him off, firm and abrupt, though her furrowed

brow suggested she was not so sure about it herself. She shook off her doubt and gave a defiant reply. 'I'm free of that place now, they can't hurt me. Why shouldn't I enjoy it like everybody else? It'll show them they can't break me.'

Moira reached out and squeezed her friend's arm. 'Thanks for looking out for me,' she said, a tear forming in her eye. 'I could have done with more friends like you when I was younger. Go and enjoy yourself with Judith and Lucy. I'll see you in lectures tomorrow.'

Hollie watched as Moira and Simon crossed the road past the Haworth pub, then disappeared up Cottingham Road again, until they were out of sight. She couldn't shake her sense of disquiet, and every instinct told her to follow them. But she'd picked up on Moira's tone; she wasn't wanted there.

Judith and Lucy would wonder where the hell she'd got to. She negotiated the crossings at the busy crossroads and walked into The Turnpike, which was positively buzzing for a weekday evening. The bar was packed with a line of students and locals, all waving five and ten pound notes, trying to get the attention of the bar staff. She scanned the room as best she could, searching for her friends in the sea of unfamiliar faces. Judith carried a mobile phone, but they were far too expensive for Hollie to consider on her tight university budget.

'You look like you've lost someone.'

An unfamiliar voice came from behind her. It was an American accent, warm and friendly. She turned around.

'I'm supposed to be meeting a couple of friends here—'

She knew the moment she saw him that she'd given the game away. He was tall, but not too tall, and had dark, well-cut hair. He was wearing an INXS T-shirt under his denim jacket, and his smile was immediately kind and welcoming. She thought it likely he was a student, too. His voice was assured and measured, and his confidence infectious.

Hollie wiped the grin off her face, knowing better than to look so obvious.

'How about we look for your friends together and if we can't find them, I'll buy you a drink, then make sure you're walked home safely?'

Hollie studied him as he spoke. His body language was gentle, his tone non-threatening; he seemed nice, his easy, instant charm washing over her. Besides, they were in a packed bar on a busy student street; what harm could it do? And if Judith and Lucy had moved on without her, she was in for a dull night.

She scanned the bar again, making one last search for her friends. Then she looked up at him and smiled. 'Deal,' she said, her eyes widening and heart fluttering slightly as she gazed at his flirtatious face. 'I'll have half a pint of John Smith's, please.'

'I'm Elijah,' he announced, holding out his hand. 'I'm at the uni – Hull, not Humberside – I'm on an exchange programme. Pleased to meet you.'

She took his hand; it was soft and welcoming, and she flicked back her hair as he smiled mischievously at her. Any thoughts of Moira and Simon were gone now. All Hollie could think about was the charming American student who was just about to turn her life upside down.

SEVEN

'I need to talk to you, DI Turner.'

DCI Osmond crept up behind her. It was more of an ambush than a request.

'Right now, boss?' she asked. Osmond was not really a *boss* kind of guy, but she felt it was time to drop the sir, to try it on for size.

'Let's stick with sir for now,' came his curt reply.

That was that then, so much for testing the water. This sounded serious, like Osmond had something on his mind. She ran through recent events, wondering if some shit might have hit the fan.

The briefing room was emptying now, and Osmond shut the door behind the final pair of officers to leave.

'Take a seat,' he instructed, pulling one over for himself. He made sure he was seated directly in front of her.

Shit, it's a take a seat job. This can't be good.

Warily, Hollie sat down and awaited his opening line, bracing herself to see what this might be about. Osmond was looking at her intently.

'I need to speak to you about a conflict of interest,' he began, his hands fidgeting.

He knew. Her mouth felt dry suddenly and she cleared her throat. Most likely, one of the team had figured it out and referred it up. That was fair enough, she'd have mentioned it herself soon enough, when the time was right.

'I've been looking over your personnel file—' he began nervously. 'I recalled something that the DCC mentioned to me after your interview.' The DCI was not good at handling the more difficult conversations; his hands were twitchy.

He let the words hang there for a moment, but before she could reply, he followed up, catching her by surprise. 'When were you going to mention your connection with the case?'

His voice was steadier now, like he'd plucked up the courage to say it, but his finger drumming on his chair arm gave the game away. Her heart sank, fearing he might be about to pull her off the case. A sweat began to form across her brow.

'You'll know I was involved in a high-profile police case here, sir, back in 1999 when I was studying at the university?'

She might as well get on with it and cut to the chase. Suddenly she was afraid; she hadn't realised how much she'd wanted this case.

Osmond shuffled in his chair. Was he delivering bad news from the brass above him? This didn't seem to sit easy with him.

'When were you thinking of telling us?' he repeated, more confident now. 'Did it not strike you that you have a strong conflict of interest with this case?'

It was her turn to shuffle in her seat now. Was this a bollocking? She couldn't tell where he was heading.

'I was looking for the right time, sir. Truth be told, I'd have raised it by the end of today probably; I just had to be certain this goes back to 1999—'

'You should have raised it the moment the conflict became clear,' he pushed, more confident that he'd got her on the ropes and that she wasn't going to land the blow which sent him flying. He stretched out his legs a little, like he was staking his claim on territory.

She swallowed hard, thinking back to the night when Moira disappeared. It could come screaming back from the past at a moment's notice, the fear and panic every bit as raw as it was back then.

'This gives me a problem,' Osmond continued. He seemed reluctant to deliver the news. 'Do we take you off the case? Can you keep a clear mind and stay detached?'

Once again, Hollie felt her heart skip a beat. As it had dawned upon her what this new case was about, she'd seen an opportunity to finally get to the bottom of what had happened to her friend. But could she be impartial?

Hollie's jaw stiffened. 'My friend disappeared at Hull Fair over twenty years ago, sir.' Her voice faltered a little, but it was emotion speaking now, not nerves. She owed this to Moira. 'No body was recovered, and she's never been heard of again, to my knowledge. It was a complete mystery and it's bothered me every day ever since...'

Hollie needed to pause. She was fighting to stay on the case here and he needed to see she'd be an asset. She pushed her shoulders back and sat up in her chair.

'In 1999, I worked with the police to help find out what happened,' she continued, picturing the reconstruction and the visits to her student house by Humberside police officers. It was all so unfamiliar back then. 'As you said, it was a high-profile case at the time, the TV reported on it, and it made a couple of the nationals. It's kind of why I'm here now; it's what inspired me to join the police.' She choked as she recalled the passion she'd felt at the time about joining the force. She'd never felt more compelled to do something in her life. It was like joining the police would somehow help Moira.

'I want nothing more than to clear up this case and I think

my intimate knowledge of what was going on in 1999 will be an asset to the investigation.'

She almost pointed her finger at DCI Osmond, such was the level of defiance she was now experiencing.

Osmond gave her an undecided look, then relaxed his body.

'I'm sorry to hear about your friend,' he said more gently. 'Investigation techniques weren't so advanced back then, there were no camera phones in those days and much less CCTV. Was the case file closed?'

'Eventually, yes. Well, not closed as such, it just went nowhere, and they pulled all the resources from it.'

Hollie softened her shoulders, and she looked the DCI directly in the eye.

'She just disappeared into thin air, sir. There was no evidence that led anywhere, no confirmed suspects and no clues that suggested what had happened to her. It was like she'd never existed. There was definitely violence involved, but no body found, and Moira was never seen again. And because she didn't have any parents – well, nobody who would advocate for her – once the police had drawn a complete blank, it died a death. But this children's home – when it was called Ambrose House – she used to be in care there. And she hinted to me once' – Hollie's throat tightened as she tried to say the words, a sense of failing her friend engulfing her all over again – 'she all but told me about the abuse when we were students, but I didn't get it – I was too immature – I had no idea how to handle it back then.'

'Damn.'

That had got his interest. Osmond sat forward, a gleam in his eye that all coppers got when they got caught up in a case. The years of admin and desk work hadn't quite knocked it out of him yet. This was time to push her advantage. She was still getting her measure of Osmond, but he was a copper through and through, and his antennae had just started twitching.

'When I knew her, she'd recently left the home and was

living independently with light-touch social worker support. She never really spoke about her life before university, but one night, she gave me a glimpse into what had happened—'

'Did she mention the alleged abuse then?'

She'd got him hook, line and sinker now. The unease in her stomach began to settle as her confidence grew. A thought struck her. Who was Moira's support worker at that time? She'd get Amber to chase it up once her connection with the case was common knowledge. There must be a record of it somewhere. That person might have some useful information to share.

'Moira didn't say as much,' she continued, convinced she was out of the woods now. 'But she didn't like the place and she was pleased to see the back of it. Something was going on, but she disappeared before we ever got to discuss it that much again.'

Hollie pictured them together, sitting on Moira's small sofa, the rain striking the windows and the dull thudding of the TV in the flat downstairs. If she closed her eyes, she could still taste the saltiness of the tears from her face and the softness of Moira's hand as she cradled it in hers. She steeled herself, pushing back her tears.

'She only told me in the first place because I saw some paperwork in her bedsit and asked about it. She was nervous about Hull Fair, too; she didn't really want to come with us on the night she disappeared. There was something about that place that spooked her. I shouldn't have let her join us—'

Hollie sniffed and took out a tissue to give her eyes a wipe. She still felt so much responsibility for her friend, even after so many years.

'So you think her disappearance could be linked to Carrick's death, DI Turner?' DCI Osmond asked, clearly uncomfortable that she'd become emotional. At least he was speaking like a copper now, not a line manager.' It seems incredible that this link should occur so many years after. It feels a bit of a stretch to me.'

He was right, it still felt a bit left of centre to Hollie. But what were the chances? There were simply too many coincidences already.

'I agree, sir. I'm still shaking at the thought of it—'

She was rocking her right leg and she forced herself to stop.

'Moira got involved with some lad she knew from the children's home shortly before her disappearance. He was homeless and she took him under her wing and let him stay in her bedsit. I didn't like it at the time.'

DCI Osmond was gripped by this story now, and he seemed to have forgotten all about the conflict-of-interest issue. His eyes widened as if he was about to open a present.

'Were they in a relationship?' he asked, anxious now to make the connections. 'Was there any suggestion he was involved in her disappearance?'

Hollie's mind began racing, the hundreds of thoughts, theories and possibilities cascading like coins out of a winning slot machine. This was such well-trodden ground for her, there wasn't a day in her life when she'd not tried to figure out what happened to Moira.

'His name was Simon Rose, and he went missing at the same time, sir. He had left her flat when the police called. There was nothing to suggest he had anything to do with it, but he was under suspicion at the time. The police just drew a great big blank in 1999.'

They sat in silence, each thinking over the implications of what she'd said. She pictured Simon's face, grubby and unkempt where he'd been living on the streets. Had she been repelled by youthful naïvety? Would she regard him differently now?

'So there's a good chance he might be our murderer?' Osmond said at last.

'It's possible, sir. And—' She hesitated, feeling that she was about to betray her friend. The words stuck in her throat, but she was a copper and she had to consider all possibilities. 'There has to be some small, outside chance that it might even be Moira, though it could, of course, be any one of the kids who were at that home.'

It knocked the wind out of her lungs, just the prospect that Moira might still be out there somewhere.

Osmond was silent as he thought over it. She intervened before he could come to his decision, anxious to steer this to a conclusion.

'I want to stay on this case, sir,' she asserted. 'I was a central part of the police investigation, a key witness. I'd followed Moira when she went rushing off at Hull Fair that night. I chased her through the crowds. They used me when they ran the police reconstruction seeing as we looked so alike. They even showed it on the *Crime Beaters* TV show at the time. It won't take long for DS Patel to unearth that information; I think we need to get ahead of this.'

Osmond shuffled in his seat. Hollie could have shaken him; she could see him dithering.

'I'm going to refer it up,' he said at last.

Hollie's entire body slumped in the chair. She'd hoped he would be convinced and make the call there and then.

'There's nothing substantive to suggest the two cases are linked at this stage,' he resumed. It felt like a judge summing up a case. 'It may just be a coincidence. Hull is not a huge city, after all, and it's not a great leap that a girl who'd spent her life in care would be at the same home that was the subject of an inquiry a couple of years later.'

His reasons felt weak, and she wondered if he just lacked the balls to make the call himself.

'Did you speak with Gordon Carrick at the time?' he said without warning. 'Did your friend ever mention him?'

'I can't recall the names of the officers I dealt with,' Hollie said, after wracking her brains. She was desperate to remember. Some things – Moira's voice, her smell, her flat, her heart-shaped locket – she remembered in minute detail.

'I don't recall the name Carrick, but it's not beyond the realms of possibility. I was a student back then, nineteen years old, and all those coppers seemed scary to me at the time. It was only the thought of being able to help my friend Moira that made me get involved as much as I did. As it turns out, it was where everything began for me with my policing career.'

DCI Osmond made some notes on a pad that he'd drawn out of his pocket. He was old school, probably a beat bobby in the days before digital devices.

Hollie swallowed hard as she watched him scribble, then cleared her throat.

'There's one more thing, sir,' she began, feeling her heart rate quicken with what she was about to share. Osmond looked at her intently.

'I was physically threatened by a man after we filmed that TV reconstruction. Somebody was trying to cover something up. I'm sure about it. But nothing was done at the time, and I didn't know how to make my voice heard.'

'What are you saying?' DCI Osmond asked, his interest reignited suddenly.

'I'm suggesting, sir, that whatever was going on at Ambrose House stinks. But worse than that, I suspect we may be dealing with a high-level cover-up. One which might even involve offi-cers who are still working on this force.'

EIGHT

Hollie looked out of the window on the drive over to meet Gordon Carrick's widow, the houses flashing by, but took in none of it.

'Is everything all right, boss?' Jenni asked. 'You've been miles away since we left HQ.'

Hollie turned to her young colleague and apologised. She wasn't quite ready yet to share details of her personal involvement with her friend: dredging everything up with Osmond had shaken her badly and she needed time to gather herself and focus on Carrick's murder. Osmond's threat was weighing on her mind; would the brass let her stay on the case? Memories from 1999 were beginning to cluster like grey clouds warning of a forthcoming storm.

The Carricks lived just outside Hull, in West Ella, part of the city's 'golden mile' for property. The redbrick house was set in mature grounds. The garden was well manicured, and the window frames and front door so recently painted that the gloss finish could still be smelled as they drew up at the doorstep. Hollie recognised DC Fran Hayes's car parked out on the spacious driveway. It reminded Hollie that she needed to chase up her resident's parking pass for her new rented place, as the street parking was so tight there.

Hollie was pleased the Family Liaison Officer had paved the way for her, as it was often easier to get some sense out of relatives once they'd had some time to adjust to the bad news.

Looking at the murder victim's home, there was no way on earth she and Léon could ever afford a place like this, even with two salaries. So Superintendent Gordon Carrick and his wife must have had some money sloshing around between them.

Hollie felt her face flushing slightly as she thought of her estranged husband Léon back in Lancaster, caring day-to-day for their two youngest kids. Noah and Lily were constantly on her mind, particularly with her eldest daughter Izzy now staying with her in Hull after concluding her world travels. She felt a sharp sting in her chest at the absence of Noah and Lily, but also shock and a little embarrassment at Léon's exclusion from those thoughts. Was she beginning to get used to him not being around?

They'd decided between them to let the youngest children stay in Lancaster with Léon after her job move to Hull, but she was beginning to envision a future life with them, perhaps choosing to live with her in Hull when they grew older. It would certainly cut down on the travel up and down the country, struggling to keep alive those close connections with the children.

Hollie shook her head slightly, shrugging it off.

'Ready, Jenni?' She turned to her colleague, her voice lowered. 'Let's see what his wife – his widow – has to say for herself. Let's hope DC Hayes has been given full kitchen access, I'm dying for a cuppa.'

Fran Hayes opened the door before they knocked, forewarned of their presence by the sound of their feet crunching on the gravel drive.

'Good morning, DC Hayes,' Hollie began, 'how is she?'

'You know the older generation; she's made of stern stuff. Come on in, she's in the lounge.'

The house was as beautiful as its exterior suggested. The furniture was old-fashioned, but the decor modern and tasteful, creating an incongruous mix of styles. It was as if they couldn't quite decide what look they were going for. Everything was in its place, with only an old tan leather briefcase tucked by a Welsh dresser interrupting the furnishing tranquillity. It was battered and well-used. Hollie assumed it belonged to Gordon Carrick.

'Good morning, Mrs Carrick, I'm very sorry for your loss,' Hollie said, walking over to shake her hand. She was younger than she'd expected and much more composed.

Jenni expressed her condolences, and the two officers took the smaller sofa, which was at right angles to the larger sofa, on which Mrs Carrick was sitting. Fran took the hot drinks orders. You could never drink enough tea at times of bereavement. Jenni prepared her phone to record their interview and took out her notebook, and Hollie made the formal introductions.

'May I call you Jane, Mrs Carrick?'

'Of course, officer.'

Her voice was steady and calm; she did not come over as a widow in mourning. Though they'd only discovered the body a couple of hours ago, and she might still be in shock. Hollie examined her face, looking for the giveaway signs. Her eyes were not red, there were no dried tear streaks down her cheeks, and she'd been in the middle of reading a *Home and Garden* magazine when they arrived.

'I'm sorry to have to come and fire all these questions at you so soon after the loss of your husband—'

'I know the drill, DI Turner.' Jane Carrick's voice was controlled and firm. 'I lived with it for thirty years of our married life. You don't have to stand upon ceremony with me. Feel free to ask any questions that you like.'

That was a good start. This woman was of the down-to-business variety. That made life a lot easier. But it didn't quite ring true. Had they been there to question her about vandalised property or a stolen car, that would all have been very well. But a murdered husband?

The hot drinks arrived. Hollie waited until Fran had distributed them on the tasteful place mats, then nodded to Jenni to let her know she was starting the interview.

'What year did your husband retire from the police?'

'In 2004. After all the scandal around that time, he was ready to go.'

Hollie knew she was referring to the allegations about the children's home. She'd get to that, but she wanted to warm Jane Carrick up first, as it would be a delicate topic to navigate.

'Are you aware of anybody who might have held a grudge against your husband?' she continued. 'Perhaps somebody from an old case, who wanted to get even?'

For the first time since they'd spoken, there was a short delay in her reply.

'I'm not aware of anything specific, detective. But you know what a police officer's life is like. Spouses don't know the half of it. Gordon never told me what went on at work. Besides, he's been out of it for two decades now, he spends – he spent – his life on the golf course and pottering around the garden. We live a quiet life here. There's nobody I can think of who might harm him.'

'What were his movements yesterday?' Jenni asked.

'I have been through this with DC Hayes already,' she replied, a momentary glimpse of impatience flashing in her eyes. She looked at Jenni and Hollie, then carried on anyway. She knew the drill all right, and it didn't look like she was going to resist it.

'Well, it started with a round of golf. It always started with a round of bloody golf—'

The three officers exchanged glances. He wasn't cold in the morgue yet and she was speaking about him in the way that she might at an all-female gathering, letting off steam at a husband's foibles.

'He had lunch at the club with his friends. And by lunch, I mean a long lunch. He came back to the house at about four o'clock then headed out to some meeting or other in the evening.'

'You don't know what it was?' Jenni checked.

'I assume it was his Youth Empowerment Syndicate, but I didn't ask.'

'Youth Empowerment Syndicate?' Hollie queried.

'It's like the Round Table, I suppose, a bunch of the great and the good doing their bit to help the needy kids in the city. My husband and I lead very different social lives – I'm more gardening and days out with friends.'

Hollie nodded.

'What time did he return last night?' she wondered.

'He didn't,' Jane replied, 'though I didn't know that until this morning. We sleep in separate rooms.'

She caught the look on Jenni's face. Hollie had clocked it, too, but kept her face expressionless.

'Yes, officers, we slept in separate rooms. You'll probably do the same when you're our age. Gordon snored badly and kept visiting the bathroom at night. We started with separate beds, then graduated to separate rooms. We all get there eventually when the inevitable prostate problems kick off.'

Hollie's mind shot back to Léon. Is that how they would have ended up if they'd made it that far? She felt a pang of regret; they'd never find out now. It seemed an unusual conversation to be having, bearing in mind this woman had just lost her husband.

'I hope you don't mind me saying,' Hollie picked up, 'but

you and your husband seemed a little' – Hollie chose her words carefully – 'distant. Remote, even.'

The reply was stern and no-nonsense. 'You're right, detective. We were two different people, living together in the same big house. Our grown-up children both live abroad, so it's just us now.'

Hollie and Jenni stared at her intently, saying nothing.

Jane continued speaking, as if she felt obliged to fill in some of the blanks. 'To be perfectly frank with you, it's been that way ever since the shit storm that engulfed us when that bloody reporter published the newspaper article about Ambrose House. Excuse my blunt language, officers, but that fucked up everything for my family. Ever since that vile stench entered our house, things have never been quite the same between the four of us.'

NINE

'How exactly did it mess up your life?' Hollie asked Jane, studying her face for any giveaway signs. 'I can imagine it must have been traumatic at the time.'

'Gordon had little to do with Ambrose House,' Jane continued, her voice remote and detached. The words were coming from her mouth, but they didn't seem anchored to her emotions. 'I can't imagine why that awful journalist ever made those terrible allegations.'

'They were dismissed, though, weren't they?' Jenni interjected.

'Yes, where do you think this house came from? Defamation pays well, officer, especially when a national newspaper makes unfounded allegations against a senior officer with an unblemished career.'

Jane looked around, as if surveying the large living room. 'All this didn't come from a police superintendent's salary, that's for sure.'

Her tone was almost derisory, not the fond memories of a grieving widow. She was tense and seemed bitter.

'Why was your husband awarded the libel damages?' Hollie

pushed her, unable to reconcile what had just happened to this woman's husband and her cold, functional reaction to it.

'That journalist fellow – Ray McGregor – suggested in his newspaper coverage that there was some paedophile ring attached to the home. It was unproven, of course. It was just because Gordon happened to play golf with Kenneth Digby—' She cut herself short, looking out of the window before finishing the sentence. This was matter of fact for her, well-trodden ground, it seemed.

'Kenneth Digby?' Jenni and Hollie both spoke at the same time, unable to hide their immediate interest in this new name. Jane Carrick exhaled.

'He was a social worker at Ambrose House at the time. I think he and Gordon had met over some incident involving one of the youths at the home. It was just some regular policing job, but the two men hit it off and they used to socialise together.'

'Where is Kenneth Digby now?' Jenni asked.

'Don't you know?'

Jane Carrick gave them a look like they ought to have understood what she was talking about. Seeing they were none the wiser, she continued, 'Kenneth Digby died three months ago.'

Hollie's mouth opened slightly, her mind going directly into overdrive.

'Of what?' she checked.

'Of an insulin overdose, apparently. He had type one diabetes. Suspected suicide. How grim is that?'

Hollie sensed Jenni tensing at her side. She was sharp and alert now. There was seldom smoke without fire when it came to policing.

'Can you overdose on insulin?' Hollie asked.

'Oh yes, it can lead to hypos – hypoglycaemia – and disori-entation, and certainly to death in some cases—'

'You seem very knowledgeable on the matter,' Jenni interrupted. 'Almost textbook.'

Jane picked up on the stares of the three police officers in her living room.

'That's because I'm a doctor – was, a doctor,' Jane replied. 'I work as a locum these days, just to keep my hand in.'

'Kenneth Digby was your patient?'

Hollie was short, sharp and matter of fact, but she wanted to know.

'Oh, no – er – no—'

Hollie exchanged a glance with Jenni. It was the first time they'd caught Jane Carrick on the back foot. That sounded alarm bells in Hollie's mind.

'You don't seem sure?'

'No, yes, I am sure, I just wasn't expecting the question. No, I never treated Kenneth Digby as a patient,' she asserted, quickly regaining her composure.

That was sure as hell getting checked out back at HQ.

'Did you treat him informally, in any other capacity?' Hollie cut in, getting a strong feeling that Jane Carrick was playing with words here.

'I perhaps had a few informal health-related conversations in passing. I didn't care for the man. But he was not on my patient list—'

'Yet you're a locum,' Hollie continued to push the issue. 'You might have encountered him while standing in at another practice.'

'I might have,' Jane corrected herself, before hesitating. Hollie could see her mind whirring. 'But I didn't.'

'What more do you know about the circumstances of Digby's death?' Hollie picked up after waiting to see if Jane might offer anything further. 'Was he in financial trouble when he died?'

'He was living in some shitty bedsit, according to Gordon.'

'They were still friends?' Jenni asked. 'After all those years and the discomfort of an inquiry.'

Hollie was pleased to see her younger colleague displaying her teeth. It would serve her well in this job.

'Yes, they stayed in touch. Although the allegations at Ambrose House were unfounded, Digby lost his job in the inevitable rebranding that followed the scandal. The break-up with his wife was much more recent, though; his marriage survived the newspaper report.'

'Did Gordon attend his funeral?' Hollie pushed, frantically working to see the connection. This situation was giving off a foul odour.

'He did,' Jane replied, clearly aware that the detectives had caught a scent. 'And it's a good job he went.'

'Why?'

'It was a sparse affair. Just his golfing buddies and a few others attended, apparently.'

'Did Kenneth Digby's wife go?' Jenni interjected.

'No, neither his wife nor his son. Imagine that.'

Jane Carrick was so cold. For a doctor, it didn't say a lot about her bedside manner.

They sat in silence for what seemed like a considerable time. Hollie was churning it all over in her mind. Something didn't add up with this woman. What was she hiding?

'What's Digby's family set-up?' Jenni asked, taking up the slack.

'His wife is Melanie, their son is William—'

'How old is William?' Jenni checked.

'Early forties, I suppose. He's divorced, so is back living with Melanie. He's a nice chap. I train first aiders occasionally, and he was on one of my courses some years ago. He's a Hull Health Responder—'

'What's that?' Jenni asked. Hollie had never heard of them either.

'They're like St John Ambulance, you know the sort of thing. First Aiders, basically.'

'Tell me more about Melanie,' Hollie picked up. 'What's your relationship with her?'

Jane was quick to reply, certain of her answer.

'We got to know each other through our husbands. We hit it off and, I suppose, got to know each other better through the inquiry. We talked a lot about it back then—'

She stared out of the window as if remembering something in her past.

'One thing led to another and once the inquiry was over, we kept seeing each other socially. Our backgrounds are quite different, but we enjoy each other's company.'

'How are your backgrounds different?' Jenni wondered.

Jane laughed.

'Melanie was very different from me when she was younger, a bit of a rebel by all accounts. She brings out the best in me, I think. Our lives are very different. She doesn't work now, due to ill health, but she was a cleaner when she was working.'

'Does... did your husband have an office space that we might have a look around?' Hollie asked, finding little of interest from Jane's replies.

'His electronics have been taken away already,' Fran updated her. 'We were planning to look through some of the personal paperwork together, later.'

Hollie knew the most likely source of information would come from his phone or his computer, but that usually took a little while to access and sift through. She lived in hope of a single damning text or email that might neatly sew up the case and save it from becoming protracted.

'May we take a look around the office, Jane? It would help me to get a sense of Gordon as a person. Sometimes I spot something which might be useful.'

'Do you want to show her where it is, Fran?'

That was good to hear, DC Hayes was on first-name terms with her already. Trust was essential in the relationships a FLO had to form, often swiftly and in times of great duress. Jane Carrick was an interesting woman. She didn't seem to be trying to hide anything, yet they felt no further forward for having spoken to her.

Fran stood up and led the way. Jenni and Hollie followed. Gordon Carrick's office was at the rear of the property, overlooking the back garden which was packed with shrubs and bedding plants. The Carricks' garden wouldn't have looked out of place on the front page of *House Beautiful* magazine.

'Just put in a call to Amber, would you, Jenni?' Hollie asked when they were out of earshot. 'I'd like to call in on Melanie Digby if we can. The timing of her husband's death seems... unusual. I want to be certain in my mind that the two deaths are not connected. And let's run some background checks on Mrs Carrick. If Digby died of an overdose, that smells fishy to me.'

Jenni took out her phone and got onto it straight away.

Hollie wanted to get as close as she could to Digby, even if he was dead.

'What do you make of her?' Fran whispered once she'd seen them inside and pulled the door to. 'She's a bit of a cold fish for a grieving widow, wouldn't you say?'

'Is she still in shock?' Hollie replied.

Fran shrugged. 'Maybe. There doesn't seem to have been any warmth between them. Maybe that's normal when you've been married for forty years. I wouldn't know. I've only been living with my bloke for nine months, so the sheen is still in the relationship. We even smile at each other when we wake up. Perhaps things get a bit tarnished after all that time.'

Hollie felt suddenly uncomfortable, reflecting on how she and Léon had grown apart. Maybe that's where they'd have been heading if Veronique hadn't arrived on the scene to shake things up. She didn't want to think about it.

'There's no suggestion she did it, is there?' Jenni checked, finishing her call. 'I mean, there's no way, surely?'

'No, I'm not suggesting that,' Fran Hayes answered, 'but I do wonder if the allegations about the children's home took their toll on them, despite Carrick being cleared. That would put a relationship under immense strain, I'd have thought.'

'She has a medical background,' Hollie interjected. 'I'd like to know more about Digby's death. Was it suspicious, for instance? We need to do some digging around her locum work. I'm really not sure about Jane Carrick yet.'

Hollie and Jenni started to walk around the room, examining the bookshelves, pulling out the drawers and looking at photographs. It was unusual that there were no images of Carrick's wife or family. She'd seen them around the rest of the house, but the framed pictures in this study were related to career highlights and male friendship groups, which she assumed were built around golfing activities.

There was one colour photograph which caused her to pause. It showed four men, three of them about the same age, one of them much younger. The fashions were dated, so it looked like the nineties from the gaudy ties that three of them were wearing. The clips at the top of the shirt collars also gave it away.

Hollie's body suddenly tensed, and she gasped to catch her breath. Her legs felt like they might give way and she reached out to steady herself on a bookshelf. Her heart thumped heavily in her chest and a light-headed sensation unsteadied her further. She'd seen one of these men before. With his distinctive red hair and eyebrow piercing, there was no doubt in her mind that this was the man her friend Moira had given chase to all those years ago at Hull Fair. The scrappy tattoos on his hands confirmed it.

'Are you all right, boss?' Jenni asked, seeing her obvious distress. She and Fran walked over, both offering steadying hands.

Hollie would have to tell them soon. The quicker her connection with the case was made known to the team, the better. She wished Osmond would get a move on clearing it with the brass.

She paused for a few moments, brushing it off with her colleagues, explaining it away as not having enough breakfast that morning. She could see from their faces that they knew it was bullshit.

Feeling stronger, her heart still protesting fiercely, she walked back to the image to study it further. The man's face sent a chill through her, and she concealed a shudder.

One of the men wore a T-shirt on which a logo was printed, and a cap, and his presence alongside the two professionals felt incongruous. He didn't appear to be one of them, even though he was in the same photo.

Jenni's phone rang and after a short conversation, she turned to Hollie.

'Melanie Digby's on. If we go there straight after this, we'll catch her in.'

'Good old Amber, she never hangs around,' Hollie replied, feeling nervous at the prospect now. Every detective nerve in her body was tingling.

Jane Carrick joined them in the office. Was she checking up on them?

'May we take this photograph out of its frame to make a copy?' Hollie asked, her voice much less steady than she would have liked. 'I'm interested in who these men are.'

'By all means,' Jane replied.

'Who's this chap with the red hair?' Hollie asked urgently.

Jane sighed. 'Well, that's Kenneth Digby.'

Hollie felt like the walls of the room were collapsing in on her. This was linked with Moira's case, there was no way she could convince herself otherwise now. This was no coincidence.

Kenneth Digby. He's the man Moira followed into the heart of the fair that night. And now he's dead, three months before Gordon Carrick. This has to be connected.

Hollie gave herself a moment before speaking again. She could almost feel the turmoil of emotions coursing through her veins, a river undammed after years of suppression. Sensing that she was distracted, Jenni picked up.

'So, we know Kenneth Digby died recently. What about these other two men?'

'That's Orsen Scott,' Jane replied, pointing to an officious looking man who can't have been much more than five foot in height. 'He was a local magistrate. I think he still does the occasional stint, but he's reached retirement age now.'

'And they're all golfing friends?' Jenni checked. 'Is that why they're photographed together?'

Hollie was gripped by fear but equally charged by the possibility that she might finally get an answer to the question that had haunted her since the night of her best friend's disappearance.

'Yes, it's a friendship group photo,' Jane continued, oblivious to Hollie's struggle. 'I guess in one way or another, they all came into contact with each other through the course of their work... with the exception of this fellow.'

She was pointing to an overweight man who was wearing the brightly coloured T-shirt and a baseball cap turned backwards. Hollie couldn't recall a time when she'd seen such a collection of mismatched men in a single photograph.

'This man joined them briefly but didn't stick around. I don't think Gordon has him in any of the other photographs.'

'Who is that?' Hollie asked. Children like the ones at

Ambrose House – youngsters like Moira – seemed easy targets for powerful men seeking... what exactly?

'That's Philip Mortimer, he was an unusual and temporary addition to the group, I always felt.'

'Go on,' Hollie encouraged her, anxious to hear where this was heading.

'He runs a charity called Splendid Days. He's a local man with a minibus who works with children's charities to take Hull kids out for special days—'

'What kind of charities?' Jenni asked.

'Kids with terminal illnesses, youngsters who have experienced trauma, that sort of thing.'

'How about children's homes?' Hollie checked.

'Yes, that's his bread and butter, I'd say. I always thought Philip Mortimer was a strange addition to the golfing group, but there it is – he was briefly one of Gordon's little gang of golfing bores.'

The shock of seeing Digby's face was superseded by the powerful urges of the detective to find answers. Hollie took in a deep breath to be certain she'd calmed herself now.

'Okay, this has been extremely useful, Mrs Carrick,' she said, taking the framed photo off the wall. 'Once again, my deepest condolences on the death of your husband, we'll be doing everything we can to get justice for you. If you think of anything in the meantime, please don't hesitate to speak to DC Hayes.'

Hollie walked towards the office door and Jenni followed her lead, back downstairs.

DC Hayes accompanied them to the front door after they'd concluded matters with Jane Carrick.

'Keep on to her about those men, will you, DC Hayes? I want to know if she shares any more information about them or if one of them contacts her. They'll all be getting house visits. I'll get DS Anderson onto it straight away. I want to speak to this journalist, too; I've a strong feeling he'll help us piece this together.'

Hollie and Jenni headed back to the car and climbed inside. As Hollie reached over to clip in her seatbelt, her phone vibrated in her pocket. She answered the call as Jenni started the car.

'It's Amber,' Amber began, her voice urgent. 'We got a rush through on the blood that Harry found on the wheelie bin.'

They must have pulled out all the stops to get that done so fast. The brass were probably taking heat because the murder had taken place at such a newsworthy and public location.

'And?' Hollie asked, praying it would be Carrick's.

'It's Carrick's blood, all right,' Amber said. 'That's how his body was moved through the fairground site without anybody giving a second glance.'

'This is excellent work—' Hollie started.

'It gets better, boss. We've got a clear set of prints on the bin. In fact, we couldn't have asked for a better set of prints.'

TEN

As Peter Andre's 'Flava' faded out and the *Top of the Pops* theme tune signalled the end of that week's show, Simon pressed the volume button on the remote control and turned to Moira.

'I reckon we're the only ones in here with good music taste.' He smiled. 'Nobody else bothers to watch *TOTP* these days.'

'Billy will be waiting for us outside,' Moira replied, fidgeting in her seat. 'We'd best get a move on.'

The communal TV room was empty except for Marvin, who read incessantly, yet never spoke to anyone. He was a regular visitor to Hull's psychological support team, and he hadn't had a whiff of fostering interest since he'd arrived at Ambrose House. Moira tried to reach out to him on several occasions, but he'd just flinch and avert his eyes.

'Okay, we're sneaking out the back way still, right?' Simon checked, looking around furtively. 'Digby is on duty from ten o'clock. We need to have our heads down before then.'

Moira knew exactly what that meant from the conversations of the older teenagers. Cross Digby and your life would be hell.

As Moira stood up to get out of her chair, Simon pulled out

a small, wrapped gift which he'd been concealing under his jumper.

'Happy birthday, by the way.' He grinned. 'What is it they say, "Sweet Sixteen" or something like that?'

Moira's eyes widened and she reached over to give Simon a hug.

'Oh, I thought you'd forgotten.' She grinned. 'All I got from the Ambrose House staff was a shitty card with "Sixteen Today" plastered on the front in pink lettering. It was faded where it had been sitting in the sunlight. I reckon they bought it last minute from the corner shop.'

She looked down at the gift he'd just handed her like it was rare treasure, turning it around in her hands, as if that was already enough without having to unwrap it.

'Open it then,' Simon urged.

Moira tore open the paper. It was Alanis Morissette's *Jagged Little Pill* CD. She let out a whoop of delight, and Marvin stood up angrily in his chair, grumpily exiting the shared TV room.

She glanced over, annoyed with herself that she'd frightened him off. Marvin didn't seem to like unexpected, sudden noises, and they'd already lowered the volume of the TV, so it didn't frighten him off.

A tear formed in her eye. It felt like Simon was the only friend she had in the world apart from Billy. They weren't supposed to know Billy, but he'd come into work with his dad one weekend and they'd all hit it off immediately. Billy wasn't supposed to fraternise with the Ambrose House kids, but when had a paternal ban ever stopped a bunch of teenagers?

'I'll hide this behind the TV and pick it up when we get back,' she whispered to Simon, conspiratorially, hugging him before concealing the brand-new CD.

'You shouldn't have spent your money on me,' Moira said, giving Simon a scolding look. His face reddened. She knew he fancied her, but she wasn't ready to invest her emotions in anybody just yet; not with her mum's ongoing problems, it was just too much.

With the CD hidden, Simon and Moira checked their route was clear, then sneaked through the hallway of Ambrose House and out the back door, which was always open at that time of the evening while the cleaning staff interspersed vacuuming and scrubbing with cigarette breaks.

They darted over the fence at the side towards where Billy was parked with his battered Fiat Panda. He was parked up out of view of the home, and the stifled thud of his tinny car radio could be heard from across the road.

His eyes lit up the moment he spotted Moira, and she was certain she detected a small grimace when he saw that Simon was trailing just behind her.

'We've got to be back by half past nine at the latest,' came Simon's stern warning. 'They'll make sure we're all in our rooms just before ten o'clock.'

'That gives us plenty of time for a bit of fun,' came Billy's mischievous reply. He waited until they were buckled in, switched on the car engine, then revved it up so that dark grey fumes belched out of the exhaust, appearing like a dense mist under the streetlight. 'Wait till you see what I've got planned.'

'I told you we needed to be back earlier,' Simon scolded, skittish and anxious.

'Did you have fun?' Billy replied, looking at Moira and disregarding Simon in the back seat.

'It was great, thank you.' Moira smiled. 'The perfect birthday treat. Thank you. Both of you.'

She liked Billy. Every time she saw him, she got a fluttering feeling in her stomach. He glanced at Simon to see if he was looking and, for just a moment, Moira thought he was going to kiss her. At seventeen years of age, Billy seemed older and wiser, even though there was only a year's difference.

There was a sudden, abrupt thump on the window at Moira's side and she jumped up in her seat, alarmed by the aggressiveness of it. Her door was flung open, and a tattooed hand reached in to pull her out.

Simon was in a state of high panic, clearly several steps ahead of her in realising what was going on.

'Get out the fucking car, you two, and go and wait in my office,' came Digby's cursing voice. His red hair was illuminated by the streetlight, which glinted in his eyebrow piercing.

'It was my fault,' Simon apologised. 'I made Moira do it, she didn't want to come—'

'That's not what Marvin said,' Digby cursed.

Billy looked like a rabbit caught in car headlights.

'They made me do it, Dad, I told them you'd be angry—'

Digby had now hauled Moira out of the car and was leaning across her vacated seat, ranting at his son. He reached out and struck Billy across the face; Moira heard the blow from outside the vehicle.

She was crying now, her birthday adventure fast turning into a nightmare.

Billy began to sob loudly, blaming Simon, Moira and anybody else he could think of for his transgression.

'Fuck off back home and if I see you sniffing round here again, I'll take this bloody car to the scrap heap and crush it myself.'

Digby slammed the passenger door shut with such force that Moira thought it might fall off.

She and Simon were standing on the pavement; Simon was shaking, almost uncontrollably, tears flowing from his eyes and in a state of high distress.

A sudden panic gripped Moira as she heard his desperate pleas to Digby.

'It was my fault, Mr Digby, please, leave Moira out of this, punish me, I'm to blame—'

Digby watched his son driving off in the rusting Fiat Panda then slowly turned to face the two of them.

'You're sixteen today, aren't you, Moira?'

She gave a small nod, fearful of crossing him.

'That shit-brained son of mine won't want to touch you again after tonight. Get your arses back to my office – I'll show you what happens when you try to take the piss at Ambrose House.'

ELEVEN

'We seem to have so much information already, boss,' Jenni remarked as they crossed the city to Melanie Digby's house. 'We've got a victim ID, fingerprints, a murder weapon, a strong motive. It's stacking up well.'

Yes, but we're still no further forward with an ID on the killer.

Hollie had just called into the office to update the team. The mallet had been partly processed but was still awaiting blood analysis to compare it with the sample taken from the bin. That seemed like a formality to her now, but it was still a vital element in piecing together the chain of events. They'd lifted a clear print off the wooden handle and were comparing this with what had been found on the wheelie bin that Harry had located.

Orsen Scott and Philip Mortimer were top of the list for home visits, and Kenneth Digby was getting the full background research treatment. Suicide seemed too convenient, given Carrick's murder. The cesspit was already beginning to swirl with names.

'You should start calling me by my first name,' Hollie

replied, changing the subject. 'I think we know each other well enough now, don't you? After all, we've starred in a viral video together. It's not many detectives who get filmed doing the karaoke on a night out in Hull.'

They shared a laugh. It hadn't felt funny at the time, in the heat of an investigation and getting called out for letting their hair down on a night out. Their office colleagues still teased them about their karaoke performance, and it prompted a shameful regret in Hollie whenever she mentioned it.

'It feels a bit wrong to use first names, boss, but I'll do my best.'

Hollie studied her colleague as she drove. There was almost no evidence now of the injuries she'd sustained previously. She thought she'd lost her friend when she was struck by the motorcycle. But Jenni was sharp and on the ball again, her scars hidden by her now regrown hair, and it was great to have her back as a full-functioning member of the Murder Investigation Team. Her colleague's ability to connect with victims was like nothing she'd ever seen in a young detective before, and she was pleased to be able to return her to a full workload.

'And try to encourage DC Gordon – Harry – to do the same, will you?' Hollie continued. 'I'm convinced he's still frightened of me; he treats me like I'm his school headteacher.'

Jenni said nothing, concentrating on the road.

'This is us,' she said after a couple of minutes, pulling up in front of a good-sized terraced house on a tree-lined street. It faced a park, separated only by a low fence.

'This is pleasant,' Hollie remarked, surveying the house with the eyes of a woman who hoped to be buying her own place soon. An adjacent property was up for sale, and she took a photo to remind herself to check out the price on Rightmove.

'This is Hymers Avenue, boss. I don't know if it's of any significance, but it's just across West Park to the Hull Fair.'

Hollie hadn't clocked that detail; she was still piecing

together the jigsaw puzzle of Hull's geography. As a student she'd walked or used the bus; it was a different city by car.

'That's interesting,' she observed, taking her phone out to check her maps app. 'So it's not far from this house to the place where Carrick's body was found?'

'If you cross the park, it's no distance, as the crow flies.' Jenni leaned over and pointed it out on the map. 'West Park has the railway line as one boundary and the MKM Stadium as another, but it's right next to the Hull Fair site if you look at it on a map.'

Perhaps it wasn't such a physical feat to have placed Carrick's body in the ghost train. Maybe he'd even been walking in the area at the time he was attacked. Was he making a house call on Melanie? None of it was impossible.

'Let's see what Kenneth Digby's wife has to say for herself. I'm interested to see what she knew about the allegations at Ambrose House...' She lowered her voice as they reached the front door.

Melanie Digby was waiting for them, answering the door before Hollie had had a chance to knock a second time.

Melanie Digby was a woman who looked like she'd endured a few knocks in life. Her face was hard, her hair cut short with purple dyed streaks, but she was welcoming enough, and Hollie didn't pick up on any hostility. Melanie's breathing was laboured, like she was struggling with asthma or something similar. It appeared to be causing her some discomfort.

'Thank you so much for seeing us at such short notice,' Hollie began.

'I knew you'd be calling the moment I heard the news this morning,' she replied through shallow breaths, with no hint of resentment in her voice. 'So, that's Gordon dead now then.'

She showed them into the living room, and they sat down on the sofa opposite her armchair. The house had the feel of being furnished from a second-hand shop, nothing seemed new.

Who was Hollie to judge? She'd just done exactly that in her new rented place. Here, clothes were drying on a clothes rack which had been placed in front of the radiator. A pair of burgundy overalls was draped over the radiator itself; she assumed someone in the house was a mechanic or in some sort of service industry, most likely her son.

Hollie glanced out of the window. As if placed there as a prop, a green wheelie bin was sitting outside in the small back garden, a mess of pruned shrubs sticking out of the top of it.

Her eye caught a small, framed photo among several other family shots. It was of Kenneth and Melanie, when they were younger. Kenneth had the red hair and piercing that she remembered; Melanie had a Mohican hairstyle which was coloured bright blue. Melanie noticed Hollie looking.

'That's the only photo I display of Kenny now. Happier days, I suppose. We were in our early twenties back then; punk was our thing. The hair got more respectable as our costs of living increased. Kenny got away with his; he was considered a bit edgy as a social worker.'

'Do you mind?' Hollie asked, leaning over to take a copy on her phone.

'Be my guest.'

Jenni activated the recording device that was sitting at the side of the table and explained what was going on.

'Just to emphasise, this is just an informal chat, you're not under arrest and you're free to end it at any time.'

Melanie had a hot drink resting on the arm of her chair already, so Hollie gave up all hope of refreshments. Melanie nodded and sat expectantly, waiting for the questions to start.

'So, firstly, my condolences on the recent death of your husband—' Hollie began, starting softly to warm her up.

'Good riddance to bad rubbish.'

The words were wheezed out rather than spoken. Hollie looked around for signs of cigarettes but saw none.

It looked like they were heading for Old Kent Road without passing Go. Jenni shuffled on the sofa, and Hollie stared at Melanie Digby, startled by the severity of her opening remark.

'Had you and your husband split up at the time of his death?' Hollie asked, attempting to draw her out. There was no point treading gently now. 'I mean, you were in love once upon a time...' she said, turning to look at the photograph on the wall.

'Yes. I can't say I shed many tears when they discovered him in that bedsit. He'd shat the bed when they found him. In life as in death, that's what I say.'

'That seems a cold thing to say about the man who you were married to for... how long?' Jennie added.

'We hadn't divorced at the time of his death. It was in the solicitor's in-tray at the time.'

It sounded like her lungs were rattling in her chest.

'Do you have children together?' Hollie checked. She knew the answer already, but it was one of her cross-referenced questions, useful for flushing out liars. This woman was intriguing her. So far, they had two widows and no tears.

'Yes, William. He lives here with me most of the time now, after his divorce.'

That confirmed what Jane Carrick had told them.

'Are you and William close?' Hollie added, keen to get a sense of the family dynamic. This was the second wife who didn't seem too troubled that her husband was dead.

'Yes, we've become closer since Kenny died.'

Hollie noted the use of Kenny. She was still using the more affectionate version of his name.

'Is there any reason for that?' Jenni wondered.

'Yes,' she answered sarcastically, 'when your son's father dies, it tends to do that. It's what a mother does.'

Hollie's mind flashed to Noah and Lily, and she wondered what they were doing at that moment, two hundred miles away in Lancaster. *It's what a mother does.* Those words landed hard, and she felt a sharp pang of guilt over her domestic situation. She'd call them if she got time to catch breath. At least their chit-chat over the Discord app kept her connected in some small way.

She looked into Melanie Digby's eyes. They were cold and angry. Did she know what her husband was up to?

'Was your husband the sort of man who'd take an overdose?' Hollie wondered. 'Had your husband ever tried to take his life before? Was there any chance he used too much insulin in error?'

'No,' Melanie replied, 'Kenny was one of life's cockroaches. I expected his heart to give out before we got old, but it seems he finished himself off instead.'

'Are you poorly, Melanie?' Jenni asked gently. 'I notice you seem to be struggling with your breathing.'

Hollie thought that might make her defensive, but she was happy to discuss the cause of her respiratory issues.

'It's emphysema and chronic bronchitis,' she explained. 'Too many ciggies in my punk rock years. It all catches up with you in the end. I'm waiting for the pharmacy to get my prescription out to me. They take forever these days and I'm all but out. I'm in some discomfort, to be honest.'

'Would you rather we did this another time?' Jenni offered.

'No, carry on. It takes my mind off it, if nothing else,' Melanie answered.

Hollie didn't know much about emphysema, but she knew enough to know that it was a life-restricting illness. There was no way Melanie Digby had moved that body across the fairground, despite her home's proximity to the murder location.

'I'm so sorry to hear that,' she sympathised, then steered Melanie straight back to business. 'So where were you on the night of Kenneth's death?'

'I was out at the bingo in the city centre,' she replied. It sounded rehearsed. 'It's something I can do to get out of the house,' she added.

'Is there anybody who can confirm that?' Hollie picked up.

'Yes, of course. I was with Jane Carrick and Jasmine Scott that night—'

'At the bingo. Jane Carrick doesn't strike me as the bingo type.'

She hadn't met Jasmine Scott yet, but also suspected a magistrate's wife wouldn't be the bingo type either.

'And what is the bingo type?' she challenged Hollie.

That was a fair cop and Hollie knew better than to dig a hole for herself.

'And Mrs Carrick and Mrs Scott will confirm this?' Jenni attempted to save her.

'Of course they will. Check the CCTV if they have it. I lost twenty pounds on bingo cards that night and won nothing. It'll be easy enough to confirm.'

Hollie looked at Jenni, but she'd already made a note in her pad.

'Which bingo hall?' Jenni asked.

'The Mecca on Clough Road,' came Melanie's confident reply.

'Do you know Jane Carrick and Jasmine Scott well? Would you describe yourselves as golfing widows?'

Melanie let out a weary laugh and shook her head, her breathing increasingly laboured. There were many times in Hollie's career when she might have sought relief in smoking. She was so pleased now that she'd never succumbed.

'We were all golfing widows, and it drew us together many years ago. When your husbands socialise like that, it tends to have a knock-on effect. I get on well with Jane and Jasmine. We have lots in common. Particularly after our husbands were hauled over the coals in the inquiry.'

Were these women colluding to kill the men? It all seemed a bit convenient, giving each other an alibi.

'Why did you and Kenneth separate?' Jenni changed the subject. It was a fair question; she was right to ask it.

Melanie sighed, then chose her words carefully.

'We just grew apart over the years. William was a difficult teenager, and he and Kenny didn't see eye to eye. We weren't at each other's throats or anything like that. I think the strain of the inquiry just caught up with us in the end...'

Hollie sensed she was holding something back, but it was Melanie's breathing that was making her pause. As if to illustrate her point, she exhaled a long, rattling wheeze.

'Did you ever discuss what had gone on at Ambrose House?' Hollie asked.

For the second time, she saw that cold, hard look in Melanie's eyes.

'You bet we did. We compared notes. They'd all given evidence at the inquiry. It was a terrible, tense time for everybody who was involved.'

'Particularly the children at the home.' Hollie had decided to lob in a grenade to see if she could raise some emotion from this woman. It did the job.

'There's not a day goes by when I don't shed a tear for those poor children,' Melanie lashed out at her, her lip trembling, her breathing becoming more strained. 'I only found out what that monster had been up to after he'd died.'

Hollie and Jenni exchanged glances again. It was the visual equivalent of a WTF.

'What had he been up to?' Hollie picked up.

'It makes me sick to say it. Those poor children. All those years. He swore to me nothing was going on at that home. And to think I shared his bed for so many years after the inquiry. The disgusting bastard.'

'Can you tell us what you believe your husband was doing?'

Hollie encouraged her. 'I understand this may be difficult for you, but it's important.'

Melanie took a long, slow breath like it was a struggle to even think about it.

'Him and Carrick, they were both in on it. And that tosser, Orsen Scott. The filthy perverts, they'd golf in the daytime and abuse children whenever the fancy took them.'

'How do you know this?' Jenni challenged her. 'Do you have any evidence?'

'You know about the inquiry already?' she checked.

Both Hollie and Jenni nodded. Hollie was pleased she'd got an early call in to check up on Orsen Scott.

'We lost our family home after that. We had to take a council property on the Gipsyville estate to pay his legal fees. And to think I believed every word he said at the time. I had to take cleaning jobs at both ends of the day to buy this house. We had a child of our own, for God's sake – how could he even think about doing something as awful as that?'

'But the inquiry absolved everybody. Gordon Carrick sued for damages and won,' Hollie reminded her.

'Yes, but did the inquiry get to the heart of the matter or was it just a smoke screen? I believed that Kenny was innocent for years, then... then, something changed. And it all suddenly made sense.'

Melanie Digby was in full flow now, angry and resentful, her eyes flashing, but her breathing increasingly laboured. She let her comment hang without adding further comment.

'Perhaps you can tell us more,' Jenni prompted.

'I think they were in it up to their necks.'

'Why all of a sudden, though?' Hollie wanted to know. 'After all those years of believing your husband was innocent. What made you change your mind?'

Hollie and Jenni said nothing, waiting for her to elucidate.

Melanie swallowed and paused before speaking.

'He reached out after Kenny's death,' she began, slowly, as if straightening out the facts in her own mind first. 'We hadn't even buried him.' Her eyes were glazed, seemingly disassociating herself from the pain. 'It was out of the blue,' she continued, her right hand shaking slightly. 'He was one of the children at the home. He told me everything.' Her words were now clipped and terse, her neck and face red. 'He told me everything that those bastards did to those poor children.' Her eyes were welling with tears, her hands clenched tight. 'That's when I knew I'd done right by kicking him out of the house.'

She spoke the words like she'd won some kind of victory for the abused children by punishing her husband. 'I like to think he choked on his own disgust with himself.'

Her malicious words flowed from her mouth like she was expelling a foul bile. 'I didn't even attend the fucker's funeral, but I bit my lip for the sake of William about the abuse. I hope he burns in Hell.'

Hollie and Jenni waited a moment, staring at each other. Often, it was the silences which encouraged the best information. But Melanie refused to oblige and said nothing more.

Hollie took a deep breath and asked the obvious follow-up question, not for one minute expecting an answer.

'Who was this man who reached out to you out of the blue?' she said.

'He was one of the kids who lived in the home. He told me everything. His name was Simon Rose.'

TWELVE

AMBROSE HOUSE, HULL, 1996

Moira hadn't felt much like talking since the night when Digby had caught them sneaking out with his son. She and Simon had barely said a word to each other, a terrible and unspoken collusion now binding them as if they'd just made a friend in Hell.

It had happened two more times since then. Moira pulled her nails down the tops of her arms, wincing with the pain but relieved to see the tears in the skin and the blood slowly seeping through the wounds. It helped the pain inside her go away.

Her body convulsed whenever she thought of that man, and the bile stuck in her throat, an unbearable feeling of nausea which she was unable to expel. Occasionally, she'd look up at Simon at mealtimes, his sad, desolate eyes staring broken at her, like it was his fault somehow.

She'd forgotten about the Alanis Morrissette CD. It was still concealed behind the TV set in the communal room. She hadn't been down there since that night, and she preferred to stay in her room now. She didn't much want to listen to music anymore; things were different now.

At breakfast, Lisa, one of the social workers, announced the annual Hull Fair trip that night.

'Simon, Luke, Tori and Moira, you're all old enough now, so you get to go on the evening trip for the first time.'

It was like an icy-cold chill had descended across the dining room.

'Well, cheer up,' Lisa urged, shrugging it off as teenage disaffection. 'You get to go to a party afterwards. Hull's Youth Empowerment Syndicate are laying everything on for you.'

There was some enthusiasm from Luke and Tori, but the room was subdued, with the exception of the younger teenagers who got to attend the earlier session.

'Mr Mortimer will be picking up the first group in his minibus after school, at five thirty; the second group get picked up at eight o'clock. Under-sixteens get dropped back here by nine o'clock; sixteens and overs get to stay out late. You'll be brought back in taxis by midnight.'

'I've heard from Billy,' Simon mumbled to Moira, like he was only half-committed to what he was saying. 'He contacted me at school yesterday. He said he's sorry for being so chicken when his dad found us. He wants to make it up to us. He's going to sneak into the party tonight. He said he'll see us at Hull Fair, then follow the minibus in his car.'

'Okay,' came Moira's lacklustre reply. She'd always enjoyed the annual visits to Hull Fair with the younger group and, under normal circumstances, would have been excited about the prospect of joining the older teenagers in care on their annual treat. Somehow, she couldn't care less now it had arrived.

As they drove off in the minibus that evening, Moira relaxed for the first time in a month, knowing she'd be out of Ambrose House for a while and safe from that abhorrent man. She'd been thinking it over during the day; she was going to confide in one of the businesspeople who hosted the trip. She was going to tell them what was going on. She had to or she was certain she'd die in that place. They'd already robbed her of her soul.

The man driving the minibus was a bit odd, but friendly enough, and he let them retune the radio to Radio One for the duration of the drive over to Hull Fair.

As soon as Moira saw the fairground lights her spirits picked up. She'd enjoy a nice night out, get to know the businesspeople who were hosting the evening, then confide in one of them at the party. Digby couldn't be allowed to get away with what he was doing; he was a monster.

She moved her hand across the double seat of the minibus and squeezed Simon's hand. He didn't turn to look at her, but he squeezed it back. When she looked up at him, he was facing the window. She could see his tearstained cheeks in his reflection. She had to find the courage to do this, for Simon's sake as much as hers. Who even knew if they were doing it to the other teenagers, too? Her stomach clamped tight at the horror of that thought; it was too unbearable to contemplate.

The people from the Youth Empowerment Syndicate all seemed like fun. They'd brought freebies too – baseball hats, T-shirts, frisbees and HMV vouchers – it was like Christmas come early.

'There'll be more presents at the after-fair party,' the man who'd introduced himself as Gordon said. He was a police officer, apparently. Moira didn't much care so long as they were paying for everything, and she wasn't anywhere near Digby.

'Who likes pizza?' another one asked. His name was Orsen or something like that, she hadn't quite caught it.

The evening passed in a haze of thumping fairground music, dazzling lights, thrilling rides and excited screams. It felt good to release the tension of the previous weeks and even better to know that she was going to stop Digby dead in his tracks after that night.

Moira wasn't yet sure who she would confide in; the

policeman seemed the safest bet, but the other man – Orsen – he was something to do with the law, too.

When they hit the dodgems, Orsen invited her into his car, seeing she'd been left without a partner. She thought nothing of slipping in at his side, throwing the flimsy seatbelt over her arm. He drove them round the track, handling the bumper car adeptly, crashing it into several other vehicles to great hilarity.

As Moira screamed with joy, she glanced over to the steps that circled the fairground ride; Billy was there, waving at her, trying to catch her attention. At that moment, Orsen touched her back in a way that made her instantly freeze; she knew that expectant, self-assured stroking and a despondent fear gripped her. This man, who'd tried to befriend her, was just the same as Kenneth Digby.

The teenagers filed out of Philip Mortimer's minibus, Tori and Luke still buzzing from the excitement of rides at Hull Fair. They'd been dropped off at a large house somewhere outside the city. Moira wasn't certain where it was.

She was frozen in her seat, incapable of moving or talking now. Simon, too, had his gaze averted, looking down at his lap, his shoulders slumped and his back rounded, as if he wanted to disappear.

As the young adults were guided through the front door of the house, and Philip Mortimer drove his minibus off along the long, gravel drive, a face peered out of the shrubbery, desperately trying to catch Simon's or Moira's attention. It was Billy, his Fiat Panda parked up at the end of the road, having trailed Mortimer's vehicle to this place.

Moira tried to avoid his gaze, not wanting him to get involved in these horrors, but she saw enough to register his disappointed face, with a look of betrayal that suggested he'd hoped to spend time with her that evening. She turned to make a face at him, to urge him to get out of there, but Orsen's hand was resting on her back again, urging her into the property.

Moira stepped into the hallway, terrified for her own safety, but out of her mind, too, that Billy might get himself caught up in this. Orsen left her for a moment and turned back at the still-open door. Moira heard him call to someone out on the drive. 'Come on in, you'll miss the party,' Orsen shouted.

Moira's nerves were overcome with the flames of panic as, to her horror, Billy stepped inside the door, welcomed by Orsen.

'Yes, sorry, they went in without me,' Billy said, stepping inside the house, looking over at Moira and giving her a beaming smile.

Moira averted her eyes; she wanted to scream at him to get away while he could. But her entire body was gripped by fear now as the other adults began to offer the teenagers alcoholic drinks.

'Come on in, son, join the party,' Orsen said, his voice that of a welcoming host. 'You don't want to be missing out on what we've got planned for you all this evening.'

THIRTEEN

After finishing with Melanie Digby, Hollie walked with Jenni up the end of Hymers Avenue and along Sunny Bank, a linking road which ran along one edge of West Park with only a low fence as a boundary. Jenni pointed out how easy it was to walk to the Hull Fair site from there.

'Let's put it this way, you'd walk it rather than drive it,' she explained.

Hollie barely said a word. Simon Rose was alive still, and that's all she could think about. While Jenni was checking to see if it was possible to enter West Park directly from Hymers Avenue, Hollie put in a call to Osmond.

'We've got to let the team know,' she pushed, more assertively than she knew she should with a superior officer.

'I'm dealing with it,' Osmond cut her dead. 'I'll update the team on this new development, but we'll keep quiet about your direct connection for now—'

'But, sir, DS Patel is sure to put two and two together—'

'My decision is final,' Osmond asserted.

That was that; she struggled to put her anger aside. She'd always blamed Simon for Moira's disappearance. It was strange how he was nowhere to be found at the time. Over the years she'd grown to hate him more and more as, perhaps irrationally, she'd figured he was the only one who could have known what happened to Moira. Why else would he have disappeared into thin air at the same time as her? The truth was she needed someone to blame – it was the only way she could live with so many loose ends.

And now, here he was, alive still, apparently. And, predictably, Melanie Digby had no contact information for him. The entire interaction had been anonymous.

As they drove through the city, Hollie excitedly typed Digby's name into the web browser on her phone, struggling to push aside her anxiety over Simon. Osmond had assured her it would be followed up, and she had to defer to him, however much it pained her.

She caught a glimpse of the scar where she'd been slashed by a kitchen knife in their most recent murder case; it had healed well but still gave her palpitations just thinking about it. She pushed the thoughts back and checked the web page; the *Hull Daily Mail* had covered the story.

FORMER HEAD OF CONTROVERSIAL CHILDREN'S HOME DIES

It wasn't a long article, just the briefest notification of his passing.

The former Deputy Head of the Caring Guardian Children's Residential Home – formerly known as Ambrose House – has died, aged 62. Kenneth Digby served at the controversial home between 1995 and 2002, when it was taken over after the inquiry into alleged child abuse. Mr Digby and other care workers employed by the home were exonerated in the report. Mr Digby is survived by his wife, Melanie, and one adult child. The deceased will be buried, pending the coroner's report.

As press notifications went, it was bland and non-committal. There was just a small photograph of him, his head now completely shaven where he'd lost his hair in the intervening years. The eyebrow piercing was long gone, too; he looked like a different person. Hollie closed down the web browser and phoned the office. DS Anderson picked up.

'Anything more on those fingerprints on the wheelie bin?' she asked.

'Yes, but it's not the news you want to hear, I'm afraid. We've confirmed that the print taken from the wooden mallet is the same as those on the wheelie bin, so we now know how Carrick's body was moved across the showground. There's no fingerprint match on the database, though, so whoever killed Gordon Carrick doesn't have a police record. It was Carrick's blood on the mallet, too, so we can get a sense of the order of events as well. Anyway, when we get our killer, it's a good, solid evidence trail for court.'

Hollie cursed under her breath; a swift ID on the prints would have been like a lottery win so early in the case. A thought struck her.

'What it does suggest, though, is that Carrick wasn't killed by someone he'd helped to lock up in jail. They'd have a fingerprint record if that was the case. So that means our killer isn't known to us; they don't have a police record.'

Jenni gave Hollie an admiring glance from the driver's seat.

'Amber's already sifting through the names of kids who went to Ambrose House around the time of the inquiry,' Anderson continued. 'We're just getting into computer records at the end of the nineties, so thank God for small mercies.'

'Great, Amber is like a human Excel spreadsheet,' Hollie joked, delighted they were onto it already. 'She'll have that sorted in no time. Tell her to let me know the moment we have names. What about the Tori named on that photograph? Did she manage to match that with her list of names yet?'

'Harry's done some more digging,' Anderson continued, his tone more positive now. 'We know she had a difficult history with mental illness before her death. It sounds to me like she may have been a victim. Unfortunately, like a lot of these kids, she doesn't have family.'

'Okay, let's keep exploring her past. This girl gives us a direct link to whatever was going on at Ambrose House.'

Hollie paused, churning it all over in her head.

'DC Gordon did well,' Anderson continued. 'He's coming on nicely, that boy. I reckon we'd have missed that wheelie bin if he hadn't sniffed it out. How about you, anything to report?'

Hollie noted the positive feedback on Harry. Anderson had had his doubts about the young detective after an early career cock-up at a crime scene, but encouraging him to be surer of his hunches was panning out well.

'I think I might have something,' Hollie replied. 'Can you run through some checks on this Kenneth Digby? The proximity of these deaths stinks. Dig out the coroner's report, will you, and check for anything unusual at the scene, particularly anything which might suggest it wasn't suicide.'

'Was he implicated in the Ambrose House allegations?' Anderson checked.

'He was working there at the time, and Jane Carrick reckons he was,' Hollie replied, picking up on his increasing sense of intrigue. 'He was also buddies with the deceased; they played golf together.'

'What did Digby use to finish himself off?' Anderson checked.

'An overdose of insulin, apparently,' Hollie answered, 'but let's check that on the post-mortem report. I reckon Digby's death is linked and I'll bet anything it wasn't an open-and-shut case of him taking his own life. I also want to know if the insulin was prescribed or if he was self-medicating—'

'You can get hold of this stuff on international websites these days; it's a nightmare for the drugs teams.'

'Tell me about it, Ben, it cropped up a couple of times in my work back in Lancaster. Let me know as soon as you have something, please. Oh, and make sure we follow up on Jane Carrick. She's a locum. I want to know if she ever treated or prescribed Kenneth Digby.' She sighed, thinking of the inevitable delays they were likely to encounter on this. It took long enough to book an appointment via the surgery switchboard, and with this, they'd have to make a formal request through the Practice Management. 'Maybe talk to Doctor Ruane and see if he might oil the wheels for us with that one.'

'One more thing,' Anderson stopped her before she rang off. 'When we contacted this Orsen Scott fellow, he was very jittery, demanding police protection.'

Orsen Scott was in the golfing photograph, and Melanie Digby had mentioned him, too.

'Is Osmond letting him have it?' she asked.

'No,' came Anderson's curt response. 'I think he's wrong.'

Hollie did, too, but she knew what a pain in the arse resourcing it would be. She kept that view to herself.

'I'll chase it up with the DCI when I'm back in the office.'

Hollie was anxious for DCI Osmond to refer her involvement with the case up the seniority chain. The sooner she got the go-ahead to declare her interest, the sooner she could release DS Patel to locate the old case notes from Moira's disappearance. That's if she hadn't done it already, since she was such a sharp detective. She'd discuss the Orsen Scott issue then, too.

She turned to Jenni, whose attention was fully on the road ahead.

'Okay,' Hollie said, sighing, 'let's go and see this Ray McGregor chap and find out what he has to say for himself. Do you know where this address is?'

'Orchard Park Estate,' Jenni replied. 'He must have fallen on hard times.'

She was right. Hollie didn't know the estate particularly well, but she knew its reputation. Bus services were often suspended after dark, shopkeepers complained that their premises were unsafe because of antisocial behaviour, and feral youths ruled at night, making regular residents scared to go out after dark. She'd have expected a former reporter to live somewhere more salubrious.

Hollie stayed deep in thought as they made their way through the city and towards the estate.

Ray McGregor's house was just like any other terraced home on a city estate. It was well-kept, with a slightly out-of-place wrought iron, waist-level fence surrounding it. It had a set-back garage and a small driveway, and the garden was well-maintained, though a couple of dog toys gave the game away that it wasn't children who played out there.

Jenni pulled up on the roadside.

'I can never figure out why these estates have such a bad reputation; I'd be happy to live in one of these places. What makes people behave like that on their own doorstep?'

Jennie switched off the engine and pulled up the hand brake.

'You and me both. I'm paying a fortune to rent a place; I'd kill to have a home like this. But I know it's not all sweetness and light here. I used to have to patrol this estate when I was a beat bobby. I had a couple of scary nights here, I can tell you.'

Hollie reckoned most cops had harrowing tales to tell. She'd draw some of those stories out of her colleague on a future occasion and probably in the pub.

They got out of the car and walked along the path to Ray McGregor's house, taking care to make sure the gate was fastened behind them in case he let the dog out. Jenni tapped at the door. There was a single bark and the sound of a man's voice.

The door opened and Hollie got her first glimpse of Ray McGregor. Everybody involved in this case so far was younger than she expected, and Ray was no exception. She reckoned he was in his late fifties, which made him in his early thirties when he tried to reveal his allegations about the children's home. His hair was still more black than grey and, most noticeably, he looked like a man who still had fire in his belly. His black Labrador waited patiently at his side.

Ray looked at the two detectives, settling on Hollie and examining her face closely like she was familiar. He shrugged it off.

'Ah, detectives, DS Patel said you were hoping to come over this morning. Can I get you drinks?'

He didn't bother studying their ID cards; he seemed like a man who was accustomed to the world and manner of the police. While Ray McGregor sorted out the drinks in the kitchen, Hollie and Jenni sat down on the sofa, with the dog taking a place in between them.

'What's the name of your dog?' Jenni called through.

'Sebastian,' came the reply. 'He'll take as much fussing as you'll give him.'

Ray was genial enough, but he showed all the signs of a journalist impatient to get on with the questions. There was little interest in the pleasantries; he was a down-to-business sort of guy. He distributed the drinks, which were served in cups from official organisations, like they'd been gathered as freebies from locations where he'd reported in the past.

Jenni started up her recording app.

'I wish we'd had all these gizmos when I was flying around this city – all my notes were taken in shorthand.'

'So, you know why we're here, Mr McGregor,' Hollie began.

'Ray, use Ray, please,' he replied.

'Okay, Ray. You know that Gordon Carrick lost his life this morning. What do you make of that?'

'Well, I'm guessing I'm on the list of suspects for starters,' he began.

Ray McGregor did have an axe to grind with Gordon Carrick, that was for sure. They'd come here for background information, but by his own admission, he had to be a suspect and Hollie needed to stay mindful of that.

'So, feel free to check and double-check my whereabouts and ask any questions you please. The TL;DR version is that I didn't do it, I was in Leeds yesterday, but I know you won't be taking my word for it.'

He touched the phone on his screen to reveal an e-ticket confirming a late-evening return journey from Leeds to Hull.

Jenni examined the ticket on Ray's phone, took a photo record, swiped across to check the first part of the journey, and took a second photo. As she handed it back to him, she gave a small nod. Hollie continued, eager to get on.

'Tell us about Ambrose House, as it was when you made your allegations.'

He sighed. This was a well-trodden path by the look of it.

'It was the exposé that ruined my career, detective. I'd crossed the i's, dotted the t's, got the legal team to check it and the moment we published it in the papers, the shutters came down and I was isolated—' His eyes reddened, and he took a long swallow. 'I've never seen such a swift and absolute closing down of a news story. It ruined my career and my marriage. I would not wish that amount of stress on anybody. I had a breakdown afterwards—' He paused; this was difficult for him.

'What was the precise nature of your allegations?' Jenni pushed.

Hollie gave a little internal smile. Jenni's use of language was circumspect, neither provoking Ray nor taking his innocence as a given.

'Can we not call them allegations?' came Ray's irritated reply. 'I'm as certain now as I was then that everything in my report is true.'

'We'll need to continue to use that word, as I'm sure you're well aware,' Hollie said, scratching Sebastian under his chin, 'but I've noted your comment.'

Ray studied the two detectives then sat forward in his chair.

'Okay, so here it is,' he began, clearly annoyed. 'If you reach over and pick up that newspaper at your side, detective, you can read my article for yourself.'

He pointed at a discoloured and well-thumbed newspaper which was perched on the edge of his coffee table. 'You won't be able to access that online now as it's all considered libellous.'

He seemed affronted as he spoke, but Hollie knew that information couldn't be left on the internet if a court had deemed it to be inaccurate or incorrect and consequently awarded damages.

Jenni reached out and picked up a browned edition of the national newspaper. It was so old that the publication was no longer available in the newsagents. It had ceased being printed several years ago. She handed it over to Hollie who noted the date: 11th September 2001.

'There is no doubt in my mind whatsoever that Kenneth Digby and Superintendent Gordon Carrick were abusing children from that home.'

Ray was completely confident in his statement; if he was lying or covering his arse, he was doing an Oscar-winning job of it.

'The inquiry said otherwise,' Hollie challenged him as she wrestled with the pages of the newspaper to find the article in the centre pages. It was a national paper, not a local one. That was interesting.

'The inquiry was nobbled,' he replied curtly, as if they should have surmised that already.

'Why do you think that?' Jenni asked. She beat Hollie to it.

'I had two informants,' Ray continued. 'They told me everything. I was able to check certain key points in the diaries of those two men, thanks to contacts in the police and at the children's home. There were more involved, but I couldn't get their names or sufficient evidence to name them in the article. I think a chap called Orsen Scott may well have been involved, too, but I couldn't prove it.'

Hollie jumped at the name. She looked at Jenni. They might just have been speaking to a reporter about a present-day case from the way Ray was talking. Orsen Scott was one of the men pictured in the photograph that they'd found hanging up in Gordon Carrick's study.

'Tell me about Orsen Scott,' Hollie replied. She scanned Ray's article. It was a hell of a punt on the part of the newspaper. Gordon Carrick was named, and Kenneth Digby was strongly implicated, but his name wasn't given. A senior member of staff closely connected with the day-to-day operations of the home was how Ray had put it. That must have set the cat among the pigeons – no wonder they rebranded the place and deployed the former staff elsewhere afterwards.

'Is there any chance you might have got your facts wrong?' Jenni challenged him. 'I know it's something you feel passionate about, but might you have made a mistake?'

'Listen, young lady,' Ray began crossly. 'These days anybody with an opinion on social media thinks they're a journalist. They publish any old nonsense and think they're somehow educating the world, whether it's based in fact or not. My generation of journalists – and I know we all seem like old gits to you – but we tested the veracity of a news story. We spoke to real people, we had contacts throughout the city, we consulted lawyers who advised us on what we could and could not say.'

Hollie could see he was emotional about it. He had a lot of his life staked on these claims.

'I don't mean to patronise you, but me and your boss here come from a time when things were different and when they were done properly. I'm as confident in that news story today as I was back then. I stand by it one hundred per cent.'

He was defiant; there wasn't an ounce of doubt about him.

'You mentioned that you had two informants,' Hollie picked up. 'Who were they? Are they still alive?'

Ray shook his head doubtfully and looked down. 'They were scared out of their wits but terrified it might happen again. Both of them were well away from it, but they feared for their lives when they came to speak to me in 1999.'

'Who were they? Do they still live in the city?' Jenni pushed.

'I can remember them as clear as day. They'd be in their forties now; I'm guessing your sort of age?' He looked at Hollie who confirmed his dates were about right with a small nod.

'They both disappeared without a trace days after they spoke to me.'

Hollie's heart was pounding hard again, a thunderous pulse warning of danger. It was beating so hard in her chest that even the dog noticed it and stirred its head, which was now resting on her lap.

This had to be Moira... and Simon?

'—they were never seen again. One of them became a high-profile missing person for a while, but the other – well, nobody seemed interested in him.'

Hollie's head was swirling; she clasped her hands tightly to hide how much they were shaking.

Was this Moira? It had to be.

Ray McGregor quickly put her out of her misery. 'Simon was the young lad's name,' he started, 'Simon Rose.'

Hollie closed her eyes, swallowing hard, an image of Simon begging outside the Jacksons store stalking her thoughts.

'—a gentle lad he was, homeless when I met him. And he came with a lovely lass, a real sparky young thing. Moira Kennedy, that's what she was called. That young girl had a fire burning fierce inside her, I'll give her that.'

Hollie felt like she was about to be slammed by a fast-approaching vehicle.

'Moira?'

It was all Hollie could say. Her mouth was dry, her throat scratchy. The word barely made it out in one piece.

'Are you all right, boss?' Jenni asked, concern written all over her face.

Ray was oblivious to what was going on, and carried on speaking, barely drawing breath.

'—and you must know about Digby, I assume?' he asked.

'What about him?' Jenni replied, picking up the tab for Hollie.

'His supposed suicide.' Ray made air quotes with his fingers as he said the word suicide.

'Why supposed?' Hollie asked, doing her best to shake the past from her mind. Moira's face was fixed there. Her poor, dear friend. She forced her emotions back down, but she could feel her eyes tearing up and the adrenaline was pumping hard now.

'Someone's killing them, one by one,' Ray continued. 'Isn't it obvious? And I'll put money on it that Orsen Scott is next.'

FOURTEEN

Hollie's head was spinning. The intoxicating possibility that Moira was still alive and the horrifying near certainty that she was the victim of those men were almost more than she could comprehend in that moment. The events of the past were waking from their slumber.

'Is there somewhere I could talk privately to my colleague?' Hollie asked.

'Of course. Use the kitchen. I won't be offended if you close the door on me. I've been around coppers all my working life; I know how these things work.'

Hollie got up off the sofa, leaving Sebastian to shuffle himself to the side and look pleadingly at Jenni.

'Sorry, Sebastian. We'll be back in a moment.'

Seeing it was useless, the dog begrudgingly settled back down, sadly following the course of the two women over to the kitchen.

Hollie pulled the door gently closed.

'Your face has gone white,' Jenni remarked, concern in her voice. 'You're not feeling ill, are you?'

Hollie paused for a moment before speaking. She cleared her throat.

'I'm going to tell you something that needs to remain between me and you for now. DCI Osmond knows, and so does the DCC.'

That got Jenni's immediate attention.

'This sounds interesting,' came her eager response. Her eyes lit up.

'I knew Simon Rose,' Hollie croaked, the words barely able to make their way out, it was so hard to say. Her hands were still shaking.

'Bloody hell!' Jenni exclaimed as she instinctively put her hand over her mouth, remembering she was in somebody else's house. 'Excuse my language. But fuck,' she continued, her voice lowered, but her entire face lit up by this revelation.

'Exactly,' Hollie replied, pleased that she'd said it but terrified at what this might mean. Her heart was thumping wildly, a combination of fear and excitement.

'How? When? What happened?' Jenni replied, a barrage of questions ready to tumble from her lips like machine-gun fire.

'When I was a student here at the end of the nineties,' Hollie began, the words flowing more easily now. It felt good, at last, to be sharing this burden. 'It would have been 1999, my second year at uni. I only met him briefly. I thought my legs were going to give way when Ray said that name.'

'Wow,' Jenni responded, grasping the enormity of this connection immediately. 'Is that just a coincidence, do you think?'

Hollie's mind was racing with possibilities; her head was aching, there was so much going on.

'I think it's a coincidence that I'm involved. I don't think it's a coincidence that Ray McGregor knew Simon. But it's my friend Moira I need to tell you about—'

'Moira?' Jenni said, a quizzical look on her face.

'She was my best friend at university. We were both studying Sociology.' As she said the words, a well-worn feeling of desolation swept over her.

Jenni gasped.

'She disappeared when I was nineteen,' Hollie continued, choking back her tears. 'She was friends with Simon Rose. They'd been at Ambrose House together—'

'Disappeared? Oh God, I'm so sorry, Hollie.'

Jenni reached out and squeezed Hollie's hand. Hollie felt an icy chill in her chest.

'Moira is still officially a missing person,' Hollie continued, pushing through the pain of saying it aloud. 'She doesn't have family and she had few possessions, so there was nobody interested enough to find out what happened to her.'

Jenni took a moment before speaking. Hollie could see her colleague's detective brain kicking in, but she was treading carefully, aware this was something close to Hollie's heart.

'Could she be dead?' Jenni asked gently.

'Unknown,' Hollie replied. 'But after all these years, I'd begun to accept that she was murdered.'

A single tear began to make its way down her cheek.

'So do DCI Osmond and DCC Warburton know all this already?' Jenni couldn't contain the detective in her; she needed to find out what was going on.

Hollie knew this information had to come out and, however unsettling for her, it was better off in the hands of her team where connections would be made and threads tied together.

'I had nothing to do with the police back then,' Hollie continued, her nerves steadying now. 'I was just a member of the public, reporting that my friend had gone missing. But it's through my involvement working with the police that I realised my vocation. I got involved in a reconstruction to help find Moira, and I worked with the police during the investigation; it captivated me. It's why I left the city soon after to return home. I knew that I couldn't care less about getting a degree. I wanted to join the police and do what I'd seen them doing when they tried to find Moira. I saw how Moira was failed, and I felt that I wanted to do better by victims. I never found out what happened to Moira, but I made up for that by solving other cases as a detective.'

There was silence for a couple of seconds as the two women looked intently at each other.

'I feel stunned by what you've just told me,' Jenni said at last. She looked it, too, like a computer unable to handle a sudden assault of data.

'I flagged it up when I came for the interview here,' Hollie continued. She'd kept this to herself for so long, it felt good to get it out at last. 'I couldn't take the DI job and not mention it. They were okay with it, they just said it's a historical case, it's no impediment to my working for the Humberside force. But when Carrick's body was found on the fairground this morning' – she paused for a moment, reflecting on the sheer coincidence of it – 'I knew it was connected, I just knew it. What are the chances?'

Jenni stared at her, a realisation dawning upon her.

'Will they take you off the case?' Her concern was palpable. She sounded as if it would be the worst thing if Hollie was removed from the team temporarily.

'I'm waiting to find out. DCI Osmond is chasing it for me.' Hollie felt her apprehension rising. 'They may decide I'm in too deep to stay on the investigation and that I can't be impartial.'

'What do you want?'

Sometimes her colleague could strike the emotional heart of an issue with a single, well-aimed blow.

'I want to stay on the case,' Hollie replied, more certain than ever that she meant it. As she said the words, she understood how badly she needed this.

'Even more so since we've spoken to Ray McGregor than I did when I arrived at the crime scene this morning. Now he's mentioned Simon... it's an opportunity to get Moira the justice she never got all those years ago. It's a chance to lay her to rest at last. The poor girl, we were so young. God, I missed her when she disappeared – I still miss her—'

Hollie was fighting to hold back her tears, picturing her friend's face. What would she look like now? What would she have done with her life? What a waste.

Jenni moved over to Hollie and hugged her.

'I know it's not quite protocol, but I feel like you need this,' Jenni said, sniffing and fighting to control her own emotions.

Hollie was relieved she'd made this house call with Jenni; Ben Anderson might not have been so sympathetic. She wiped her eyes and rallied herself.

'There's another thing, too,' Hollie began, cautious and timid, hardly daring to admit what had happened to her. 'I was threatened back then, physically threatened, and it scared the life out of me. I've never forgiven myself for not speaking up, but I was so young and it was so damn scary...' Her voice trailed away, and her legs weakened as the sheer terror of the attack came screaming back through her memories.

Jenni didn't say anything. She just waited with Hollie while she composed herself again.

'I just needed you to know that before we asked Ray any more questions. I've only ever told the interview panel about that, I never discussed it with friends or colleagues – not even Léon—'

She forced her way through her faltering voice. She had to fight this – she could not allow the past to intimidate her.

'I want you to make sure I'm not skewing things or missing

anything. If you think I'm getting it wrong, tell me, Jenni, I won't be offended. But I couldn't hold this information back from you any longer. Please keep it to yourself, just for now. I'll tell the team as soon as I know what the DCC has to say about it.'

'I won't say anything,' Jenni assured her, reassuring in her tone. 'Will you let Ray McGregor know?'

'No. I don't want my involvement to be a distraction from the case,' she replied, more assured now. 'If anything, it gives me a unique insight. I was in the city at the same time as Ray. I met some of these people.'

Hollie spent a couple of minutes filling Jenni in on the background from 1999, sharing everything related to Moira's confessions about Ambrose House and her chance meeting with Simon Rose at Jacksons cash machine.

'When I saw that picture of Kenneth Digby, it sent a shiver through my body,' Hollie continued. 'He was the man who Moira followed into the darkness on the night we went to Hull Fair together. I only caught a glimpse of him then, but I knew it as soon as I saw Carrick's photo. I'll bet anything he knew what happened to her – but now, now he's dead—'

Jenni gave her another hug.

'Let's see what else Ray has to say,' she suggested gently. 'He's just the kind of person we need to be speaking to.'

'How's my face?' Hollie checked, concerned that her eyes might give away the emotional nature of their conversation.

'You're fine,' Jenni reassured her, moving some hair away from her friend's face to be sure.

They returned to the living room, and Sebastian was instantly alerted by their return.

'Sorry about that,' she apologised to Ray McGregor, who seemed completely unperturbed by the short interruption.

'Now, where were we? You were telling us about Simon Rose and Moira Kennedy. What do you think happened to them?'

Ray gave a cynical laugh.

'They got to them, that's what happened,' came Ray's bitter reply. Hollie watched as his fists clenched.

Hollie sat down, shocked by the certainty of his reply.

'Who's they?' Jenni asked.

'Well, Gordon Carrick for starters,' he answered, his face reddening, his eyes welling with the sheer emotion of what he was suggesting. 'And whoever else was involved in what was going on at that home.'

His pent-up rage was oozing through every pore now, his fists pounding the side of his armchair.

He was looking at Jenni, a menacing demeanour, his body contorted with barely suppressed rage.

'I'm not some conspiracy theorist, I promise you. I can see it on your face,' came his angry outburst, without warning, an unexpected eruption.

Hollie looked over at Jenni, who'd been taken aback at the hostility of his unprovoked attack.

'I don't think you are,' Jenni said, nervously looking directly in his eyes.

As if realising he'd stepped over a line, Ray sighed and relaxed his body; immediately he became less threatening.

'Look, I'm sorry. I'm just so used to being dismissed as some nutter who couldn't let it lie. Look, look what I have to write these days to make ends meet.'

Ray's hand reached to the side of his armchair, and he pulled out a copy of *People's Friend* magazine. It was opened at a one-page story: 'Her Last Glimpse'.

'I have to write crime stories for their specials these days, because nobody was much interested in my journalism after that. They stole my career, they wrecked my marriage, and they ruined my life. And believe me, I've spent so many years despising those men, I'd have quite happily killed them myself.'

FIFTEEN
HULL, 1999

'Help, please, I need help—'

Hollie felt the panic closing in on her as she forced her way through the dense crowds, Moira's soft toy in her hands, desperately looking for patrolling police officers or somebody official who could help. Her friend had disappeared into the night, suddenly fixated by something – or someone.

The pounding music thudded all about her as she forced her mind to focus.

'What's up, luv? You look like you're upset.' A middle-aged man, walking with what looked to Hollie like his wife and grandchild, stopped at her side, concern written all over his face.

'I've lost my friend,' she spluttered, relieved at last to find someone – anyone – to help her.

'It'll be okay, my dear, she'll turn up somewhere, she'll just have wandered off,' the lady tried to reassure her. The couple exchanged a glance that suggested they thought she was worked up over nothing.

She had to let them know.

'No, look,' she urged, more forceful than she had ever been

with strangers. Hollie held up the soft toy, splashes of blood flecked across its yellow, fluffy exterior. She wanted to scream.

'Oh my god, is someone hurt?' the woman said, suddenly grasping the seriousness of the matter.

'Yes, it's my friend,' Hollie continued hurriedly, frustrated that she couldn't articulate her urgency fast enough. 'Something's happened to her—'

'All right, luv, you stay here with my wife by the candy floss stall, and I'll come back with some bobbies.'

He disappeared into the crowds, and Hollie lost him in a moment. It was like the fairground was swallowing him up; had it done the same to Moira?

The child picked up on the level of distress among the adults and the woman did her best to distract her. She bought a toffee apple from the stall. That did the job.

'Try and stay calm, my darling, I'm sure she's all right,' the woman attempted to soothe her.

Her platitudes were well meant, but the knotting deep in Hollie's stomach indicated the truth of it. Her best friend was in terrible danger, and she needed to find her fast.

'I've got to go,' she said, unable to wait any longer. Her mind was a confused mess, not knowing what to do for better or worse.

'No, dear, please wait here,' the woman urged. 'The police will need to speak to you.'

The incessant booming of the music was becoming oppressive. Hollie wished she could just switch it off.

'I'll be over by the caravans, directly behind the Fun House,' Hollie said, rushing away.

She'd been foolish looking for help. Anything could be happening to her friend. If she'd hung around shouting, it might have frightened off whoever she'd followed. She pictured Moira lying on the ground, blood seeping out of her head; her imagination was tormenting her.

Tears began to flow as frustration and helplessness took a hold of her body. She dropped the soft toy, ducking out of the crowds behind the Fun House ride and running over to the caravans. Her heart pounded as she left the well-lit area and stepped into darkness and shadow.

'Moira!' she called, cursing herself for running off to seek help. 'It's Hollie, the police are coming.'

She hoped the threat of imminent backup might frighten off whoever it was who'd taken her. Then, momentarily, doubt entered her mind. Was that blood on the toy? Was she making a fool of herself? Would the police find Moira safe at home and think her a ridiculous, neurotic young woman?

She didn't care, she'd take the risk. Hollie stepped into a row of caravans, searching in the darkness, aware of every noise around her. A light was on in one of the units. She ran up to it and banged at the door. There was movement inside.

'Help, please! My friend has gone missing.'

The door to the caravan opened and a young girl, dressed only in a nightie, was standing there with a toddler in Bob the Builder pyjamas, nervously lurking behind her.

Hollie realised what she'd done and immediately regretted it. The two children looked terrified, as if the last thing they'd expected was for some strange woman to come knocking at their door while they were sleeping.

'Oh, I'm so sorry,' she apologised, backing away from the door. 'It's all right, I'm sorry I disturbed you. Please go back into your caravan and make sure you lock the door behind you.'

She felt awful, frightening a couple of kids like that. She heard male voices, and torch beams flickered through the gap between two of the caravans.

'I'm over here!' Hollie shouted, knowing it must be the help the man had gone to summon. As she stepped through the gap, she exhaled a long breath as she saw two uniformed officers, one of them holding the discarded toy.

'Are you the young woman whose friend has gone missing?' the first one asked.

'Yes, yes, I lost her somewhere around here. She was following someone.'

'Okay, now calm down, my dear, what's your name first of all?'

'Hollie. Hollie Turner.'

'How old are you, Hollie?'

'I'm nineteen. I'm a student at the university. Humberside University.'

'And what's the name of your friend?' the other constable asked.

'She's called Moira, Moira Kennedy.'

'What does Moira look like, Hollie? Can you tell us what she was wearing?'

Hollie wanted to scream at them. *Just find her, will you?* But even in her panic, she knew they were right, they had to know who they were looking for.

'She's got shoulder-length, auburn hair. Sometimes people say we look alike from a distance. She was wearing a patterned scrunchie. Her coat is navy blue. She was wearing jeans and a University of Humberside sweatshirt.'

'That's perfect. Now, I need you to stand somewhere safe while we're searching for your mate. That gentleman who came to find us is over there waiting by the Fun House. Please stay put where we know you're safe, and we'll go and find your mate, is that okay?'

Hollie nodded and turned towards the ride.

'She was following somebody. He had bright red hair—'

The second officer interrupted her. 'Let's just find your mate, shall we? This fairground is packed with people. You can't possibly know if she was following somebody or not—'

His mate gave him a look, but he was shut down before he could say anything.

'I want to look for her—' Hollie began.

'Look, if something's happened to her, you're safer somewhere more public,' the first constable chided her. 'Let's concentrate on finding your friend, that's the most important thing.'

'I'll go with her,' the middle-aged man said. He'd walked over to join them while they'd been talking.

The police officer didn't seem sure, but to Hollie's relief, he agreed.

'You go that way, Terry, I'll sweep along the second row. You two search over there.' He indicated by pointing to a separate cluster of generator lorries.

They took off in different directions, Hollie rushing ahead of the man.

'I'm Leonard, luv,' he said. 'Best not rush ahead too far – the officer asked us to stick together.'

They walked in the darkness through the lorries and the small group of caravans. Hollie's eyes were adjusting to the lack of light now, and it was becoming much easier to see. She scoured the ground and all around her, nervous about what she might find.

Did Moira get away? Was it possible she just lost sight of her friend in the crowd? She wished she could be in two places at once. Perhaps Moira was back at her flat already, oblivious to all the worry she'd caused. Maybe she didn't want the stuffed toy and had carelessly discarded it. But something deep inside told Hollie she wasn't wrong. What Moira had confided in her a couple of nights ago, her sudden skittishness at spotting a stranger in the crowds, the way she'd just rushed off like that – something was up, she felt it; Hollie knew it.

She walked around the lorries, even looking underneath them. There was a TV on in one of the caravans. This time Leonard tapped gently at the door. A woman opened it; she was elderly.

'You haven't heard anything going on out here, have you, my darling?' he asked.

The old woman seemed annoyed to be disturbed. Hollie could hear the laughter track from a TV comedy. It sounded like *French and Saunders*. Moira liked *French and Saunders*, she said she liked their ridiculousness.

The woman shook her head, closed the door, and left Leonard standing in the darkness.

'There's nothing here, my love. We'd best head back to the Fun House and meet back with those coppers. Try not to worry too much, it's a busy site, she won't have gone far.'

'We haven't checked those two caravans over there.'

Hollie pointed across a patch of grass to where two units were pitched out on their own. Leonard looked over and attempted to stifle a sigh.

'I'll need to be getting back to my wife and grandchild,' he began. 'We're supposed to be having some quality time.'

He looked at Hollie, but she could tell from the look of resignation on his face that he'd already given up any hope of continuing their pleasant evening out at the fair.

Hollie walked over determinedly. Both of them were in darkness. She was immediately alerted by one of the red gas canisters at the rear being knocked over, which seemed unusual. They were tall and heavy-looking.

Hollie stared down at the canister; was that blood on the side? There was something splashed on it, but it was so damn difficult to make out anything in the darkness.

She stepped between the caravans and surveyed the grassy area on the far side. It was in shadow there, and much more difficult to make anything out. Hollie was about to give up when she spotted something in the mud. Normally, she'd have ignored it, but there was something about it that made her want to investigate further.

'Come on, luv, let's leave it to the bobbies,' Leonard said, coming up behind her.

'Call them over, I've found something,' she replied, rushing over to the object on the ground.

'It's nothing, luv—'

'Call them over!' Hollie snapped. She'd never talked to an adult like that in her life before.

She knelt and picked the item out of the mud. She knew what it was before the police officers even got there with their torches.

'Shine your torch on it, I need to check the colour.'

The two officers had rejoined her now, summoned by Leonard's reluctant calls.

The first officer shone his torch directly on the object. It was just as Hollie had feared. It was Moira's patterned scrunchie, the same one Hollie had watched her wrap around her hair earlier that evening.

SIXTEEN

'I know it's a hike from here, but we need to take a look at the children's home before we return to HQ. Could you head there, please?' Hollie said urgently. She reflected on their meeting with Ray. The journalist definitely had motive when it came to finishing off Gordon Carrick.

Ray McGregor had promised to search his loft for the cassette of Moira's and Simon's revelations. Hollie couldn't believe that she might hear her friend's voice again after so many years. The prospect both thrilled her and terrified her.

'No problem, boss – Hollie,' Jenni replied, indicating to take the next turnoff. 'I know roughly where it is from what was said in the briefing, but maybe you could glance at Google Maps and get a road name for me?'

Hollie was grateful for the distraction. She took out her phone and began scrolling through the maps app.

The thought of Simon Rose still being alive was incredible to Hollie. In her darker moments, she'd felt that he might have been responsible for Moira's death. From what Ray was telling them, they were about to spill the beans on something big; is that what led to their disappearance? Had they fled? And if

Simon was still alive, what about Moira? Might she still be alive?

'Head along Holderness Road and turn right at the roundabout where the Health Centre is located. I'll talk you in from there; it's up a side road.'

Jenni drove on, and Hollie churned over her thoughts, desperately trying to piece it all together.

They parked outside the Caring Guardian Children's Residential Home and surveyed the building before getting out of the car.

'I prefer Ambrose House as a name,' Jenni remarked, 'though if half of what Ray McGregor is alleging is true, I think they'll be needing another rebrand sometime soon.'

The fabric of the building seemed like it was seventies or eighties, but the windows were modern and double-glazed, and the roof looked like it had been recently replaced.

'We should have called ahead really,' Hollie said as she moved to unbuckle her seatbelt. 'But let's chance our luck and see if we can learn anything. Make sure you have your ID at the ready.'

They walked across the road to the well-signed entrance and tried the door; it was locked.

'They've got camera-based security,' Jenni observed, pointing.

'Is that to keep the kids in or out?' Hollie whispered grimly.

She pressed the buzzer and moved her face in alignment with the camera that was embedded in the casing. She fumbled in her pocket and held up her ID card.

'DI Hollie Turner from Humberside Police. We'd like to ask you some questions about a case we're investigating.'

'*Come in, officer,*' a voice came over the intercom. There was an electronic click in the door frame, and Jenni gave the door a push; this time it opened.

A lady wearing jeans, trainers and a flowery blouse was

standing in reception, and it looked like she'd been chatting to the receptionist.

She stepped forward and held out her hand.

'You just caught me in time,' she said, a concerned look on her face, her body tense. 'I'm about to go onto a conference call, but I'll do what I can to help. I'm Verity Mitchell, by the way. I'm the day manager.'

She shook both their hands, checking their IDs, and led them to some chairs in a waiting area to the side of the reception desk. Verity took a seat, too, but she appeared on edge, sitting forward in her chair, an agitated look on her face.

'So, I'm guessing you want to know about Ambrose House and the historic allegations, am I right? I heard the news about Gordon Carrick on the BBC bulletin. What a terrible thing to happen.'

Verity was saying the words, but they didn't appear particularly heartfelt to Hollie. Why was there so little love lost over these dead men?

This was better than Hollie had expected for a cold call. She was braced for evasion and a barrage of confidentiality and safeguarding spiel, but it did not come.

Verity carried on speaking, with the delivery of a corporate presentation. All that was missing was the slide deck.

'Okay, so this place changed its name from Ambrose House in 2002, after the inquiry, which I'm assuming you know all about already?'

Hollie nodded.

'The council offloaded it to private ownership in 2005. It's been the Caring Guardian Children's Residential Home ever since. Those allegations are long behind us now.'

'How long have you worked here?' Jenni asked.

'I've been here for nine years, working as a manager for the past three. I can't tell you much about what happened back then. It was a storm in a teacup as far as I know. We have these things to deal with from time to time, officer. We're dealing with vulnerable young adults; sometimes they make spurious accusations, and then all hell breaks loose.'

'Do the children still go on an annual visit to Hull Fair?' Jenni asked.

Verity paused before answering, her face reddening a little.

'No, they were organised via a local charity group, and it was thought best to end them after the inquiry ended,' she began, choosing her words carefully. 'I do know that much. I suggested reintroducing the Hull Fair visits when I took charge here, but there was strong resistance to it because of what – what it was claimed – had happened.'

So, this is historical child abuse, not current. Thank God for small mercies.

'How were the trips organised, do you know that information?' Hollie pushed, relieved that there was, at least, some news that wasn't terrible at last.

For the first time, Verity seemed furtive. She checked her watch as a reminder that she was short on time.

'A fellow called Philip Mortimer picked them up. He's done local charity runs for years. The older kids came back in taxis, paid for by the local business group which laid on the trips. They used to take the kids on for a night out afterwards. As I said, the inquiry found nothing at the time, but the trips were discontinued when the home rebranded.'

'I take it Philip Mortimer and the accompanying adults from the charity were all police checked?' Hollie verified.

Verity shuffled in her chair. 'Well, detective, the Children's Barred List has always been a part of my working life, but something called List 99 was used before that—'

'What's that?' Jenni asked.

'It was a register of all people convicted or suspected of child abuse,' Verity explained. 'It became the Children's Barred List after that.'

'So, if you hadn't been found out yet, you were free to just carry on abusing young people?' Hollie interrupted, more angrily than she would have wished. Verity didn't make the rules, but the topic always triggered strong emotions in her. She thought of the secure family life her own three children had experienced, even now in the midst of marital break-up. An instant rage fired up inside her whenever she had to contemplate the horror of adults preying on children.

'Of course, but hasn't that always been the case?' Verity answered defensively. She was prickly now, and Hollie was annoyed with herself for provoking that.

'And could the older teenagers just come and go as they pleased?' Jenni asked.

Hollie ran through the dates. Moira had left the home when she was eighteen – an adult. She knew enough from her informal dealing with children's homes that the youngsters were given more freedom as they got older.

Verity seemed offended at Jenni's question and her reply was curt.

'Of course they could, they're not tagged or monitored 24/7, officer. Were you monitored all the time when you were seventeen? It's a home, not a prison.'

Verity checked her watch again and sat further forward in her seat. Hollie could see they'd irritated her and that they were now on borrowed time.

'About the allegations,' Hollie continued, 'could something like that still happen, if it were true?'

'It was found not to be true,' Verity replied emphatically, hardly concealing her annoyance. 'But yes, you've seen the news, these things happen. And before you ask, we are inspected by Ofsted under the SCCIF framework.'

Hollie hated acronyms.

'You'll have to tell me what that is,' she interjected.

'The Social Care Common Inspection Framework. They're watching all this on your behalf, detective.'

Hollie would look it up later. Thank goodness for Google.

'If that's everything, my Zoom call awaits,' Verity said impatiently, getting up from her chair.

'Yes, thank you, you've been very helpful,' Hollie replied, following Verity's lead. As she did so, she caught sight of a cluster of photographs which had been gathered under brightly coloured lettering:

CARING GUARDIAN IN THE COMMUNITY

Hollie's attention had been instantly drawn to an image in which an overweight man in a baseball cap and bright T-shirt was standing in front of a minibus, holding a giant cheque, surrounded by children, she assumed from the home.

She recognised him instantly – Philip Mortimer, older and heavier now – and the photo was dated 2023.

Hollie's stomach churned as she turned to face Verity Mitchell. She felt like she'd just been rinsed out, as the horrific realisation dawned on her.

'That man is Philip Mortimer. He was the man who was transporting the children to Hull Fair in 1999—'

'Yes, so what?' Verity asked, impatient to get away to her meeting. 'He's a local, approved contractor.'

Jennie had seen it now, and she was taking a photograph of the framed image with her phone.

Rage surged through Hollie's veins once again as she thought back to the photograph on Carrick's wall, showing Mortimer with the group of potential abusers. This time she made no effort to conceal her anger.

'Can't you see what that means, Ms Mitchell? You may have long since ceased taking children on the Hull Fair trips, but the same man is providing transport services to you after all these years. Is Philip Mortimer ever left alone with the children?'

Verity Mitchell's face blanched and she looked at Hollie with the fear of a manager whose careless oversight was causing considerable discomfort.

'Yes, officer,' she answered, as if the words were leaving her mouth with some difficulty. 'Philip Mortimer does spend unsupervised time with our children.'

SEVENTEEN

'Damn, I could have done without this today,' Hollie cursed as she checked her phone. She'd been thrown off by the visit to the children's home and now this. 'I've got a couple of media interviews to do with the DCC on the fairground site this afternoon. I'm doing it live on the radio at five o'clock then the TV channels are recording an insert for the evening news programmes.'

She clenched her jaw and closed her eyes momentarily, forcing herself to focus on the next matter in hand.

'Rather you than me, boss.' Jenni grimaced from the driving seat. 'I don't fancy having to deal with the media – that scares me silly.'

Jenni checked her mirrors and pulled away from the kerb outside the Caring Guardian Children's Residential Home. An impatient Verity Mitchell, fifteen minutes late for her Zoom call, had provided the paperwork confirming that Philip Mortimer's service had been providing day trip transportation for the home for almost three decades. He was fully police checked, but to Hollie he was a remaining link between the dark allegations made in the inquiry and the present day. Verity was rightly embarrassed and squirming as she confirmed the contractual information.

'So, any thoughts about Ray McGregor yet?' Jenni asked, appearing to sense Hollie's agitation. Perhaps it was the way her fists were tightly clenched that gave it away.

Hollie exhaled a slow, deliberate breath to calm herself down. This is what DCI Osmond was afraid of – of emotions and personal involvement interfering in the case.

'I think he's earnest,' Hollie replied at last, 'but it did occur to me that he's a man with a strong motive.'

'Do you think so?' Jenni replied, clearly not of the same opinion. 'I think he's got a point to prove, but he strikes me as the kind of man whose revenge would be best served in the centre pages of a national newspaper.'

Hollie considered that.

'I agree with you, but let's not discount him. Let's hope he finds those old shorthand notebooks and the cassette up in his loft. I'm looking forward to our follow-up interview with him. I'll bet he has all sorts of names and contacts he can throw our way.'

'And what about Verity Mitchell?' Jenni continued. Hollie felt like she was being sounded out, like Jenni wanted to compare notes and see if they concurred.

'I think she's just like any other manager who's subjected to the scrutiny of inspection teams. Their lives are dominated by public-facing reports and interference. Who knows if you can tell what's really going on in a place from a cursory inspection? I say we need to be speaking to all the people who were running these charity trips, and Philip Mortimer just moved right to the top of my list.'

Hollie was dialling the office even as she said the words.

'Hi, DS Patel,' came the answer, swift and professional.

'Oh, hi, it's Hollie, what have you got for me, Amber?'

Hollie heard DS Patel shuffling her notes at the other end of the phone line.

'Forensics have the wheelie bin from the fairground and will get the detailed report to us ASAP. DCI Osmond did some leaning to move it through faster.'

Hollie still hadn't got a handle on DCI Osmond, but he had his uses, and she was grateful he'd made a priority of the bin.

'Oh, and Doctor Ruane says he won't be able to finish his work on the body until tomorrow morning. He sent his apologies, they're up against it, there's been an unrelated fatal stabbing in the city centre and he's under pressure, apparently.'

It felt like they were constantly having to do their jobs with fewer resources. She was sick and tired of hearing about backlogs.

'Are there any initial findings to mention?' she asked, pushing the negativity away from her. If she got down-mouthed about it, it would rub off on the team. There was no substitute for a good copper, and she had an office full at her disposal.

'I've got us a list of names of youngsters who were placed at the home, 1990 to 2001,' Amber continued. 'I emailed it over to you as soon as it came in.'

Hollie checked her phone and saw she had a couple of unopened messages waiting for her. She'd missed them coming in while she was engrossed in the earlier interviews.

'Talk me through it, would you, Amber?'

She placed the call on speaker phone, so Jenni could hear.

'OK, boss. It makes distressing reading, I'm afraid.'

Hollie's jaw tightened. Surely she must have Moira's name by now. Osmond needed to get a move on clearing her for the case, as it wouldn't take long for the penny to drop. She was ready for when they found out. It would be a sensation for five minutes, then they'd all get on with the job in hand.

'Go ahead,' they both said at the same time.

Amber took a long breath; she was bracing herself for something.

'Fifteen per cent of the people on this list are now dead,' she began.

Hollie did the maths; most of them would be her sort of age now.

'Do you know why yet?' Jenni asked.

'Suicide and substance abuse mainly,' Amber replied. 'I know these kids had troubled lives, but that can't be right, can it?'

Hollie shook her head; is that how Moira would have ended up? Her friend had been turning her life around at university. Hollie hadn't understood the monumental effort that must have taken back then; she did now.

'Of the other names I've been able to trace so far, several have ongoing issues with mental health, drug or alcohol use and the usual list of suspects. Ambrose House wasn't turning out that many well-rounded individuals, it seems.'

No mention of Moira and Simon yet.

'This is great work, Amber. Keep running through that list.'

By the time you get to Moira and Simon, DCI Osmond should have got his arse into gear.

'I take it we're interviewing the people who said Ray McGregor's newspaper article had legs?' Hollie added.

'Yes, a couple of interviews have been conducted over the phone, and we've dispatched detectives to the local calls. It's all been updated in the case log. I'll let you know if we get any bites.'

'What about the magistrate, Orsen Scott?' she wondered, recalling the photograph on Carrick's wall.

Amber let out a small laugh.

'Mr Scott is still a magistrate in the city, but he's significantly reduced his availability now he's older. He was pretty rattled when DC Gordon spoke to him on the phone. He demanded police protection.'

That made Hollie's ears prick up.

'Did he give any reason why he's so afraid?' Hollie asked.

'He's on the board of trustees—'

'Still?' Hollie's heart had just started protesting again.

Amber seemed thrown by that. 'Why, boss?'

'For fuck's sake!' Hollie struck the door handle on the passenger side with her fist.

There was a pause from her colleagues, and she instantly regretted her sweary outburst. Perhaps DCI Osmond was right to be circumspect; she was finding it much harder to control her emotions than she'd anticipated.

'I'm sorry, Amber, Jenni, but are these people stupid? Has Orsen Scott had his home visit yet? If not, boot one of the DCs out of the office and get them down there ASAP.'

Amber waited until she was sure it was safe to continue.

'DS Anderson has sent Philpot and Norton over there. Carrick was also on the board, by the way, before the scandal, but he stood down immediately afterwards. These guys seem to wear positions of authority like badges.'

Hollie sighed. She could never understand why, in spite of screening procedures, so many paedophiles still managed to slip through the net. If Orsen Scott had been involved, or even implicated, how the hell was he still on the board of trustees?

'Have you managed to locate this Philip Mortimer yet?' She changed the subject. She heard Amber shuffling her notes on the other end of the line.

'Philip Mortimer runs Splendid Days – it's a small-scale community transportation business, providing services to local charities with several contracts placed with the council. It's a man-with-a-van type of affair, basically.'

'Now I think about it, I reckon I've seen that guy in the papers,' Jenni remarked. 'He always strikes me as one of these odd characters, a salt-of-the-earth do-gooder who looks like he'd be better suited to following random women along dark, lonely streets. You know the type.'

Unfortunately, Hollie knew the type only too well.

'The lady at the children's home says he has a current DBS check, or he wouldn't be allowed to work with children, but let's bring him in anyway. I want to find out how a man like him ends up playing golf with the local paedophiles – alleged paedophiles, I mean.'

Seeing that they were now close to the fairground, Hollie brought Amber up to date with their visits, then started to wind up the call, mindful that she needed some time to check the briefing notes that the Press Office had sent over via email.

'Is that us up to date?' she checked with DS Patel. It was growing darker already. The clocks hadn't changed yet, but several of the rides were operating now, no doubt making the most of the younger children who were out of school at that time. The day had flown by since she'd been there in the early hours, and she was looking forward to getting home and catching up with Izzy. She might even squeeze in that Face-Time call with Noah and Lily.

'There's one last thing I forgot to mention that Doctor Ruane passed on,' Amber said, her voice focused and intent.

'I hope you're saving the best until last, Amber?'

It never ceased to amaze Hollie how much her colleague could achieve over the course of a day.

'Maybe,' DS Patel replied. 'He said he'll talk you through it when you come to look over Carrick's body. But Doctor Ruane said he was on the scene when Kenneth Digby's death was called in.'

'Oh yes, that's useful. What did he have to say?'

'He made sure it was recorded in the coroner's report at the time. But in the official report, Digby's death was given an open verdict rather than death by suicide. Doctor Ruane said that suicide was suspected and there was nothing to suggest otherwise, but evidence of intent was lacking, and it was not one hundred per cent conclusive at the time.'

Hollie let it sink in. *So it might have been murder*.

'One more thing, boss, you're gonna love this—'

'Go on, Amber.'

'I was digging into the case files. Remember Harry found that Polaroid image of Tori Bellingham at the fairground this morning?'

'Yes, yes, go on,' Hollie encouraged her, sensing the excitement of Amber's discovery.

'It was discounted at the time, but uniform found an old Polaroid camera that had been smashed against Kenneth Digby's bedroom wall when his body was discovered. There has to be more than a passing chance that that was the same camera that took the photograph of Tori, given what we now know about those men.'

EIGHTEEN
HULL, 1999

The table in the interview room at Osbourne Road police station was covered in names and messages written in pen or scratched into the wood. Hollie hadn't expected that. For some reason, she'd always thought an interview room would be better than that. It reminded her of the graffitied desks at school, their surfaces desecrated, chewing gum stuck underneath.

Her nerves were in overdrive. Just being in that place made her feel guilty, or responsible in some way, like she was in the spotlight.

There were posters on the walls, too. Most advised on how to prevent bicycle thefts, shed break-ins and purse snatches. There was a Crimestoppers notice there and a wanted poster, which Hollie thought only existed in Western movies. Humberside Police were hunting for a man in connection with a series of violent assaults on sex workers. It made her shudder.

This was a sinister world from which she'd been protected throughout her life; had it now claimed Moira as one of its victims?

Somewhere in the building, Judith and Lucy were going through the same thing as she was. It was intimidating sitting there, waiting for the police officer to return. Her hands were shaking, and she forced them between her knees in order to steady them before someone came in. They'd think she was involved in Moira's disappearance the way she was reacting.

She jumped as the door opened and one of the officers who'd attended to her at the fairground came in with a plastic cup filled with water. He placed it in front of her, saying nothing, and took the seat opposite.

'So, I need to take your witness statement, as Sergeant Maxwell said,' he began. He sounded like he'd done this a million times before and approached it in the same manner she might have tackled one of her university essays – with a look of resigned boredom.

'All I need from you is an exact statement about what happened this evening. You're not in any kind of trouble, this is standard procedure. The more details you can give us, the more likely we are to be able to find your friend.'

Hollie nodded. She was already uncertain of some of the details of what had happened, it had all played out so fast. Her mind was clouded by uncertainty and doubt. It seemed so formal now, having to write it down, and she didn't want to make a mistake. She wished she could stop her hands from trembling. Her throat was dry, so she took a sip of water. Her gulp sounded loud to her; would he read that as suspicious? Why did she feel so guilty when she'd done nothing wrong?

As the officer took down her basic information, she relaxed a little, the questions simple and routine. He then asked her to explain in her own words what had happened.

She hesitated, anxious not to mess this up for Moira's sake.

'Moira hadn't wanted to go to the fair, but something made her change her mind.'

The officer wrote as she spoke. She tried to read his scrawl upside down, but it was too far for her to see clearly.

'We separated from Judith and Lucy after a while, because we liked different rides.'

'Was that at your request?' the officer asked.

'What?'

That seemed an odd question.

'Was it you who wanted to split off from your group?' he rephrased.

'No, we just liked different rides, and it seemed most sensible if we were going to make the most of the evening.'

He scribbled something down, and she tried her luck at working out what he was writing again, with no success.

'Carry on,' the officer encouraged her.

'I thought Moira was having a good time, it seemed that way,' Hollie continued. 'But then, just as we'd come off one of the rides, everything changed suddenly.'

'Had you argued?' he asked, looking up at her, searching her face.

'No!' she responded, prickly and annoyed. 'We were laughing and having fun. Then the mood changed.' Hollie waited for him to challenge her again, but he said nothing. 'Moira went rushing off. She'd seen somebody – a man – with red hair.'

'Did you recognise this man?' The officer's interruption seemed urgent this time.

'No, he could have been anyone. But I'm sure that's who she was following.'

'How sure?'

Why was he pushing her on this?

'I'm certain. He had red hair—'

'And it wasn't just the fairground lights?'

His eyes were on her now, fixed and cold.

For a moment, she doubted herself. 'I suppose...' she began hesitantly. 'Well, yes, it might have been the lights from the rides. But I don't think it was. I'm as sure as I can be that his hair was red.'

Is this what the police always did when they took statements? She was growing increasingly less sure about the details of what she'd seen.

'What happened next?' he asked, matter of fact now, the seeds of doubt sown in her mind.

'I followed her into the fairground. It was dark behind the rides – the show people pitched their caravans there. I called out for Moira and knocked on one of the caravan doors.'

'Had they seen or heard anything?' the officer asked.

'No, no. They were children. I think I might have frightened them, actually.'

The officer stopped writing, gave her a disapproving look, then set his pen to paper once again. As she continued to recount the details, he rephrased what she was saying and read it back to her. It was her account, but in his words. She assumed he was doing that for clarity, but she'd expected a witness statement to be only her words. It was all so unfamiliar to her that she went with the flow.

They were interrupted by a knock at the door, and it startled her again. She'd seen so many police officers that evening, she was finding it difficult to work out who she'd seen already and who was new.

'Hollie, we've checked out your friend's house and nobody is there.'

She felt her heart sink and she was unable to complete a swallow. She reached out for the cup of water once again. Her hand was shaking, and she almost knocked it over. Both officers noticed it, too.

'We'll leave a police vehicle there overnight, in case she comes back,' the second police officer continued. Then he hesitated, suddenly uneasy. 'I hate to ask you this, but is there any chance she might have...'

Hollie could see the police officer was bracing for something. What was he going to suggest? Her mind was frantic, terrified at what might be coming next.

'Is there any chance she might have gone off to see a boyfriend or maybe met someone there?'

She couldn't put her finger on it, but the tone had suddenly changed, and she didn't know why. It felt like they were trying to fob her off, perhaps even find an excuse not to take the matter seriously. She would not let them do that.

'Moira didn't have a boyfriend,' she replied, steadying her voice.

Was Simon a boyfriend, or just a friend? Moira had invited him to stay over at her flat. It hadn't felt like that kind of arrangement at the time. Was she being naive?

'Something distracted her, like I just told you. She saw someone she knew. That's why she walked off. You saw the state of her soft toy.'

The police officer studied her for a moment.

'Okay, I'll let you know if there are any updates,' he said at last, like he'd decided to give her the benefit of the doubt for now. He leaned down and whispered something in the other officer's ear. He nodded his head and grinned.

'Oh, one more thing,' the second officer said, turning back to face Hollie. 'We found your Student Union card tucked between the cushions on Moira's sofa.'

'And?' Hollie challenged, immediately alerted by his accusative tone. 'I must have dropped it there when I visited last time.'

'There was something else.'

Hollie looked at him; could they hear her heart pounding?

'There was a broken cup on the floor. It looked like it had been thrown against the wall.'

Hollie knew she was giving him a vacant look, but that's how she felt: clueless.

'There were splashes of coffee up the wallpaper, too,' he continued.

Where was he going with this?

'It looks like it might have been thrown in anger.'

He stared at her, as if he was expecting her to say something. Had Simon and Moira had a disagreement that night?

'Did you and Moira have an argument?' the first officer asked. They were working as a team now. It felt like they were trying to corner her.

'Where did you say you found Moira's scrunchie, Hollie?' the second officer asked. 'It wasn't in your pocket all the time, was it?'

Hollie's throat was dry, she could barely speak. Her chest felt tight and her clothing clammy.

'Look, I didn't hurt Moira,' she protested. Why was she having to defend herself? She was trying to help her friend. 'Judith and Lucy will tell you we were at the fairground together. They'll tell you we hadn't fallen out.'

The second police officer gave her a cold stare; it felt like he was searching the very depths of her soul.

'I have to ask you this, Hollie. We have to cover all the angles. Did you hurt your friend, Moira? Did the two of you have a fallout which resulted in you harming your friend at Hull Fair this evening?'

NINETEEN

Hull Fair was in full swing by the time Jenni parked the car. In complete contrast with Hollie's morning visit, the rides were now active, and the early evening crowds were making their way around the multitudinous attractions. There was a crackle of eager anticipation in the crisp autumn air.

'Do you want me to stick around, boss, or will you hitch a lift back to HQ afterwards?'

Jenni looked like she was hoping to hang around. She'd missed out on that morning's visit to the newly discovered crime scene, and Hollie couldn't blame her for wanting to take a look for herself and sniff around a bit. She was always happy to have new eyes in a case, on the off chance they spotted something that had been missed.

'Come with me and see how it works with the press. It'll be good for your personal development. We've got time to check out the crime scene first, though. Have you done media training yet?'

'A bit,' Jenni replied, fidgeting in the driver's seat, her voice wavering at the prospect of facing a wall of journalists. 'The thought of it horrifies me.'

Hollie climbed out of the car and checked her phone to see where she was supposed to be meeting for the press briefings.

'The media is a big part of a case like this,' she continued, looking around to get a sense of direction. She started walking and Jenni followed close by. It was a vast site and even harder to navigate with all the noise and bustle. 'This place will be buzzing tonight with people talking about the death. Anderson's got extra officers all over speaking to members of the public, and we need to keep an ear out in case anyone saw anything.'

They made their way through the crowds, which seemed busy for the early time of evening. Already music was blaring from speakers, show people were encouraging passersby to dip their hands in their pockets and try the stalls, and the smell of frying food was wafting in all directions.

'Here it is,' Hollie said, having successfully located the ghost train where Carrick's body had been found earlier that day. The ride was now completely cordoned off with fencing and police tape, and a witness appeal poster citing the Crimestoppers number was attached to the front of it. A couple of bobbies were stationed there, standing next to an 'A' board on which were written the words:

CAN YOU HELP?

'You're not going to be able to see much now it's all blocked off,' Hollie continued, 'but be my guest, take a walk around, see if you can come up with anything that the rest of us might have missed. We've got ten minutes before I'm needed by the press team. We're meeting over by the big wheel at the far side of the showground, so if I lose you, meet me there.' Hollie pointed into the distance, and Jenni followed her track. She felt like she was letting a blood hound off its leash.

The sight and sounds of the fair brought 1999 roaring back

into Hollie's mind. If she closed her eyes, she could see herself –
nineteen, young, naive, and with her whole life in front of her.

She looked around for Jenni, who'd disappeared into the
darkness, and a sudden spark of fear engulfed her as she
recalled Moira disappearing into the night just like that. She
shook herself out of it; Jenni knew what she was doing, this was
her job.

Hollie headed over to the big wheel, making her way
through the crowds. Soon enough, the BBC and ITV vehicles
appeared up ahead; they were parked at the far end of the showground, away from some of the noisier rides. The DCC was
there already, chatting to a BBC reporter, as well as a woman
from the Press Office who spotted Hollie walking over.

'Hi, I'm Lisa Courtney,' she introduced herself. 'You've got
two TV interviews and three radio interviews, I'm afraid. The
DCC was keen to roll out the big guns seeing as Hull Fair is
such a big deal. The council are concerned that a murder might
be bad for business, so it's a case of steadying the horses and
letting the city know that it's all under control. Did you get your
briefing notes?'

Hollie had scanned them briefly while they were driving
over, but Jenni had been keen to press her on Moira and what
had happened to her back in 1999. There wasn't much new to
say to the press, and she wanted to withhold the information
that she'd gleaned during the day until they'd had a chance to
consider it as a team at the next day's briefing.

DCC Warburton had spotted Hollie and was walking over
to join them.

'Would you excuse us a moment, Lisa? I just need a
moment with DI Turner alone.'

Lisa took her cue and walked over to chat to the reporters.

'Just walk this way, I don't want them overhearing us,' DCC
Warburton said secretively.

Hollie followed her lead to the rear of a doughnut van,

intrigued now. The smell from the van was divine, and it reminded Hollie that she was hungry.

'I just wanted to catch you about your personal involvement in the case,' the DCC began. 'DCI Osmond gave me a full briefing.'

Hollie held her breath, hardly daring to guess what was coming.

'I want you to remain in charge,' the DCC began, and Hollie exhaled slowly.

'Your knowledge of what happened back then could be crucial to this case. You're uniquely positioned. It may not link back to when you were here as a student, but if it does, we might end up solving two cases at once.'

DCC Warburton's face was straight. She'd given this some serious thought.

'If you're certain it won't compromise us in any way, ma'am?' Hollie asked, feeling immediately foolish for seeking further approval. This is what she wanted. This is what she needed to get justice for Moira.

'If you're up to it, I'm more convinced than ever that you should stick with it,' Warburton continued, earnest and emphatic. 'We should tell the investigations team at tomorrow's morning briefing and get it out of the way.'

Hollie pictured herself in the briefing room, explaining it to the team. There'd be some open mouths the next day, that was for sure.

'We'll need to brief the press immediately afterwards so they can't hijack us with it at a later date. We'll go for complete transparency. If at any point in the investigation we feel you may be compromised, I'll ask you to step aside, and DS Anderson can assume the lead role. How does that sound?'

Hollie's pulse quickened as she dared to imagine some resolution to Moira's disappearance after so many years. She owed this to her friend.

Hollie and DCC Warburton rejoined Lisa and the various journalists, and one of them with a BBC Radio Humberside emblem on her microphone stepped forward and commandeered Hollie.

'Hi, Hollie, I'm Rachel Elliot, thanks for agreeing to speak to us today. Would you just put on a set of headphones, there's some audio you need to hear before we do the interview. It's live, by the way, so we need to keep going whatever happens.'

The sight of the microphones and the TV cameras took her back to the reconstruction two decades previously. Facing that reporter, with the fairground to their side, music pounding, lights flashing, shrill voices filling the nighttime air, she felt like a teenager again, scared about what might happen next.

Her hands shaking, she placed the headphones over her ears, and the sound of the radio station's output could be heard on one side, and comments from the producer coming from the BBC Radio Humberside studios on the other. The studio presenter began to introduce the news item.

'A retired superintendent from Humberside Police was found dead on the Hull Fair showground in the early hours of this morning. He's been named Gordon Carrick, aged sixty-eight, from West Ella in West Hull.'

Hollie thought back to Carrick's corpse, bloodied and cowed, the victim of what must have been a revenge attack.

The presenter carried on reading the introduction.

'In 2001, Mr Carrick received damages amounting to two hundred and fifty thousand pounds after he won a libel case connected to unfounded allegations at what is now the Caring Guardian Children's Residential Home in the city. In a moment, we'll cross live to Hull Fair where our reporter Rachel Elliot will be speaking to the detective leading the murder investigation. But first, here's Rachel's exclusive report on what's been happening today.'

A pre-recorded report could be heard on one side of her

headphones, and the producer's voice appeared on the other side, informing them that the recorded item lasted three minutes, after which Rachel should pick up off the back of it.

'You might want to listen to the last minute,' Rachel said. 'I'm going to ask you about it in my first question.'

Hollie jolted at that remark. What did that mean?

She focused on what was playing through her ears, listening intently as the Ferris wheel began to turn just ahead of them. It was massive – she estimated at least fifty metres in height. When did Ferris wheels treble in size? They all seemed as high as the London Eye these days.

The report outlined the details of the case, with interviews from show people and a councillor expressing concern that a scare like this might keep the crowds away. It was the staple fare of the press so far.

Her heart skipped a beat as she listened to a piece of audio which she hadn't heard for well over twenty years. Her nerves were on fire as it started to play.

Hollie didn't even know how they'd managed to lay their hands on it. She thought her legs might give way. The report ended and Rachel introduced her. They knew. How come they knew already?

She imagined she saw Moira, disappearing behind the caravans, a soft hue from the fairground rides colouring her silhouette.

They were now live on the radio across the entire Humberside region.

'Thanks for joining me, DI Turner,' the reporter began. Hollie swallowed hard, fearful that she would be unable to find her voice.

'So, you heard the audio from the *Crime Beaters* TV reconstruction, which was recorded in 1999, and in which you played the role of nineteen-year-old Moira Kennedy who disappeared from this very showground twenty-five years ago.'

They'd found out before they had a chance to stage manage it. How would this make Humberside Police look now? The reporter carried on as Hollie braced herself for a hijack. Her imagined image of Moira disappeared into the nighttime and her emotions flared as the first, inevitable question came.

'Is it right that you should be investigating a case in which it's very likely you have an intimate personal involvement? I mean, you were there at the time, weren't you? Surely you could also be a suspect?'

TWENTY

Hollie was shaken but not entirely surprised by the BBC interview. Her one consolation was that her secret was now well and truly out there. It didn't get more public than a live interview on the BBC.

It was dark now, the city drive-time traffic was slow and, knowing she'd got Izzy waiting at home for her, she ordered a Chinese meal as she left the office, which was just being dropped off as she walked up to the front door.

It was fitting that Izzy was back in the city for the first time since they'd left it together over twenty years previously. At that time, Hollie had dropped out of her course, determined to join the police. Her parents had offered to look after Izzy while she trained. It had been tough, but they'd managed it. It was something they'd shared together, even though Izzy was far too young at the time to remember much of it.

As soon as the front door was closed, Hollie placed the brown paper bag on the hallway carpet, and Izzy walked over to greet her. Hollie's stomach grumbled.

'I'm famished – that chicken chow mein is calling to me.' She smiled. 'Did you have a quiet day?'

'Yes, just a couple of callers at the door, mainly delivery guys wanting me to take in parcels for the neighbours. There was another guy, too—'

Hollie interrupted by asking her daughter to grab a couple of plates from the kitchen. As Hollie carried the takeout boxes into the dining room, her preoccupied mind distracted her from what Izzy had been trying to say. Settling into chairs at the worn table, they busied themselves opening up cartons, and between them, they spread out the Chinese food. It was all still piping hot.

'I don't know how these delivery firms get it dropped off so fast,' Hollie remarked, crunching on a prawn cracker. 'I don't think I could cook it any quicker myself.'

They tucked into the food.

'That was a long day at work, Mum,' Izzy said, chewing on a spring roll as she spoke. 'I see they're still grinding you into the ground.'

There was a hint of concern in Izzy's voice as well as a tinge of resentment. This is what her daughter had known all her life.

'It's always the same on a new case,' Hollie replied, reluctantly delaying the devouring of a delicious prawn that was perched on the end of her fork. Her mind returned to the BBC interview. They'd known everything about what happened in 1999. Sometimes the press seemed further ahead than the police. They'd put her under a lot of pressure as to whether she should be involved in the case; at least she'd had a great practice run for that in her chat with DCI Osmond.

'There's a lot of pressure with this one,' she replied, trying to shake off her worries about the interviews. 'I'll be on the telly in a couple of minutes, do you want a laugh?'

She was attempting to shrug it off, but it would be a good chance to see how she'd handled it. In the moment, she had felt like her jaw had dropped to the ground. She hoped it wasn't as bad as that in reality.

Izzy was more than keen to watch her mum's performance.

Hollie found the remote and switched on the small, flat-screen TV which was still perched on a large cardboard box. She'd bought what furniture she had in the new rented house via a charity store. Not only had she part-furnished her new home for under five hundred pounds, but she'd also contributed to the very heart research charity which might help save her life when all the bad eating finally took its toll. As far as Hollie was concerned, it was a win-win situation.

As the TV presenters ran through the evening's main news stories, the two women fell silent, and Hollie noticed how Izzy was seemingly preoccupied by her thoughts.

'What's on your mind?' she asked, observing how much her daughter had matured since her foreign travels.

Izzy began speaking then stopped before she'd formed half a sentence. She paused and picked her words carefully.

'Watching you come and go from work these past few days, it's made me think about things,' Izzy started again, returning to her theme.

It sounded to Hollie like she had something to get off her chest.

'I wasn't fair to you.' Izzy placed her fork on the table. 'You brought me up on your own when I was tiny, and you had Noah and Lily to cope with later on, as well as your job. It was easy for Dad.'

Hollie always liked the way Izzy called him Dad. He was, and always would be, her dad, in terms of what he'd done for her. Never once had he treated her differently from the other two children. She had to remember that Léon was a good man, however angry she felt with him over their recent split. He was an excellent dad and had been the perfect male role model for her eldest daughter – prior to the extramarital affair.

'So,' Izzy continued, her cheeks slightly flushed now and her eyes moistening. 'I'm sorry for giving you such a hard time.

I've had a lot of time to think about it while I've been travelling. I've got to figure out how I'm going to start earning my living now I'm back, and it's made me grow up a bit, I think.'

This was new territory for her daughter, but it marked a welcome softening for Hollie after some of their problems during her teenage years. She hoped they could reestablish the closeness they'd once enjoyed when Izzy was younger. Policing was not the best job to have when you had a pubescent daughter who was railing against everything her mother said or did. It seemed to Hollie that the first teenage pimple that appeared on Izzy's face signalled the end of the easy relationship that they used to have. It was as if Izzy was so angry with her all the time, but she couldn't articulate what it was that Hollie had done wrong. It was one of Hollie's greatest wishes that they'd get things back to how they'd once been, and what Izzy had just said to her was a great start.

There was a time, in Hull, when it had just been the two of them against the world. Her mind drifted as she remembered Elijah. She'd rarely thought about him since leaving Hull, he'd long since been consigned to the cast of bit-part actors in her life. It was so long ago now, she barely remembered his face. He'd most likely be bald and overweight by now. Izzy had only ever known Léon.

'It's on now, look.' Hollie pointed. 'There's that reporter at the fairground.'

She turned up the sound on the TV so they could hear it properly.

'You look so cold,' Izzy remarked as she dipped a prawn cracker into a small tub of duck sauce.

Hollie hated watching herself on TV but knew the best way to learn how to improve her performance with the press was to cringe her way through it and take the lessons on the chin. What she wasn't prepared for in the TV version was the film footage of the reconstruction.

Izzy gasped when she saw it. Hollie felt stunned, like she'd just caught a reflection of her younger self in the mirror.

'Is that you?' Izzy exclaimed.

Hollie felt the weight of lost years on her shoulders. All the time it was buzzing in her mind – there was something ethereal about it. But seeing her younger self on the screen like that transported her back in time to being that scared, overwhelmed teenager, desperate to find her missing friend.

'I was three years younger than you are now.' Hollie grimaced. She'd not seen this film footage since she'd first sat down to watch it with her friends in their student house. Listening to the audio of it in the earlier radio interview had helped prepare her a little, but seeing herself there made her want to cry. All that lost time, and still no word of Moira.

'Look at that hair!' Izzy teased, looking at her mum like she couldn't believe she'd had a life before her. 'You look so old-fashioned now.'

They kept quiet as the old *Crime Beaters* TV footage showed Hollie – dressed to look like Moira had on the day of her disappearance – walk through her friend's last-known movements.

Izzy sat in silence. She stopped eating her food as if she was entranced by seeing her mother all those years ago.

Hollie was grateful to be able to watch it quietly; it had a more profound impact on her than she could have possibly expected.

Watching the TV reconstruction was like reliving those moments all over again; the fear of what had happened to Moira, the frustration of finding someone to help her, the slowly descending realisation that she'd disappeared and then – the nightmares about what happened to her.

A shiver ran through her as she felt that same sense of desolation that she'd experienced when the police came to tell her that they were scaling down the investigation.

At least Rose Warburton gave the reporter a robust defence of the reasons for keeping her on the case. It felt good to have the DCC in her corner.

'We all want this murder solved fast for everybody's peace of mind,' she'd said, 'and with DI Turner heading the investigation, it's like having a consultant with unique historical experience at our fingertips.'

Hollie was grateful for the vote of support but simultaneously pressured by the extra expectations that heaped upon her to bring the investigation to a swift conclusion.

With Hollie's pre-recorded insert out of the way, the camera was now off her and turned on to DCC Warburton, who was assuredly answering questions about the children's home investigation, the potential links with Moira's disappearance and the possible reasons why somebody might want former Superintendent Gordon Carrick dead.

'It's one hell of a case,' Izzy interrupted as the report diverted from Hollie. 'I can see how you get so caught up in this stuff.'

She must have caught the look on Hollie's face. She squeezed her mum's hand.

'I'm sorry, that was insensitive of me,' she spoke gently. 'You lost your friend that day. I can't even begin to imagine what that's like. You never spoke about it. I wish you had.'

Izzy was growing up at last. She'd finally realised life wasn't all about her.

As Rose Warburton was speaking on the TV, two images flashed up on the screen: one of Moira and one of Simon Rose.

The change of view on the screen caught Hollie's attention, and Izzy followed her gaze. Izzy's eyes widened momentarily before the images disappeared from the screen.

Izzy seemed agitated; she had an odd, puzzled look on her face.

'What's up?' Hollie checked.

'I want them to put the photo of that guy up on screen again.'

'Why?' Hollie looked at her, intrigued and a little nervous at her urgency.

'There was just something about him... you know I said we had a couple of callers at the front door today—' She didn't finish her sentence but, instead, was transfixed by what was on the TV.

The images were flashed on the screen once again, only for a few moments, but it was all that Izzy needed.

'It is him!' she exclaimed.

Hollie was trembling now, unable to grasp what her daughter was trying to tell her, but aware that whatever it was had sparked something connected with the case.

'What's this about?' Hollie pushed, desperate to know, but fearful of what was coming.

'Bloody hell, do you know that guy in that photo?' she asked.

'Yes, he's Simon Rose. Why?' Hollie replied. 'What the hell is it, Izzy?'

'I know that man,' she began.

Hollie's heart thudded deep in her chest.

'You can't—' she protested.

'I know him!' Izzy interjected. 'He's older now, of course, but I'm telling you, sure as day, I've seen that man. He was one of the people who called at the front door this afternoon.'

TWENTY-ONE

HULL, 1999

'Action!'

Straining not to look at the camera or the assembled journalists to her side, Hollie walked from the Hook-a-Duck stall, moving hastily towards the crowd of people, and then ducking behind the caravans, just as Moira had done. They'd dressed her as closely as they could, right down to her friend's distinctive scrunchie. They'd found the packet in Moira's flat; there were four left, excluding the one Moira had been wearing that night.

'And cut! Perfect, Hollie, well done,' the producer shouted over to her, and she walked back towards the small filming team.

'We'll add in the sounds of the fair in the edit, as we have to be careful not to obscure what you're saying,' he explained. 'Take a break in the mobile cabin and we'll set up the cameras at the back of the caravans. You're doing well, Hollie, thank you.'

She felt a glow of pride as she headed over to the police cabin that they were using for changing clothes and rests between filming. She'd been sick that morning before leaving home, yet strangely didn't feel ill.

The two officers who she'd dealt with on the night Moira

disappeared were in the small cabin, speaking earnestly to the researcher. It was intimidating seeing them there so relaxed and assured, but she stepped inside nevertheless and greeted them all nervously.

She tried to recall their names; PCs Dennis and Mac-something if she remembered correctly.

'They seem to be playing down the man's distinctive hair,' she remarked, hesitant, addressing the producer rather than the police officers.

'We discuss this stuff with the police and focus on what's likely to bring in the best response from the public,' the young woman explained. 'I can talk to the director if you're not happy with anything.'

It wasn't that Hollie was unhappy, she just wondered why they weren't making more of it.

'Take a seat, Hollie,' the PC she thought to be Mac-something said before she had a chance to reply. Her stomach still wasn't right, but she put it down to anxiety.

Hollie did as she was told, unwilling to force the issue too much, but reluctant to let it drop. This was all about finding Moira, after all.

'Can you describe this man for me again?' the PC began, looking at her. Hollie felt like she was about to get ticked off by the teacher.

'He had red hair,' Hollie replied.

'What else?' he pushed, aggressive and dismissive.

'He was normal height. Just an average man, really,' she faltered. 'And he had the piercing, as I told you. And tattoos on his hands.'

'Was the light from the rides reflecting on him?' came Mac-something's swift and irritable reply.

'Yes,' Hollie whispered. She could feel her face burning and her hands starting to shake.

'What colours were the lights?' the second PC interjected,

accusative and challenging.

'You know—' Hollie spluttered. Her face was burning, her stomach in an uproar. 'Red, yellow, blue, green—'

'So, if he had blond hair and a fairground light reflected on him, it would look red?' Mac-something confronted her, seemingly oblivious to her discomfort.

'Yes. But that isn't how it was.'

Hollie felt a rising panic now. Every time she spoke to these men, they made her doubt herself, causing her to question what she knew had happened that night at the fair. She hung in there – for Moira – though she just wanted the room to absorb her.

'How sure are you about that?' PC Dennis chimed in, like he was the bully's diminutive buddy, following the leader. They were a tag team and appeared to take pleasure in it. The female producer shuffled in her chair; she was finding this as difficult to navigate as Hollie.

'Why don't we get some coffees?' the young woman asked, seemingly eager to get out of there.

'Sure,' PC Dennis answered. 'I'll come and help you carry the drinks.'

They left, leaving PC Dennis's previous question unanswered. The second cop was still waiting for his answer.

'I'm as sure as I can be,' Hollie ventured, feeling like her memories were being scrambled by this interaction.

His cold eyes were fixed intently on her.

Hollie hesitated. In the heat of the moment, with Moira not fifteen minutes out of her sight, she'd had no doubt. Now though, two days afterwards, challenged by this police officer, she was not so sure.

'Are you so certain about this guy's hair that you'd gamble your friend's life on it?' the PC pushed. He was beginning to make her feel like she was the guilty party here. 'Please tell me, Hollie, because that's what you're suggesting we do here.'

The blows kept coming, and she barely had time to recover in between them.

'No,' she answered, softly, feeling small and stupid.

'Only, you seem so sure of yourself, Hollie. You seem to know more than two experienced coppers and that TV director out there, who told me he's worked on *Crime Beaters* for eight series. If you think you know better, I'm happy to get them to wipe all the tapes and we can shoot all over again. Is that what I should do, Hollie? Tell them they've just wasted hundreds of pounds because you think they got it wrong?'

He was making an act of getting up off his chair like he was prepared to march out there and then to disrupt the production schedule on her behalf.

Hollie wanted the ground to swallow her up. The officer looked at her and smirked. He returned to his seated position.

'How old are you, Hollie?'

His tone was friendly now.

'Nineteen.'

He'd relaxed his body, so that it was much less adversarial. She, in turn, relaxed a little. The ordeal seemed to be over.

'I'm twenty-one, a similar age to you,' he said, like the previous hostile exchange had never happened. They might have been chatting in the pub.

He shuffled his chair, so he was sitting directly opposite her. He glanced back towards the door.

'You and I should be friends. We shouldn't be fighting.'

As he spoke the words softly, he moved his hand over and placed it on her right thigh. Hollie's stomach clenched tight; she felt sick, yet she was paralysed. What was he doing? Was this just him being friendly? Why didn't she just push him away? She couldn't find her voice to challenge him. Was this how a fly felt in a spider's web?

'It'll be much better for everybody if we can get along, Hollie.'

His words made her flesh creep, her face burned with the discomfort, and she thought she was going to vomit.

There were voices outside the door. All Hollie could do was to stare at him, a stunned animal in car headlights, waiting for the inevitable.

'We got your drink.' It was the producer and PC Dennis.

She stepped back into the mobile cabin. The police officer withdrew his hand and stood up.

Surely they could see it on her face. Hollie was unable to say anything, so stunned was she by what had happened.

'Good timing, we're finished here,' he said, brazen, taking a drink from the young producer. He stood up, held his stare on Hollie, then moved towards the cabin's exit.

'I've just set young Hollie here right on matters.' He sneered. 'You really need to leave these things to the police, young lady. You can trust us completely, we've got everything safely in hand.'

TWENTY-TWO

Hollie choked on the mouthful of food she'd just taken.

'What? No- no, that can't be right,' she stuttered. She placed her fork back in the foil takeaway tray, as her hand was shaking too much to continue eating. 'He'd be in his mid-forties now. He'll look nothing like that. He was a teenager when that was taken.'

Her chest felt like it might implode. If Simon was alive, perhaps Moira was still out there? It was difficult to swallow; her head was swirling with the thought that she might come face-to-face with Moira. But the sight of Simon, very much alive and well, threatened to overwhelm her; it was too much out of the blue.

'I'm telling you, it was him. I've never been surer of anything in my life,' Izzy protested.

Hollie looked at Izzy, clutching her arm with her right hand. She wouldn't joke about something like this.

'What did he want?' came her faltering voice.

'He just asked if you were in.' Izzy gave her a concerned look. She was old and wise enough now to read her mum's face.

'I assumed he was a neighbour. He sounded pretty casual about it.'

Hollie's head was thumping, as if there was so much going on in there she could barely contain this new information.

'You must be mistaken,' she challenged, shaking her head, trying to convince herself it couldn't be so. 'How would he even know where I lived?'

'Well, you're the copper, Mum.' Izzy smiled at her. 'You and I know it doesn't take that much working out. Besides, you've got that fancy doorbell outside. You've probably got a lovely photograph of him sitting on your laptop.'

Hollie hadn't thought to check the doorbell app. Her stomach twisted as she realised what Izzy was suggesting. She'd have images of Simon as he looked now. That would be a massive leap forwards in the investigation.

She'd been reluctant at first, but a bit of basic security on her new home seemed to make sense. A man had come round to set it up for her. By the time she'd been alerted for the sixth time by a parcel deliverer ringing her bell because a neighbour was out, she muted the alerts and had resolved to have the thing removed. However, it was probably still capturing images, even if it was no longer disturbing her every time someone called at the house.

'You can tell you've got a copper's genes,' Hollie said, reaching over to pull her personal laptop from the far side of the table, her cop's instincts pushing her fears aside now. She fired it up and accessed the website which was linked directly to the doorbell.

'For Christ's sake, look how many files there are already,' she pointed out to Izzy. Her eyes widened as she scanned more than seventy thumbnail images of short videos which had been recorded each time somebody rang the bell. Sometimes they were holding large parcels, most times they wore fluorescent vests or quarter-length shorts.

'What time was it when he called?' Hollie checked urgently.

'It must have been three o'clock, something like that,' Izzy answered, picking up on her mother's excitement.

'Jeez, two more delivery people have called since then,' she sighed. 'It's constant. It's a long time since I lived in a row of terraced houses, but this is a new phenomenon to me. It's the curse of the delivery driver. They must constantly be in search of a safe place to leave parcels.'

'The last one is you and the food deliverer,' Izzy observed. 'Open up that file, Mum, that's him.'

Hollie double-clicked on the video file, and it opened on her screen. She made it full-size. The outside light was poor, but Izzy had the hallway light on, and the man's face was clear.

She recoiled from the screen when she saw him, as if a spirit had just appeared before her. It was like seeing a ghost; she'd never expected to see this man again. She felt her face flushing as her anger and resentment began to flare up within her, a burning coal that was not yet ready to fade. She had to keep her copper's mind alert here; Simon might be the key to all of this.

She stared at the video. It was him, without a shadow of a doubt. He was older, of course, and there was grey in his hair. He looked quite well-to-do and poised now, but there was still the distinctive Hull lilt to his accent. It was exactly as Izzy had said. A brief exchange, perfunctory almost. He said he'd call again at another time. Just like he was a neighbour. When she closed her eyes, and listened to his voice, it was 1999 once again and she was a floundering nineteen-year-old.

'Look, he'd been here before,' Izzy observed, pointing to another thumbnail image.

'Damn, he was round here two days ago,' Hollie responded angrily. 'That's just before Carrick was killed.'

Hurriedly, Hollie double-clicked on the thumbnail. The video opened and she watched as the man – Simon, she was certain of it now – rang the doorbell a couple of times, waited, cursed, then turned away. As he turned, he took his mobile phone out of his pocket and dialled a number. All the time he was in front of the doorbell's camera, it continued to record him, audio and video. The picture quality was excellent.

As a street bobby starting work in the early noughties, Hollie had been constantly frustrated by the poor quality of video-based CCTV systems. These days, what with DNA advances and vast improvements in both the number and quality of surveillance systems, she wondered why the crooks even bothered getting out of bed in the morning.

The man pulled out a piece of paper, on which she could see the name of her lettings agent was printed. Simon walked away from the video; it had ceased sensing his presence and the video recording came to an abrupt ending.

'Dad warned you that that photo of the flat would lead to trouble,' Izzy said.

Hollie tapped in a couple of search terms into Google and an online newspaper article came up outlining the details of a previous case which had since made its way to court. Her son's abduction had been mentioned in the article, and to illustrate the point, the reporter had taken a photograph of the large building which contained her former flat in Pearson Park. A lettings board was attached to the window of the unit which she'd rented. It didn't take a genius to put two and two together, especially if Simon was keen to find her. Why not get in touch via work, though, surely that would have been easier?

'I think that bloody agent must have given them my new address,' Hollie cursed, her eyes flashing. 'For fuck's sake, everybody gets uppity about data protection and GDPR these days, but once they've got the announcement on their website and headed paper, they take no further notice of it. I shall be calling Larry Bolton Lettings and having a word with him.'

Hollie ran her hands through her hair, so roughly that it

tugged. As a cop, she did her best to have a zero imprint on social media. She was connected with her kids and parents, of course, but her privacy levels were locked down tighter than Léon's emotional response whenever she'd said she loved him at any time in the previous year. There were no holiday images, no pictures of the kids, not even an artful snap of her dinner. Hollie was a ghost on social media. She knew what nutters were out there and she had no intention of ever answering the door to one of them. However, when it came to other people's lax behaviour, she was stuffed.

'Who is he, Mum?' Izzy asked, picking up on her tension.

'He disappeared in 1999, at the same time as Moira. For a long time, the police thought he might have been responsible for whatever happened to Moira.'

It felt funny referring to them as the police. It was hard to remember a time when she hadn't been one of them. That was in the distant past now.

'We need to get the old files dug out on Moira's case. If Simon's back on the scene, that's one of our chief suspects back in the city. I want him hauled in ASAP.'

The adrenaline had gripped her now and her mind was running away with her. Was Simon the killer? Had he come back to finish off the men who'd tormented them in the home? Was Moira with him? She wanted to do a million things at once.

Izzy was smiling at her.

'You know, I'm beginning to understand why you get so obsessed with all this stuff,' she began.

'This is my past – my friend,' came Hollie's choked reply. She fought the tears that were forming in her eyes and lost the battle. 'After all these years, I might find out what happened that night.'

The thought of it made Hollie light-headed, her breaths coming fast and shallow.

Her mind snapped back into work mode. Izzy had been

speaking to a potential killer. Thank God he'd not harmed her. Where had he gone; was he watching the house? The flames of anger began to course through her once again.

Her head started swimming as the cocktail of danger and possibility began to take a hold of her. She tapped on her laptop and stared intently at her daughter.

'You're going to have to get out of the house for a while for your own safety. I'll pay for you to stay in town at the Royal Hotel, by the railway station. We need to get you booked in now.' She reached for her credit card and handed it over to Izzy.

'But Mum—'

Hollie held up her hand.

'No, Izzy. You're not staying here while that man is out there. For all I know, he killed Moira. I'm not risking it. Get yourself booked in and book a room for me, too. I'll run you over in the car.'

Izzy didn't argue; she knew that tone of old.

Hollie grabbed at her work phone as she watched her daughter navigating to the hotel bookings page.

She dialled into the office, praying that Anderson was still there. She was right; she'd rung through direct to his desk and he picked up almost immediately.

'Hi, boss, what have you got for me?'

It was as if her sudden urgency had been transmitted along the phone line, a potent spark of electricity that would ignite her colleagues.

'Simon Rose called at my house today. I'm going to email over some photographs. I want every damn available copper in this city looking out for that man.'

Hollie was shaking now, Simon Rose's sallow face taunting her mind. He'd been standing on her own doorstep face-to-face with her daughter. Her legs felt suddenly weak, her top clammy, as the terrible possibilities of what might have happened piled up before her. What if he'd hurt Izzy?

A rush of anger engulfed her, and her mother's protective instincts kicked in. If that bastard had anything to do with Moira's disappearance, he wasn't getting within an inch of her daughter ever again. Her hands tensed into fists.

'You're sure it's him?' Anderson ventured on the other end of the phone line.

'I'm sure it's him,' Hollie asserted, not a drop of doubt in her voice. 'And if that man is back in Hull, I can guarantee he's tied to Carrick's death in some way.'

TWENTY-THREE

Hollie was still thinking about Izzy when she pulled up at the morgue. Whenever she appeared on the local media, whether it be at a press conference or in an interview, she immediately felt like everybody was looking at her all of a sudden, trying to figure out where they knew her from. Simon was out there, too; he'd have got a good look at her on his TV screen or mobile phone. He now knew exactly what she looked like. Even worse, he'd spoken to her daughter.

'Would you like a coffee?' Doctor Ruane asked as he walked over to greet her from his office. He looked fresh and alert, which was more than Hollie could say for herself. 'Did you read my notes yet?'

She'd been up since the crack of dawn, catching up with the case notes, desperately seeking the thread that would tie everything together. She'd skimmed his email but preferred to discuss the details of the body in person, as it was easy to get distracted by all the forensic detail. She liked the *Reader's Digest* version first, before getting embroiled in the specifics.

Ruane sorted them both out with coffee, then led her to the area where the bodies were kept. He got himself suited up as they chatted and then walked her over to where Carrick's body was stored. One of his assistants had prepared the corpse for viewing, and he thanked her, and she left them to it.

Doctor Ruane shrugged on his overalls. 'So, my usual warning, it's not a pleasant sight, look away now if you don't want to see the results.'

He moved over to the cover and removed it carefully. Hollie screwed up her face as she got her first complete look at Carrick's body in proper light.

'I know, it's grim, isn't it?' Doctor Ruane remarked.

Hollie shook her head. 'Somebody was very angry with Gordon Carrick,' she replied.

'Looking at him, you'd say the cause of death is obvious, wouldn't you?' he continued.

'Yes. I'd guess the blows to the head did it.'

'Not necessarily correct, I'm afraid,' Doctor Ruane teased her. He certainly knew how to get her attention. 'Gordon Carrick may have had something injected into him before his body was mutilated—'

'What?'

'Yes, take a closer look here,' he said, pointing to Carrick's hip.

'What am I looking for?' Hollie asked, confused.

Doctor Ruane positioned a mounted magnifier and invited her to look again.

Hollie shook her head. 'Sorry.' She shrugged. 'I don't know what I'm looking for.'

'I believe the head injuries and body mutilation may have been done post-mortem. I suspect those are hypodermic needle entry points, but they've been obscured by the tissue damage. That may well have been intentional. Gordon Carrick might have died of an overdose, but I'm running toxicology reports, so I won't be able to confirm that until they're done.'

Hollie could barely take on board what she was hearing.

Her mind immediately shot to Jane Carrick. She was medically trained – how the hell would her husband OD... unless...

'Do we know if he was on any medication?' Hollie checked.

'Not that I'm aware of,' Ruane confirmed.

'Well, that throws the cat among the pigeons,' Hollie replied, reaching for her phone. 'Excuse me one moment while I call the office.'

She walked over to the far side of the room and took out her phone.

DS Patel answered.

'Do you ever go home, Amber?' Hollie asked.

'Occasionally,' came her resigned reply. 'It's so expensive to heat my place these days, I stay at work and let Humberside Police keep me warm on their buck.'

Hollie laughed but wanted to keep things brief. 'I'd like you to send Anderson over to see Jane Carrick as soon as he shows his face. Make sure he reads Doctor Ruane's report before he goes. I want to know what she has to say about it. She didn't mention anything about Gordon being on any medication when we spoke to her yesterday, and I want to know if he'd been prescribed anything by her or anybody else. And are we any further forward on finding out if she ever treated Kenneth Digby? The mere whiff of two injected overdoses is too much of a coincidence.'

'Like you said, boss, it's an admin nightmare getting access to medical records – they seem up to their ears at his medical practice. We're still chipping away at it, I'm afraid.'

Hollie finished off her call with DS Patel, then rejoined Doctor Ruane, who'd now covered up the body and was waiting for her. 'Thanks for trying to move things on over Kenneth Digby,' she said.

'Sorry I couldn't do more,' he replied, obviously disappointed he'd been unable to help. 'There's something else I wanted to tell you,' he picked up. 'If these men are linked by this case, I'd have to flag up potential anomalies with both their deaths. I concluded that Kenneth Digby had likely overdosed on insulin, but I was unable to confirm that. If Gordon Carrick died from an injection of drugs into his body, then my concerns over Mr Digby's death may be confirmed.'

'Might we be looking at an exhumation of Digby's body?' Hollie wondered, thinking it over as he said the words.

'In an ideal world, a second examination might be prudent. However, Kenneth Digby was cremated as soon as we were done with the body here.'

'At whose request?' Hollie asked.

'At Melanie Digby's. She couldn't wait to get him cremated the moment we released his body.'

'We'll pay for the taxi, there's no problem,' Shirley, the researcher, offered.

'No, honestly, it's been such a long day, the fresh air will do me good,' Hollie replied. 'When will it be on the TV?'

'It'll be on next Tuesday at nine p.m. You did a good job today, Hollie, well done. I'm sure if your friend is still out there somewhere, it'll help to find her.'

The two women were standing on the pavement outside Radio Humberside's Chapel Street studios. She'd just been there to record a remote interview with the *Crime Beaters* presenter who was still in London.

It was fully dark now and the early evening cold air was refreshing and invigorating. Hollie was keen to clear her mind and the walk along Beverley Road was a fair distance, but she wanted the alone time. Judith and Lucy would pounce on her the moment she opened the front door, as the prospect of her being on the TV had caused great excitement.

Hollie walked Shirley through the town centre, as far as the crossing opposite the railway station.

'Just head straight across the road and you'll see the platforms directly in front of you when you walk inside.'

They said their goodbyes and Hollie watched the young
researcher cross Ferensway until she disappeared into the
entrance of Paragon Station. She'd arranged to meet the rest of
the team there, where they'd catch a train back to London.

Hollie turned and headed out of the city, walking past
Hammonds and its brightly lit windows. Inside looked so warm
and inviting, but her mind was whirring after the day's events
and it was nice to be alone, even though the cars were beginning
to queue along Ferensway on the rush home from work.

As she made her way towards Beverley Road, Hollie
thought she caught a movement behind her. She glanced
around but it was still early evening, and everybody was making
their way home from work. She must have been mistaken – that
damn policeman had rattled her.

Beverley Road was at a crawl, and she crossed over just after
the Hotel Campanile, to the side of the *Hull Daily Mail* offices.
As she passed by the Banks Harbour pub, she looked down
Wellington Lane towards the nightclub entrance.

As Hollie progressed along the road, she wondered whether
to splash out on a bus to the junction at Cottingham Road. She
was beginning to wish she'd taken up Shirley's offer of a taxi
now as she was starting to tire. As Hollie crossed the small side
road to the site of the derelict Rediffusion building, she caught a
shadow at her side, moving fast towards her. Before she had
time to turn and check, someone had grasped her arm and was
pulling her towards the unlit doorway.

'Don't say a word,' a male voice said. It sounded familiar,
though whoever it was tried to conceal it.

She froze, her body tense with panic.

The abandoned building stretched some way along
Beverley Road and had what used to be a small parking area out
front, so it was set back from the path and road. She was pushed

into an unlit entrance area, where the old boards nailed across to secure the structure had been pulled away by vandals so that it was now accessible.

Hollie couldn't move, so taken aback by the speed of the man that she had no time to act or think. She took a gasp to shout out, but the rumble of the engines in the back-to-back cars and the revving of a nearby bus in the bus lane would have made it futile.

Whoever had taken her arm pushed her deep into the dark entrance area, her feet kicking discarded cans and bottles as she stepped deeper into the darkness. He turned her so her face was directly against a wall and his hand moved up to her neck, so he was pushing her face sideways against the brickwork.

'Keep your mouth shut. Just listen.' He was whispering in a husky voice, a clear attempt at obscuring his identity. His hand was covered with a leather glove.

Hollie's entire body was shaking, her legs weak with terror. She moved her eyes from side to side. On the left, the traffic continued to crawl along the road, oblivious to her plight. On her right was smashed glass and broken door frames, the once proud entrance to a prosperous Hull business.

'What do you want?' she stammered. 'I don't have much money on me.'

The man moved up close to her right ear and all she could hear was his breathing, close, intimate, threatening.

'No, please,' she pleaded. She ran through the list of things she'd been told to do at the Street Safety student briefings. Shout, scream, get the attention of a passerby. Scratch him and make a mark so he could be identified. It had seemed so simple when the Student Union reps demonstrated it, but now, in the heat of the moment, her voice failed her and all she could do was wait to see what he would do next.

He said nothing, just breathing close at her side, his hand firm on her arm but moving no further. It was as if he himself was working out how far he would go to terrorise her, a hesitant assailant.

'Please, just let me go—' she begged, the tears coming now.

He pushed his hand a little harder on her neck. It was hurting her nose, and the brickwork felt like it was grazing her skin.

'You're hurting me. Please, just let me go, I won't say anything.'

'Listen and listen well,' he whispered. She still couldn't make out if she knew the voice – it was a Hull accent, that was for sure, but there were no more clues to pick up on.

'You need to keep your mouth shut about your friend. There are powerful people in this city, and they don't like you blabbing off. Understand?'

'Yes – yes, I understand, I'm sorry.'

'If the cops ask you anything, tell them about your friend, but keep your mouth shut about the rest, okay?'

Hollie thought her legs were going to give way. She'd never been so scared in her life.

'Okay!' he repeated, pushing her harder against the brick wall. She just wanted him to go, as she was fearful he might threaten her further.

'I promise, I'll say nothing. Please, just leave me. I won't say a word.'

'If you do, you'll piss off some powerful people. Who knows what might happen?'

His hand had moved to her skirt now, his gloved fingers clutching its hem as if he was about to push it up.

'Please, no,' she sobbed. She felt sick at the thought of what he might do, and she began to retch.

Still, he kept his other hand pressed firmly against her neck.

'And don't think of calling the police. There are eyes and ears everywhere. A lot of bad things might happen to a nice girl like you.'

Suddenly, his hand was away from her skirt and the pressure released from her neck. He darted out of the dark doorway, leaving Hollie panting hard from a panic attack, the tears of relief and fear cascading down her face.

She stepped out of the terrifying darkness towards the light thrown off by a nearby streetlamp. There was no sign of him, either up or down the road. She stood by the roadside, sobbing, Hull's commuting drivers completely unaware of the ordeal she'd just been through.

TWENTY-FIVE

When Hollie entered the briefing room, she immediately noticed the still-frame photo that had been pinned up on the whiteboard. It had been taken from her reconstruction video and showed her youthful, nineteen-year-old face in a close-up. Somebody had drawn red hearts on the page.

As the senior investigating officer, she had a couple of options open to her, but she already knew which one she was taking. She could either go all-out ball-breaker and insist the person who'd put it there see her immediately in her office for a thorough dressing down. Or she could shrug it off, laugh it away and put it down to team building and camaraderie.

She knew better than to opt for her first choice; that way resentment and conflict lay. There were some things you had to take on the chin in the police force and this was one of them.

'Okay, everybody, let's get started,' she began, steeling herself. The room settled into silence, and Jenni Langdon darted in at the last minute, clutching a piece of paper.

'So, I take it we're all aware now of my personal connection to this case?'

Somebody at the back wolf-whistled; she let it pass.

She hadn't spotted DCI Osmond at the rear door, and he stepped into the room, clearing his throat to get attention. The wolf-whistler didn't venture further comment.

'Just for clarity, DI Turner's continuing involvement with the case comes with the go-ahead from DCC Warburton,' Osmond began. 'Between us, we have set up a protocol for if the DI feels she is compromised on the case, but we have decided that the background information and detailed knowledge that she can supply is, overall, more beneficial to our inquiry. Please continue, DI Turner.'

'Thank you, DCI Osmond.'

He was a man who was difficult to get a handle on. But he'd proved useful to her on more than one occasion.

'Twenty-five years ago, almost to the day, my university friend Moira Kennedy disappeared at Hull Fair. She was never located, a body was never found, and Humberside Police were unable to find out what happened to her.'

She looked around the room. The photo of her younger self might have created some amusement, but their heads were fully on the case. That's why a bollocking would have been wrong. The teasing was just a release.

'Moira had been raised in care at Ambrose House – now known as the Caring Guardian Children's Residential Home. Her friend from the home, Simon Rose, also disappeared at the same time.'

She searched in the clutch of papers that DS Patel had handed her in readiness for the briefing and held up one of the images taken from her doorbell camera the previous night.

'This is Simon Rose as he looks today. He called at my home last night. Simon was one of the suspects when Moira Kennedy disappeared, but no evidence placed him at Hull Fair on that night, or even in the city. We've issued an alert to all mobile units to be on the lookout for this man, and we'll be bringing him in ASAP if he makes another appearance. And, needless to say, I have the alerts switched on from my doorbell, so if he calls at my home again, I'll be able to speak to him directly via the speaker facility. This man is our prime suspect, and as far as I'm concerned, he's dangerous and a potential threat to anybody who was caught up in the Ambrose House allegations.'

It was possible that he was also a threat to her, but Hollie forced those thoughts out of her mind. Izzy was safe at the Royal Hotel now. She pressed on.

'Although I didn't know any of this twenty-five years ago, I believe Moira may have spotted Kenneth Digby in the Hull Fair crowd that night. At the time of his death, Digby had shaved off what little was left of his hair, but as a young man he had a full head of red hair and a distinctive piercing in his eyebrow, as well as scrappy hand tattoos.'

She held up two more photo prints, one of Digby in the group image taken from Carrick's office and one used in the newspaper for his obituary.

'The link between these men is strong,' Hollie continued. 'Ray McGregor is convinced his news reports were factually correct, and Moira and Simon were talking to him in confidence before their disappearance. Moira never confided in me the full details, but I believe she and Simon both had traumatic experiences at Ambrose House. Whatever it was I got myself caught up in back in 1999, I think it was brushed under the carpet when Gordon Carrick won his libel damages. I suspect at the very least he and Digby knew about what was going on or at most were directly involved.'

Amber Patel raised her hand. Hollie gave her the nod.

'On those child abuse allegations made at the time, I've managed to secure the transcripts from the inquiry interviews, and they've been distributed to everybody via email just before the meeting.'

'Can you give us an overview, DS Patel?'

'Yes,' she continued, consulting her notes. 'Carrick, Digby, Mortimer, the minibus driver, and the magistrate, Orsen Scott, were all implicated, as well as some others. Those four were cleared. Carrick pushed for damages, and Scott and Digby let it lie. Philip Mortimer seemed to be dismissed as a suspect very early on.'

'What sort of allegations were made?' Hollie asked, turning back to Amber. 'I mean, what were the specific allegations?'

'Sexual activity involving minors off the premises, boss, which is why it was so hard to pin it down.'

Hollie's stomach knotted. She'd had a hint of this already from Ray McGregor. How could Moira have been involved and not given away the horrors of her life before university?

'What do you mean, off the premises?' Hollie asked, hardly daring to step off this precipice.

'The youngsters were taken on day trips and then moved on to third-party locations where it's alleged the abuse took place.'

Hollie felt the rage blazing inside her. She wanted to scream. But more than anything she was desperate to reach back through the years and do things differently with Moira.

'I'm guessing Hull Fair was one of those places?' Anderson interjected.

'Remember, these are allegations, dismissed by the inquiry,' DS Patel reminded them. 'But yes, it was claimed that the youngsters would be taken on an annual trip to Hull Fair. At the end of the trip, the kids would – allegedly – be taken to some well-to-do home, where they would be passed around the various men there.'

Hollie sighed, her heart sinking, a queasy feeling in her stomach. She could see where this was heading. If it involved Moira, a part of her wanted to be shielded from this information. A fiery indignation burned deep in her heart, and she had to take a moment to compose herself.

'Why did the inquiry dismiss the allegations so readily?' DC Norton asked.

'It was written off as hysteria and rumour at the time,' DS Patel explained, clearly angered. 'And several of the youngsters withdrew their allegations at the last moment, saying they'd been encouraged to lie by some of the older youths who wanted to stir up trouble. It relied on the testimony of two teenagers in the end. One of them committed suicide shortly after the inquiry, the other died of alcohol poisoning five years ago.'

There was silence across the room. Brains were working feverishly, as was Hollie's. The anger inside her was glowing like the furnace of a steam train, and with every horrifying suggestion made by the team, the flames spewed higher and more fiercely. She was shaking, as if her body could barely contain her sense of rage.

'This has all the makings of a cover-up,' Hollie said at last, having fought to steady her voice.

Poor Moira. She should have been a better friend.

'Are you all right, Hollie?' DS Anderson asked softly.

She shook herself out of it.

'Yes, I'm sorry.'

Her heart felt leaden at the thought of Moira on her own, dealing with such horrible things in her life.

'I'll bet any money she saw something going on that night and she was trying to prevent it—'

Hollie couldn't even think about the officers watching her there; all she could think of was how she'd let down a friend.

'How about you take a minute?' Anderson said, his voice kind and gentle.

She sat down and Anderson picked up her thread. His face was flushed; they were all feeling acutely the deep betrayal that these youngsters had been exposed to.

'I think this just goes to show that the brass made the right call on DI Turner's continuing involvement in this investigation. This stinks of a cover-up of historical abuse. There's plenty of motive here, any number of people might want Digby or Carrick dead. But the question is, all these years after those events, why the hell would somebody wait so long to get their revenge? What – or who – would draw them out of the shadows after so many years?'

TWENTY-SIX

'Thanks for taking over, Ben,' Hollie said as the briefing room emptied. 'Sorry for getting so distracted.'

'No bother, boss, I can see this is all still very raw for you,' Anderson replied with uncharacteristic empathy. Maybe he'd been taking notes from Jenni's book.

'I want a private word with you, actually,' he continued, an expectant look on his face.

'Sure,' Hollie replied, switching back into detective mode.

Private words with DS Anderson were always of interest. Whereas some members of the team used side conversations to bitch or carp, Anderson always saved them for something juicy. He walked over to the briefing room door and closed it.

'I'll start with the simple stuff first—' Anderson began.

'Before you do,' Hollie interrupted him, not wanting to forget, 'would you see if there are any photographs from when Kenneth Digby died? Were any items retained, were photos taken of his body, that sort of thing? Something Doctor Ruane told me is bothering me. Can you chase that for me? I want to see it for myself.'

DS Anderson noted down her request, and then carried on with what he'd come to say.

'We've done some digging on that Polaroid camera – well, DS Patel has. Apparently, it's a Polaroid OneStep 600 Express, and it was released in 1997, which coincides with our timeline. These things took instant pictures; they didn't need to go to the chemist to get developed. Frankly, they were a paedophile's dream come true.'

Hollie sighed. It wasn't the first time she'd encountered these instant cameras in abuse-related cases, and she was certain it wouldn't be the last.

'I've also been reading the old case files from 1999,' Anderson continued. 'I've spotted something which might, potentially, become explosive.'

She studied his face. The annoying thing with Anderson was that he was just as likely to be setting up a fart joke as starting to share some useful intel with her. As it turned out, a fart gag was far from his mind.

'Have you read them yet?' Anderson continued, looking like he couldn't wait to spill the beans.

'No, I haven't had time. DS Patel only told me she'd laid her hands on them when I came in this morning. What have you found?'

'Do you recall the names of the police officers who inter-viewed you at the time?'

Anderson was building it up – where was he heading with this?

'No, it was a blur,' Hollie replied, even though a tiny spark had just crackled in her mind. 'They all looked the same to me back then. Why?'

'It might be something, it might be nothing—'

'Go on. Don't hold back on my account,' Hollie encouraged him, picking up on his excitement.

'The officer who took your statement on the night Moira disappeared had the surname MacKenzie.'

Hollie's heart pounded in her chest, her forehead felt warm and clammy.

'What – as in DI Bryan MacKenzie, my predecessor?'

She recalled dealing with a Mac-something, but few names were given to her at the time and the officers that she was dealing with then were now just a blur in her memory.

Anderson looked like the cat who'd just got the cream.

'Yes, exactly. My former boss and your predecessor. What are the chances of that?'

'It's just a fluke, isn't it?' Hollie challenged, sensing already that it was anything but. That young copper had given her a hard time and tried to steer her evidence. But she had to be certain. 'I mean, like you, he worked here all his life. I might have encountered you, too – were you policing at that time?'

'No, I started a couple of years after, probably just before you.'

He was right about that. And it was MacKenzie who had pressured her all those years ago. He'd been lazy, even trying to obfuscate details. He'd been gaslighting her; she could see it clearly now.

'Okay, now you've got my interest.'

Hollie's mind was on fire. Her palms were moist with sweat, and she was struggling to slot the pieces into place.

'You reckon MacKenzie was caught up in something, don't you?' she suggested, still reeling from the prospect of him being involved in the Ambrose House case.

'Yep, I'm sure as anything. I don't know what it was, but casual killers don't chop off heads and limbs.'

He grimaced as he said the words. Anderson had discovered MacKenzie's body after his brutal murder in the line of duty. It had shocked every police officer in the city. But MacKenzie's death had looked like a contract killing; it was not the work of a ne'er-do-well out of his depth.

'That copper who interviewed me – I don't remember him as MacKenzie – but that police officer leaned on me to adjust my statement.' Hollie struggled to say the words, picturing herself as a young, intimidated student, scared to rock the boat too much.

'How?' Anderson pushed.

'I wanted to—' Hollie stopped and tried to swallow, her mouth gone dry. She coughed to try to clear it.

'Are you all right? You look like you're getting upset again.'

'That fucker—'

It was still so difficult to say the words. She thought back to that time when she'd been so young, vulnerable and naive. The words stuck in her throat.

'That bastard touched me. He ran his hand up my leg. He as good as told me to shut the fuck up.'

'Damn.'

Anderson looked genuinely stunned and there wasn't much that shocked a cop with his air miles in the job. 'Did you tell anyone at the time?'

'Nineteen years old, silly young girl, out of her depth, intimidated by all the police officers and terrified her friend was dead. I'll give you one guess.'

She felt the bitter resentment of having been humiliated by a bully. Even after so many years it stung.

Anderson was silent.

'I'm so sorry. I never knew he was like that. I once called him... a friend.'

Now he was struggling for the words. It appeared that they'd both been deceived by this man.

A shiver ran through Hollie's body as her memories transported her back two decades to that portable cabin, alone with the young PC MacKenzie.

'I liked MacKenzie,' Anderson said, struggling to say the words. 'I knew he could be a difficult bugger, but behaviour like that – fuck. I don't know what to say. Did you ever talk to anyone about it?'

'Who would I talk to? I was fucking angry afterwards, I can tell you that.' She was struggling to contain that anger even now. 'I was furious with myself for not kicking him in the goolies, and I was mad at him because I wanted him to find Moira. But he convinced me that I was confused about what I'd seen. As for the touching, to a certain extent, I just assumed it went with the territory.'

She could barely believe there was a time when she'd thought that; that inappropriate touching was just something that she almost expected. At least some things had moved on for the better since she was young.

'I just don't know what to say—' Anderson seemed as enraged as she felt. 'You might want to record this moment on video, as it doesn't happen very often.' He attempted to shrug it off.

Hollie laughed. She needed it, she was wound up tightly and wanted a release.

'Do you think he was involved?' she said at last. 'In a cover-up, I mean.'

Anderson paused a moment before answering. 'That's what I was just thinking. You said you saw a red-haired man; you've just told me he tried to distract you from that information. And now, two decades later, it seems that if they'd found that man it might have led them directly to Kenneth Digby. And that, in turn, might have led to the alleged abuse at Ambrose House.'

'Jesus, Ben, sometimes I feel like a shit magnet. I've spent my adult life thinking about Moira every day, wondering what happened to her, desperately wishing she was out there some-where. And now it seems like MacKenzie might have been up to his ears in it.'

'Do we tell the brass?' Anderson asked. His voice was lowered like they were colluding.

'Why wouldn't we? I mean, it's not like it can do any damage to his career now, is it?'

'What if this goes higher up, though? MacKenzie was just a PC back then, though he was a DI when he died. Gordon Carrick had seniority in the force, and Orsen Scott has local influence and contacts, too. This Ambrose House case feels like it runs deep to me. It hints at dark forces and hidden threats.'

'You'll be putting tinfoil on your head next,' Hollie teased.

But his face told her he was deadly serious. 'I mean it, boss.' His face was straight and earnest. 'MacKenzie's death was professional; it was a hit. This Ambrose House inquiry has all the makings of a stitch-up. And then there's your friend – what did she know? Was she silenced back in 1999? The whole thing stinks to me.'

'But why not tell the brass? If MacKenzie was compromised in some way, they need to know, surely?'

'What if the brass are in on it?' Anderson suggested, after some consideration. 'It only takes one bad apple.'

Hollie felt her body freezing, like a morning frost was stealthily engulfing her. She thought it over. It wouldn't be the first time a cop had got caught up in something bigger than they could handle. And Anderson was right: MacKenzie was just a DI at the time of his death, high up enough to be involved, but not so high up that he could call all the shots. If he was up to his ears, who else knew?

'Look, none of this impacts the case so far. MacKenzie is dead, so it's not like we can suspend him or anything like that. But if he was involved in a cover-up, even if he was just a tiny cog, we can't protect him from this. But for now, we can keep it between ourselves. It's not going to take long for Amber Patel to put two and two together when she trawls through those notes, and any number of people in that office are perfectly capable of making the same connection that you just did.'

Anderson nodded. 'So, what next, boss?'

'I want to speak to Orsen Scott directly. Everything we've discussed today puts him directly in the line of fire. I want to find out what he knows about the abuse of those children – and why he thinks he might be next on our killer's to-do list.'

TWENTY-SEVEN

HULL, 1999

'It's on, it's on!' Lucy screamed.

The ominous music of *Crime Beaters* began to blare through the TV speaker, and the flashing light of a police car took up the screen, followed by an animation of crime scene tape criss-crossing from corner to corner. The faces of the two presenters appeared on camera, and Hollie's sense of nervousness intensified as she realised that this was it and if she'd made a fool of herself, it was about to be seen by millions of TV viewers.

'You won't want to speak to us when you're famous,' Judith teased.

Hollie smiled, but even she knew it was hollow. She hadn't told the others about what had happened along Beverley Road yet. She was still too terrified to relive it in her mind, let alone articulate it with words. Every time she thought of that horrible man, she shuddered, and her body froze with fear. Who was he? Why was he following her? Why did he even care what she said?

'Coming up tonight, we'll have an exclusive reconstruction of a worrying case in Hull which has Humberside Police baffled.

A young girl, attending the city's annual fair, went missing without a trace...'

The girls quietened as the bare bones of what had happened were repeated in the show rundown. Despite the excitement of Hollie being on the TV, they were brought to heel by the heartbreaking reality of their missing friend.

The female presenter was seen behind the scenes with the police officers who were on the phones. Hollie spotted a couple of officers that she'd met already. They were down in London, answering any phone calls from the public which related to Moira's case.

A phone number flashed on the screen. The lines were busy already, but other cases were being covered in the programme, too, so it might not be of any use to them.

Hollie's short film was second in the running order.

'And now we turn to Hull, where nineteen-year-old Moira Kennedy went missing at Hull Fair just under two weeks ago.'

Moira's face flashed up on the screen, a photo which was not particularly flattering, but one of the few pictures the girls had of her. Hollie tried to push back her tears; she didn't want to get upset again. The presenter, Nicky Mason, continued with his introduction.

'In a moment, we'll be speaking to the officer who's leading the investigation in the city, but first, here's a short report from the showground which we hope will jog some memories about what happened on that night.'

Hollie's face was on the screen; she cringed at the sight of herself. It seemed unreal, watching herself in Moira's flat, looking like she was getting ready for a night out. They'd shot the footage in reverse order – it all made sense on the TV, but it felt odd to her knowing how they'd filmed it.

'You did great,' Lucy complimented, struggling to contain her excitement at the sight of her friend on their small black and white television screen.

'Thanks,' Hollie replied. She'd got an odd feeling in her stomach which she'd put down to nerves. She'd felt sick that morning, too. It was all catching up with her. Her breasts were sore as well, and it was beginning to concern her.

The report segued into the interview which Hollie had recorded with the presenter at the BBC Radio Humberside studios and, if she hadn't known better, it looked like she was doing it live. At the end of the interview, the female presenter picked up and ran through some key information.

'So, did you see anything at Hull Fair that night? If you did, the number to call is at the bottom of your screen right now. Were you the person Moira ran over to see, or do you know who that person might be?'

Hollie retched, unable to restrain her instinctive panic as the details of Moira's disappearance were recounted once again.

'Are you okay?' Judith asked.

'Yes, it was just a crisp going down the wrong way,' she lied. 'Sorry about that.'

A veil of fear engulfed her suddenly and she began to shake in her chair. Would taking part in the programme place her at risk from that man who threatened her? Would they come for her in the house? What would they do to her? Part of her wished she'd never got involved with the TV show.

As the programme continued, now as a drone in the background, she wondered if Moira had simply left with Simon, to start a brand-new life away from Hull. Perhaps she should have kept her mouth shut. Maybe Moira didn't want to be found.

'Hollie! Hollie!'

She tuned back to what was going on in the room.

'Look, they've made a breakthrough! You look like you're a million miles away!'

Hollie glanced at her friends and then towards the TV again. Both presenters were sitting alongside the officer who was leading the investigation into Moira's disappearance.

'This sometimes happens on a live TV programme; we've just had a significant development in the case of Moira Kennedy. DCI Redgrave, talk us through the call one of your detectives just took off-air.'

The DCI looked as pleased as punch, a man who'd finally got a much-needed break in a frustrating case.

'Five minutes ago, we received a phone call from a call box, purporting to be from Moira herself.'

Hollie went cold, a shiver passing through her. The girls were completely silent.

'This young woman sounded very distressed, and she didn't have enough money to stay on the call very long.'

'Do you believe the person making the call was Moira Kennedy?' the female presenter asked.

'We can't say just yet. But she shared information about the case which we believe only Moira could have known. That will remain confidential for obvious reasons. But I have a message for you, Moira, if you're still watching. Or, if you know Moira, please tell her to reach out to us in complete confidence. Moira, we understand that you're scared. But please contact us again, so we know you're safe. You're not in any trouble, Moira. The people who love you just want you to come home.'

TWENTY-EIGHT

'If it's any consolation to you, boss, I thought you looked like a natural in that old *Crime Beaters* video.' DS Patel smiled as Hollie approached her desk.

'Less of the old,' Hollie replied, 'but thank you. It's years since I've seen it myself. It just makes me feel ancient, to be honest with you. I don't know where all that time went.'

'Do you want some good news?' Amber smiled.

Amber's good news usually meant a breakthrough of some sort. Hollie's eyes widened.

'Go ahead, make my day.'

'It's Philip Mortimer – the van man,' Amber began. 'He prefers Big Phil apparently. He's just rocked up in the car park with his minibus.'

'Bloody excellent,' Hollie exclaimed, placing her hand over her mouth as she checked to see who might have caught the expletive.

This was good – everything was lining up nicely.

'Is this the guy who runs Splendid Days? The business sounds like something Jimmy Savile might think up. Someone needs to have a word with him about his branding.'

'Yes. His wife rang him while he was doing a drop-off job this morning. He came around here of his own volition, as he was busy with contract work today. He's downstairs if you want to talk to him.'

'What's your workload like?' Hollie asked, thinking she'd like Amber in on this. It was good for her to step out from behind her desk. 'Fancy using your legs and seeing what he has to say for himself?'

'Well, my workload currently stretches to the sun and back.' Amber grinned. 'But I reckon Mr Minibus should jump to the front of the queue, don't you?'

Hollie agreed this was a man of particular interest in the investigation, and it was convenient that they didn't have to chase him to the ends of the earth to get to speak to him.

The two women made their way through HQ to the reception area where Big Phil was waiting.

'Now my secret's out I need to add one more thing to your list,' Hollie began, as they made their way through the building. 'My friend, Moira, had a support worker when she was a student. They must have known a fair bit about her. Will you try and track them down?'

Amber took a sharp intake of breath.

'Twenty-five years ago... it's a long-shot, but I'll keep my eyes open while I'm combing through the files. I'll let you know as soon as I know.'

The name of their minibus driver – Big Phil – was apt. Philip Mortimer was an overweight, sweating hulk of a man, whose shirt had come untucked from his trousers and looked like it might burst its buttons at any moment; never had a piece of stitching come under such immense strain.

The man had ballooned in size since the golf photo from Gordon Carrick's wall had been taken. He was wearing a Splendid Days baseball cap, which sported a logo of three smiling children, each holding an ice cream.

'Good morning, Mr Mortimer,' Hollie began.

Big Phil looked up at her and held out his hand which seemed uncannily small compared to the thickness of his arm. It looked clammy and wet, and she didn't want to shake it, but she took one for the team and it was as unpleasant as she'd anticipated.

'My wife tells me you want to speak to me about the children's home excursions,' he began. He had a thick Hull accent and sounded breathless as he spoke.

'Yes, we'll have a chat with you in one of the interview rooms rather than out here in reception,' Hollie said, glancing out of the reception window and across to the car park. 'Before we do that, can we take a look at your vehicle? I take it that it's out in the car park?'

The minibus stood out like a sore thumb among the sober police vehicles and staff cars.

'Yeah, it was a bit of a struggle to get in what with your security and whatnot, but the kind detective here sorted it for me.'

He gave DS Patel a bashful smile, and she pretended to be looking at a pot plant to deflect it.

'Lead the way, please,' Hollie said.

Even walking across the car park was a physical struggle for Phil, and Hollie decided they should take the elevator on the way back to the interview rooms; she did not want a dead witness on her hands.

The minibus continued the theme which had begun on Phil's baseball cap, emblazoned with images of children having a great time and mostly, it seemed, fuelled by confectionery which would be stuffed with sugar. The words *Splendid Days* were liveried on the front and back and both sides, though the subheading helped considerably to make it all a little less creepy: *Fun Trips for Disadvantaged Children*.

When Hollie read that, she felt a little ashamed of herself for making such snap judgements about Big Phil. For all she knew, he was a well-meaning man who was doing good work in the community. She resolved to give the man a fair hearing before jumping to further condemnations. For all she knew, the Big in his name referred to his big-heartedness.

'This is the Phil-Mobile,' he began.

It was going to be a struggle to remain impartial, but she could do it; she was a professional.

'Basically, I take disadvantaged kids on special days out to concerts, fairgrounds, leisure centres, theme parks, the seaside – whatever kids like doing, I'll be there to help.'

Hollie and Amber glanced at each other. Hollie wondered when working with children had become an instant flag for suspected paedophilia. There was a time when Scout masters, soccer coaches and children's entertainers could go about their work without comment. These days, all those jobs came with the inevitable jokes about misguided intentions. As ever, it was the few bad apples that had upset the apple cart for all those poor people who genuinely felt passionate about working with children and encouraging the next generation.

'I believe you've done some work with the Caring Guardian Children's Residential Home?' Amber asked.

'Yeah, I've worked with them for years,' Phil answered, not at all rattled by the question. 'I know what this is about. I followed it in the newspaper at the time, and they came sniffing round me and my van like you are now. And now Gordon Carrick's dead... well, it figures this will all come back again.'

He sounded like he was deeply wounded by any suggestion he might have been involved.

'Every year they took a group of kids to Hull Fair on the Thursday night. It's not been done since the inquiry and, funnily enough, it would have been tomorrow if those trips were still running. I started this business thirty years ago.'

'How did you get involved with Ambrose House?' Hollie wondered.

She studied the man as he spoke; she was struggling to decide what she made of him.

'A guy called Kenneth Digby used to be a manager at the home. There's a small group of them who arranged the trips and had done so for years. They want to give something back to their community. He took a chance on me when I was a young man.'

Phil opened the minibus doors as he was speaking, back and sides, so the two detectives could take a closer look. It was a regular minibus; it had seen better days and some of the seats had been repaired with gaffer tape. Inside was decorated with stickers of pop icons, film stars and cartoon characters.

'What did the Ambrose House trips involve?' Amber asked, moving on.

'They were quite straightforward really. I drove to the children's home and picked up the kids in two shifts. The younger kids went first, then I took the older teenagers later in the evening. Gordon Carrick and Orsen Scott and some other local men from the business charity would meet us at the fairground. They were from a Hull group of businesspeople who used to help the city's underprivileged youngsters. The kids were taken for an all-expenses-paid night of a lifetime.'

'What did you think of the accusations in the papers?' Amber asked him, short and sharp.

He looked at her with a *this again?* look on his face.

'I just did a job. The kids never said anything to me. I thought they were going to some pizza and soft drinks party to finish off a good night out. I never saw anything.'

'What about Kenneth Digby?' Hollie asked.

'Well, as you know, Kenneth took his life earlier this year. He never came to the fair.'

Hollie's heart sank a little. If Digby wasn't at the fairground or the parties, that made placing him with the other men more problematic.

'Didn't he lose his job at the home?' she pushed.

Big Phil sighed, a rattling wheeze continuing long past the exhalation of breath.

'Well, he was redeployed rather than losing his job. And remember, nothing was proved at the time.'

There was a pause for a moment while they all reflected on what had been said.

'We saw a photograph of you with several of the accused men in golfing gear,' Amber remarked.

Big Phil's face screwed up as she said the words.

'Oh, yeah, that was a one-time thing. It was a thank you day out at their golf club. I'm not a golfer and besides, I've got Cushing's syndrome, which makes life difficult, you know.'

Hollie felt like a shit. She didn't know much about the syndrome, but she knew it accounted for Phil's excessive weight. Sometimes she cursed herself for putting people in boxes too fast, though she never seemed to learn even as she got older and, supposedly, wiser.

'What did you do while the kids were at the fair?' Amber continued.

'I'd wander off, get myself some food, look around the stalls and generally kill time. I'd leave them to it. I always had to show my face at nine o'clock, as they'd arrange for the local press to take a photo of everybody standing in front of the bus. It was good for their image and publicity, I reckon. They'd stay until the fair closed then I'd drive them on to their next destination.'

'Wasn't that back to the children's home?'

'No. They were all older teenagers, mind, and it was a Thursday, so they made a night of it. I'd drive them over to a private house, where some kind of reception had been laid on for them.'

'You have the addresses of these houses?' Amber picked up.

'No. It was twenty-five years ago. They used to tell me where to go on the night.'

'Did you stay?' Hollie pushed.

'Nah. That was the end of my contract. I got paid in cash and sent on my way after that. They never invited me in. It would have been nice to get a soft drink and a slice of pizza as a thank you. I got a bit funny about it once. That was the year they took me out golfing. I shut up complaining after that because it almost killed me walking around that bloody golf course.'

'How did the kids get home?'

'Taxis, I think. These guys aren't short of a bob or two, and I'm guessing it was part of the treat.'

'What were the kids like on the drive over?' Hollie wondered.

'Quiet. Always very quiet and subdued.'

'Why was that?' Amber continued, picking up on Hollie's line of thinking. 'Doesn't that strike you as odd?'

The wounded look was back on his face.

'Think back,' Hollie urged him. 'Were there any signs at all?'

'I always put it down to tiredness,' he began, then faltered.

'What is it?' Hollie said.

'Something just came back to me. It was odd, but when I asked Digby about it, he just told me to stop being stupid. I can see how you're looking at me, officers, you think I'm daft, too, just because of the way I look—'

'No, not at all—'

'Oh no, of course not—'

Hollie and Amber spoke at once, unable to reassure him quickly enough.

'Carry on, Mr Mortimer,' Hollie encouraged, keen to move on.

'I once found a piece of paper on the floor when I was cleaning out the bus after one of the visits. It had youthful hand-writing on it.'

'And what did it say?' Hollie pushed, eager to get to the point.

'Three words – "Please send help" – scrawled on a serviette from a fast-food order.'

'Did you do anything about it?' Amber interjected, barely concealing her irritation.

'Yes, of course I did. I rang Kenneth Digby from home as soon as I got back. He was angry with me and said it was just mischievous children screwing about with me and that if I made a meal out of it, I could say goodbye to my contract.'

'So, what did you do next?' Hollie asked.

'Nothing.' And a look of shame flashed over his face before he continued, 'I needed the work. I took his word for it.'

TWENTY-NINE

'This is my least favourite part of a case,' Hollie observed as Ben Anderson pulled the car up at a red traffic light. 'All we get is a handful of threads and it's difficult to know which to pull.'

'You can say that again,' he agreed, his eyes on the lights and his foot poised on the accelerator, ready to move on. He seemed as agitated as she felt.

'If you asked me to bet, I'd say Big Phil has been shut out of the inner circle,' Hollie theorised. 'I honestly think he's just a do-gooder who's running errands for the devil. I reckon they were bullying him when they took him on that golf day. It was a sort of fuck off to him. The poor guy didn't stand a chance on a golf course.'

'Have we heard any news of Simon Rose yet?' Ben asked, as if it had just occurred to him.

Hollie took a sharp intake of breath.

'Nothing,' she replied, instantly becoming irritated by the lack of progress. 'Sometimes I wish I could kick some uniformed arses. You'd think he'd have been spotted by now. I'm hoping he's going to turn up at my house again. He's unlikely to pull up outside HQ like Big Phil did. There are so many directions this case could go.'

'How do you mean?' Ben wondered, changing up the gear.

They'd reached Hessle now and would arrive at Orsen Scott's house shortly. She wanted Anderson with her for this visit. They hadn't got any basis on which to arrest Scott yet, but she wanted him to know they were breathing down his neck.

'The obvious candidate for killing Gordon Carrick is Simon Rose – if only we could lay our hands on him. Also, was Digby a suicide or not? And we still have no actual proof that anything was going on at the home. I mean, it's me against an official inquiry at the moment. I suspect that won't play out in my favour.'

Hollie scraped fingers along the surface of the door handle at her side. She immediately ceased her irritated action, fearing she might break a nail.

'Okay, so using my years of experience as a detective to sum it up, we know fuck all so far and we have a shit storm of contradictory information.'

Ben Anderson had a knack with words.

'Eloquently put. But yes, that's about it,' Hollie sighed. 'How about you? Any theories you'd like to share with me?'

'I'm suspicious of Jane Carrick and Melanie Digby, but then, if your hubby turned out to be a child abuser, how would you feel about it?'

'I'd smash him in the nuts and punch his lights out,' Hollie answered, seething inside. She couldn't think about child abuse without it enraging her. 'And that would just be the warm-up.'

'Yes, and that's exactly what happened to Gordon Carrick,' Ben continued. 'I'd say that's sexual predator revenge 101, wouldn't you?'

He was right, but there was not enough evidence to go making arrests.

'But he was absolved of that. He was so damn confident, he

even sued for libel damages. You've got to have some arrogance to do something like that.'

She was scratching at the car door again. She placed her hands between her knees to prevent herself from destroying the interior of the vehicle.

'Agreed. Anyway, we're here now,' Ben announced as they turned off the road, Hollie becoming aware of the crunching of tyres on gravel.

'Jeez, look at the size of the house,' he erupted. 'Where do these buggers get their money from? I've still got an avocado bathroom suite in my divorced dad's flat.'

Ben pulled up the car in the drive. A large black electric SUV was charging there. The garden was immaculately kept, though being October, the colours were fast receding. They got out of the car.

'Have you ever thought about getting one of these things?' Ben asked, pointing disparagingly at the SUV.

'They cost a fortune,' Hollie replied. 'And it's so big, it must be twice the size of what I drive. I thought they were supposed to help us save the planet, not eat up twice the resources of a regular vehicle. But that aside, I'm happy to plug in a hair dryer and I'm happy to plug in an electric lawn-mower, but I refuse to plug in a car. It's like a grown-up's version of a Scalextric car.'

'I see you've given it some cursory thought then.' He smiled.

She had got on her soapbox a bit.

'Can I help you?'

A woman carrying secateurs emerged from the side of a large shrub.

Hollie felt her face colouring. She had to have overheard her appraisal of the family car. Sensing his colleague's unease, Ben stepped in.

'Hello, Mrs Scott. I'm DS Anderson and this is DI Turner. I think your husband is expecting us?'

The look on her face conveyed her distaste at the mention of him.

'He's expecting you. He'll probably have a heart attack when you come in the house. He's been very jittery ever since Gordon's death.'

'Why do you think that is?' Hollie asked, recovering herself.

'The past is catching up with him,' she mumbled under her breath. Then, she gave her official reply at a more audible volume: 'I think it's made him realise that he's dealt with several people as a magistrate and there are probably a lot of them who'd like to give him a piece of their mind.'

'Anybody in particular?' Ben asked.

'You'd best ask my husband,' she said, placing her secateurs in a nearby bucket and opening the front door.

'Be careful of the charging lead for the Scalextric car,' she cautioned.

Hollie cringed but said nothing. If she tried to explain herself, she'd dig an even bigger hole.

'Orsen! Visitors!'

The coldness of her voice would have frozen the atmosphere inside the house even if the heating was on.

'I'll leave him to you. I'm Jasmine, by the way. I would say I'm pleased to meet you, but I think we all know that would be stretching the truth a bit, don't we?'

She walked back to her shrubs, not bothering to introduce them to her husband.

Orsen Scott was a skinny man, of average height, and he wore the sort of thin-rimmed glasses that made him appear studious. He had a worried look on his face as he approached the front door.

'Are you getting me some police protection at last?' he asked, his voice frantic. 'All I've had so far is a patrol car driving by every couple of hours.'

'Do you need protection?' Ben replied, blunt and accusing.

Hollie showed him her ID card and Ben Anderson followed suit. Orsen beckoned them in, impatient, a man accustomed to being listened to.

He showed them into the kitchen and took a chair. He left them standing for a couple of seconds before Ben took the initiative and grabbed a seat without being invited.

'So, you're here about Gordon,' Orsen Scott started.

'Do you have any ideas who might have murdered him?' Hollie asked, sitting down with slightly less assurance than Ben.

'No doubt one of the same people who tried to stitch him up previously.'

'And who would that be?' Ben asked.

'You'll have done your research already, I'm sure. If you haven't, you should piss off back to your office and play catch up.'

Perhaps DCI Osmond had done the world a favour denying 24/7 police protection to this man.

'There were a couple of names from back then who made accusations,' Orsen continued. 'Some of them got anonymity due to their age. It'll be one of them, no doubt, trying to squeeze him for cash, making baseless accusations.'

'Were they baseless?' Hollie challenged him.

'Of course they were!' he protested, barely pausing for breath. 'Gordon Carrick carried out generous, charitable works throughout this city for many years, and those little shits tried to bite the hand that fed them. The inquiry upheld Gordon's version of events, and they were sent packing with their tails between their legs. I only wish I'd sued for defamation of character myself.'

His face was fiery red, but there was nothing threatening about this man. Off the record, Hollie might have described him as a bit of a shit.

'So why should this happen now, so many years after the

inquiry?' Anderson asked. 'It's all come out of the blue, hasn't it?'

'Maybe the press coverage around Kenneth Digby's suicide attracted some attention. Perhaps it was Gordon's recent award that did it—'

'Award?' Hollie and Ben both replied at the same time.

'His MBE – he was recently made a Member of the Most Excellent Order of the British Empire. I was one of his nominees.'

Of course you were.

'When did this happen?' Hollie asked. Nobody had thought to mention it so far.

'He was in this year's New Year's Honours. It got a mention in the papers and on the radio. I'm surprised you don't know that.'

I'll bet that pissed off a few people.

'Are you still involved with the children's home, Mr Scott?'

'I am. I'm on the board as a non-executive director—'

FFS, it's true.

'So you continue to have direct access to the children there?' Ben Anderson provoked him.

Orsen Scott seemed annoyed and slightly flustered.

'I don't know what you mean—'

Hollie's phone suddenly began to emit a loud, abrasive noise, like a doorbell sound. She felt as agitated as Orsen Scott looked. She fumbled for her phone and tried to work out what was going on; it didn't sound like a regular call. She activated the screen and clicked on a new notification.

'Excuse me, I need to handle this in private,' she said, getting off her chair.

'Everything all right, boss?' Ben asked.

Hollie showed him the screen, which was showing the view from her doorbell at home. Standing on the doorstep at her house was Simon Rose.

THIRTY
HULL, 1999

Simon dug his hand deep into his pocket, checking the twenty pounds in notes that Moira had given him was still there, alongside the cassette. He'd insisted she keep the money, but she wouldn't see him spend another night on the street without having the means to check in at a cheap B&B if things got too bad.

He'd taken it, determined to hand it back to her the next day, but there was no way he was risking that cassette not finding its way into Ray McGregor's hands.

He rearranged the flattened cardboard box that he'd picked out of the Aldi industrial bins, and shuffled himself into as comfortable a position as he could manage.

An owl hooted in an overhead tree and, if he fixed his gaze long enough, he could make out the shapes of bats scouring the night for insects. He'd long since ceased being frightened of such things; his greatest fear on the streets was gangs of men kicking or urinating on him. He tended to avoid the city at night – it was safer.

Tired out now, Simon drifted off into the half-sleep that had to suffice for rest among people in his position. He could hear the traffic along Beverley Road still: its constant hum was soothing and soon lulled him into a drowsy state.

Suddenly, without warning, a bright light shone in his eyes. It caught him unawares. He'd drifted off, and he hadn't heard anybody approaching.

'You stupid fucker,' came the hateful voice of Kenneth Digby through the darkness. Before Simon had time to respond, a solid boot struck the side of his face and he reeled, fighting to recover himself in case it was followed by further blows.

'That stupid tart that you call a friend has really screwed things up,' he cursed as he picked up Simon by his coat and threw him back down on the ground, his head striking the trunk of a tree. Simon moved his hands and legs as fast as he could, desperately trying to get traction so he could get away. He thrashed about for something to throw. His right hand found a crisp wrapper then tapped against something harder: a discarded bottle.

'So, you're planning to tell that McGregor chap everything,' Digby seethed. 'Did you tell him you little shits were asking for it?'

'How did you know?' Simon began, staggered at the ferocity of the attack.

'My contacts have eyes and ears everywhere,' Digby sneered.

Simon had been on the receiving end of this man's spite before. A vision of him lying on top of him, the bristles on his chin rubbing against his face, the smell of cigarettes on his breath, made Simon heave. Just as he'd been powerless then, he felt his body numbing, the protective armour of the abused, ready to shut off mentally and physically from the atrocities that were about to be inflicted on him.

Digby drew back his fist. In the home, they never bruised them, not on the outside anyway. There was never anything to show, just the broken, damaged souls which resided lifeless in their bodies, resigned to their desolate lives.

'She tried to call me out at the fair tonight. Well, the stupid whore bit off more than she could chew. She told me about your little recording while she was begging for her life. So where is it? Where have you hidden it, you shit?'

His fist crashed into the side of Simon's face.

'It was good having my fun with Moira this evening,' he taunted. 'She was always a bit feisty, that one. I like it when they wriggle a bit—'

'You bastard!' Simon screamed, grasping the top of the bottle at his side and crashing it on Digby's head. It smashed but didn't draw blood. Digby was momentarily shaken but recovering quickly. Simon scrambled to get his footing, hauling himself up from the ground using the branch of a bush.

Digby lunged at him, but Simon twisted away, avoiding his grasp. Simon ran along the semi-lit footpath, hardly daring to look back. He was sobbing uncontrollably now, screaming inside for poor Moira, terrified for his life, his mind in a million places at once.

He couldn't stay in the city, he had to flee. They knew what the two of them were up to now, and they wouldn't stop until they found them. He ran into the night, away from the city, along Victoria Docks and towards the port.

Simon spent that night hiding in a large drainage pipe alongside the Half Tide Basin at Victoria Dock. He waited it out through the night, his stomach grumbling with hunger, his mind frantic over what they'd done to Moira.

He was woken in the morning by the sound of a horn; it was the overnight ferry coming into dock. In that moment, he saw his escape route.

Fumbling in his pocket he felt for the notes that Moira had given him. It was plenty for a foot passenger without an overnight berth, but what about his passport? As his fingers found the creased-up notes, his heart jolted as he realised the cassette was gone. He checked his other pockets, turning out his coat and trousers.

Panicking now, he checked again, making sure it hadn't fallen out into the concrete drain. It was not there; he'd lost it.

He screamed out loud within the drain, the agony and impossibility of his situation tormenting him.

That night, under cover of the early evening October darkness, having spent a day keeping his head down in the docks area, Simon sneaked onto a lorry which was boarding for that night's sea crossing. He concealed himself in an empty crate and did not move until he felt the lorry pulling over at a motorway stop in what he knew must be close to Zeebrugge.

When he was convinced the coast was clear, he jumped out of the lorry and exchanged a five pound note for Dutch currency, having found an English family in the motorway service station happy to make the swap. He picked up the copy of the previous day's *Hull Daily Mail* that the family had been reading over breakfast. He read the headline, his heart pounding so ferociously he thought he might die.

Search For Missing Student At Hull Fair

Moira's picture was on the front page.

Panicking, he scanned the article, searching for a name or contact number. A hotline had been set up, so taking one of the Dutch coins that he'd been given, he found a public phone and began dialling.

His fingers shook as he pushed the numbered buttons, and he waited as the dialling tone established. It was answered almost immediately, and he was passed to one of the PCs who was working alongside the detectives newly assigned to the case.

'PC MacKenzie, how can I help you?'

'My name is Simon Rose. I've got important information about the student who went missing at Hull Fair.'

There was a sustained silence at the end of the line.

'Hello?'

'Simon Rose?' came the voice at the end of the line.

'Yes. I'm a friend of Moira's.'

'Where are you, Simon? I have some friends who'd like to speak with you.'

His voice was cold and threatening.

'I-I-I'm not telling you that...'

'I hope you're a long way away from Hull, Simon,' came the deadly, whispered voice. 'Because if we ever see you in this city again, you'll end up just like your girlfriend.'

THIRTY-ONE

'Hello, Simon. It's a long time since we spoke.'

Hollie was trembling, part desperate for this encounter, but also terrified of what the outcome might be. She reached out to rest her free hand on the edge of a chest of drawers which had been placed in the Scott's hallway. Having steadied herself, she moved over to Orsen Scott's kitchen door, muted her phone and waved Ben Anderson to join her in the hallway.

Simon seemed confused at first. Hollie watched him on the video feed on her phone, and it took him a few moments to figure out where her voice was coming from. She was relieved Izzy had agreed to stay with her at the Royal Hotel. She didn't yet know if Simon was dangerous.

Hollie unmuted her microphone and placed the call on speaker, motioning to Ben that he should close the kitchen door behind him. She adjusted the volume so the two of them could hear, though Orsen Scott would be excluded from the conversation.

'Get a patrol car round there to pick him up,' she whispered to Ben, who already had his mobile phone out having seen who was on the call.

'*Is that Hollie Turner?*' Simon continued over the video link. '*Probably not Turner anymore, I'm assuming?*'

The signal was choppy, the audio poor quality. Simon was trying to sound confident, but his shaking voice gave the game away. Hollie's throat felt tight and dry, but she pushed through it. She had to remain in charge here.

'No, I still use my maiden name at work,' Hollie answered, pleased that he couldn't see her. She'd had a long time to think about what she might ask this man if he ever showed his face again. Now that time had come, she felt overwhelmed.

'Yours is a face I never thought I'd see again, Simon,' she began. 'Why are you in Hull? What do you want?'

She'd only ever spoken to Simon once, outside the Jacksons store on Beverley Road. Now here he was, a quarter of a century later, potentially holding all the secrets to her friend's disappearance.

'*Well, it's been a few years,*' he continued. '*Things have changed. You took some tracking down, but thanks to the inter-net, here I am.*'

Hollie cursed her video doorbell. It was difficult to hear Simon if a car passed by on the street behind him, but also the wireless internet signal meant that his words often dropped out at the beginning and end of his sentences.

'*When I saw that Kenneth Digby was dead, I decided to risk coming back. I've got something that I want to deliver directly to your hands.*'

'What is it, Simon? Why not drop it in at police HQ?'

Ben Anderson gave her a thumbs up, and Hollie muted the phone again.

'Patrol car on the way,' he confirmed. 'DCs Philpot and Gordon are heading over, too. There's some traffic snarl up in town, so keep him talking as long as you can.'

Simon was still speaking.

'*I've got an old notebook here which I want to deliver*'

directly into your hands. It has to be somebody I trust. You'll find everything you need in there to see what was going on at Ambrose House.'

'Just post it through the letterbox,' Hollie urged. She had to repeat herself because Simon was struggling to hear her standing out on the street.

'No, I don't trust anybody, not even your police colleagues. This goes from my hands to your hands; these people are too powerful. They stopped us telling our story once, but never again. People need to know what happened—'

Simon's voice cut out on Hollie's phone, and she cursed. Anderson showed her a text that he'd just received on his phone from Harry Gordon.

Roads are congested, nothing moving. Can you get a foot patrol over?

Hollie checked her phone was muted before answering.

'Do whatever it takes but get someone over there now,' she whispered to Ben urgently. 'This damn doorbell of mine is barely hanging on. I should have paid for a better broadband package when I moved in.'

Simon's voice was back again.

'Moira never stopped talking about you, so it's good that you're back in Hull. I hope I can trust you, Hollie. I know Moira certainly did.'

And there it was: Moira. That's who it was all about. Perhaps not directly, but it all led back to her.

'What happened to Moira, Simon?' she asked gently, almost choking on the words. It was the question she hardly dared to ask; she wasn't sure she even wanted to know the answer. It felt like the truth might spring up at any moment, like a jack-in-the-box, and catch her by surprise.

'That's what I'm hoping to find out.'

Hollie felt a sudden rage; was he here to goad her?

'Then why call at my house if you have no intention of telling me, Simon?' she shouted. 'Is this just some sick little game to you?'

After so many years of wondering what happened to her friend, of longing for a resolution, she felt a desperate urge for the torment of uncertainty to end.

Simon held up an envelope and looked around, surveying the street. Had one of the patrol cars got there at last?

'It's all in here. I'll get this to you, somehow—'

'Is she still alive?'

The words were difficult and slow, like they didn't want to leave her mouth. Her eyes welled as she spoke the words.

Please tell me she's alive.

'I don't know.'

Simon was equally choked up. He spoke the words like it was a personal failure.

'I honestly don't know, not yet.'

Simon was looking directly at the camera on her doorbell now. It was like making a Zoom call to her past.

'I read on the internet that you're a copper now.'

His voice was unsteady still, and she wasn't ready yet to change the subject.

'It was Moira's disappearance that led to that. It shaped so much of my life after we lost her.'

She said it almost defiantly, like becoming a police officer had been the only thing she could do after letting Moira slip away from them.

'At least something positive came from it.' Simon shrugged.

Simon was resigned. He didn't seem like a crazed killer, but then she'd thought that about suspects a number of times in her career.

He changed his tone, as if remembering why he'd wanted to contact her.

'You'll appreciate I can't risk being apprehended at this stage

*of the game. I know you'll all be looking for me after what
happened. You have absolutely no reason to believe me, but I
promise you I did not harm Moira. I tried to save her—'*

'Then why don't you come in for questioning, Simon? If
you've nothing to hide, prove it to me. I know Moira was your
friend, too. Let's find out what happened to her together.'

For just one moment, Hollie thought he was going to accept
her offer. If what he was saying was true, he, too, must have
spent a part of every day of his life wondering if Moira was still
out there.

'Come in and speak to me, Simon.' She was almost pleading
with him now.

*'I can't. If you charge me, I'll be banged up and out of circu-
lation. I can't let that happen. I've got things to do still—'*

Hollie felt a sudden rush of impatience.

'If you're innocent and can prove it, you could be a real
asset to solving this case.'

He paused, then seemed resolved in his course of action.

'Somebody is killing them all,' Simon continued enigmati-
cally. *'I need to find out who that is, in case the truth slips away
from us once again—'*

'Who, Simon? Who's killing who?'

Hollie was finding it hard to hide her frustration now. She
felt so close to getting some answers, but he was holding back.

Simon shook his head and did not offer a reply. Hollie was
desperate to push him for whatever information she could, but
could see he was doubting himself, looking around for the
returning police officer and ready to bolt if he had to.

The video feed from the doorbell was becoming increasingly erratic. Hollie couldn't remember if it was connected to
the mains or powered by a battery. If it was battery, it wouldn't
be built for long conversations like this. If it was mains, perhaps
the wi-fi was messing about again. She had to secure some

better way of communicating with Simon before they were cut off.

'Simon, look, we need to speak—' she pleaded.

'We can't – do – that yet – not until I've – had time to find out who's—'

It was breaking up fast now. Hollie cursed the technology that provided amazing things but also screwed them up just as often.

'Who's doing what, Simon? What are you trying to find out? Let me help—'

'I've – got – to – find – out—' The video was buffering; his voice was beginning to sound like a robot.

'Who's killing them off? Simon? Simon!'

'Damn you – you – sent – coppers—'

Simon was looking off to the distance, in a panic now. The connection terminated.

'Fuck it!' she shouted as she slammed her fist against the wall of Orsen's hallway. A framed picture jumped off its hook and landed on the tiled flooring, smashing the glass.

'Get onto the control room,' she half shouted at Anderson. 'See if they got him.'

Ben was straight on his phone, his face deadly serious and focused. He had to wait a few moments while Control updated him on the details as they were relayed over the radios from the two Specials who'd made it on foot first to Hollie's house.

She saw from his furrowed brow that it was bad news.

'Sorry, boss, he saw them coming from up the road and made a dash for it. He's still on the run.'

THIRTY-TWO

'Simon Rose is now my number one priority,' Hollie barked down her mobile phone, more ferocious than she knew she should have been. 'I want that man arrested and in an interview room ASAP.'

She softened her tone. Amber was an excellent team member; she had to control her impatience with the uniformed officers.

'I'm sorry, Amber, that rant was not meant for you, I hope you know that.'

'No problem, boss, I know how frustrating it can be. To help soothe your nerves a little, I found out what happened to Moira's support worker. She retired to New Zealand of all places. I'm tracking her down via her son who still lives in the UK.'

That gave Hollie the chance to send some praise Amber's way. She ended the call. They'd just pulled up outside Ray McGregor's house, having hastily concluded things with Orsen Scott. Hollie had called DCI Osmond enroute, adamant that Scott now needed police protection as a matter of priority, despite him protesting his innocence. She'd finally convinced

Osmond to sanction posting an officer at his house. If Orsen Scott was murdered, it was possible that none of those men would answer for what they'd done in this life.

'For fuck's sake!' Hollie exclaimed as she ended her call back to the office. 'Bloody uniform sit on their arses all day and amble over there like they've got all the time in the world.'

Ben Anderson pulled up nearby and switched off the engine. He paused and turned to Hollie.

'Maybe we should take a moment, boss. I know you're pissed that he got away, but we'll find him. He can't last long out on the streets without somebody spotting him.'

Hollie drew in a long, deep breath and exhaled slowly.

'I'm sorry, Ben, I wouldn't curse like that in front of our younger colleagues. Maybe I am too close to this case. But we had him right on my doorstep and still we couldn't get our hands on him—'

'I know, it's frustrating as hell,' Ben agreed with her. 'But we're almost there now, Hollie. We know who we're looking for, and Orsen Scott is finally getting the protection he needs. It'll all play out now, we just have to be ready for it.'

There were times, and they were rare, when Ben Anderson said exactly the right thing at the right time. This was one such instance. If it was a numbers game, he was bound to strike gold every once in a while.

'Thank you, Ben, you're right, of course you are. I've been waiting over twenty years for this. I need to steady myself and focus, you're right, we're almost there. Let's see what Ray McGregor has for us. This is the detailed work that will help put those bastards behind bars.'

Lance Fairclough from the digital forensics team had sorted them out with an old tape unit which had been used for recording interviews prior to the arrival of digital files. It was a relic from Hollie's policing past, and it made her feel nostalgic for simpler times when she saw it.

Even Sebastian, McGregor's dog, had picked up on the tense atmosphere in the room, and had slunk off to his basket, confident in the knowledge that there would be no fussing today.

Ray McGregor had just handed Hollie a C60 cassette. It was years since she'd seen one.

'That's my handwriting,' Ray replied. 'You can see the date, too: Friday, the first of October 1999. Hull Fair was just getting set up and this was recorded several days before Moira's disappearance. She said she'd opened up to a friend and felt it was time to let the truth be known.'

Hollie felt the cold chill of the past running through her body. Had Moira confided information to her that night in the flat that led to her disappearance? Were she and Simon plotting to expose their abusers? Was Moira killed to protect somebody's secrets?

Hollie shivered, her friend's last words ringing in her mind.

If I could burn Ambrose House down with the staff inside, I would.

'Oh, and you'll want to see this,' Ray continued, reaching over for a brown envelope. 'It was pushed through my letterbox sometime last night while I was in bed. It's almost as if someone knew we were meeting today.'

Hollie reached over to take it from him, her hand trembling a little in anticipation of what it might be.

'I didn't think not to handle it,' Ray apologised, 'and besides, Sebastian will have been all over it before I picked it up, so any fingerprints will be long gone. I'm sorry.'

Inside were three Polaroids. Anderson's eyes widened as she showed him what was inside. Using a pen to turn them over her heart almost stopped; it was Moira, just as she remembered her, and Simon Rose, exactly as he'd appeared to her that night outside Jacksons. Their faces were gaunt and haunted; Simon had the streak of tears across his face.

Hollie struggled for breath, it felt like her body was shutting down.

'Can I get you a glass of water?' Ray asked. 'I see you've recognised who's in the pictures.'

He got up and walked to the kitchen anyway. Hollie tilted the two images towards Anderson, who sighed as he studied them.

'Send them over to Amber, will you?' Hollie asked, trying to figure out what was in the third Polaroid. It appeared to be a picture of a park, with a lake of some sort in the distance. Some long object or structure cast a shadow, so whoever had taken the photograph, the sun was behind them. A small arrow, drawn in pen, had been scribbled above one of the far-off trees.

It seemed like it had been included by accident, and the Polaroid image appeared to have no bearing on the other two photographs.

'What do you make of this?' Hollie asked McGregor and Ben as she took the glass of water with her spare hand. 'Any idea where this picture was taken?'

Ray shook his head.

'Sorry,' he answered, 'I've already tried that. It's an old photo, and wherever it is has changed.'

Anderson shook his head as well.

'No idea, sorry, boss. I'll send it over to Amber with the other two Polaroids, let's see if she comes up with anything.'

Hollie calmed herself as Ben took care of the images. She was grateful for the pause. To see her friend like that – hollow, frightened, scared – it made her want to scream. They had to press on; somebody had leaked this information, somebody wanted these abusers exposed. Was it Simon?

She checked the envelope again, to make sure she hadn't missed anything. She had. There was a torn-off piece of paper lodged in the corner, which she coaxed out with the pen in case there were any fingerprints preserved. It looked like it had been torn off a 'with compliments' slip because a small part of a logo had been left at the top. Scrawled on the paper in block capital letters were the words:

THEY MUST ALL PAY

'Is this Simon's work?' Hollie exhaled, shaking her head. She cursed the uniformed officers once again. Simon Rose seemed to have the run of the city right under the nose of Humberside Police.

She and Anderson bagged the items after sending images to Amber back in the office. If this is what he'd handed over to Ray McGregor, what on earth was left to reveal in that notebook that he wanted to deliver to her personally?

'Shall I see if this piece of junk still works?' Ben asked at last, holding his hand out to Ray for the cassette.

Hollie read the handwritten label.

Moira Kennedy/Simon Rose interview/ref: Ambrose House. Friday, 1st October 1999

Anderson pushed the cassette tray shut and pressed the PLAY button. A swishing sound came through the small speaker at the side of the tape unit, and they waited for the audio to begin.

'Where was this recorded?' Hollie asked.

'They wouldn't meet me at the *Hull Daily Mail* offices. We recorded it in Moira's flat. I think Simon was staying there at the time. She was very nervous about it, swearing me to secrecy and making me promise not to share anything until she gave me the say-so.'

'And did you stick to that?' Anderson asked.

'Of course I did,' McGregor replied, annoyed. 'There was a time when you could trust a journalist's word and we would protect our sources to the grave.'

The poor-quality audio recording began to play.

'Interview with Simon Rose and Moira Kennedy at 11.13 a.m. on Friday, 1st October 1999. The interviewer is me, Ray McGregor.'

Ray's voice sounded much younger than he did sitting in front of them, and in spite of the defunct technology, it was clear enough.

'So, Moira and Simon, in your own time, tell me what you wanted me to know about Ambrose House. Start by explaining your connection there, please.'

Ray had several pads of shorthand notes on the coffee table in front of him and he picked one up, flicking over the pages. It looked like he was following it through as he'd written it down.

And then she heard it: Moira's soft, earnest voice, a ghost from the past.

In an instant, Hollie was nineteen again, sitting with her friend in the university coffee bar, laughing about the lecturer's caustic remarks on her essay, picking the flakes out of their hot chocolate drinks.

'I came to the home in 1992 and left in 1998 at the age of eighteen,' Moira began.

Hollie wished she could reach through time and warn her friend to be careful. Tears formed in her eyes; so much time had passed and so much had been lost.

'I arrived at the home soon after Moira, in 1993. I left a year after her. I ran away and ended up sleeping rough. Moira adjusted well and got a flat and some help to get used to life as an adult.'

'We were always pals,' Moira picked up. *'We used to talk to each other about what was going on there—'*

Moira's voice faltered, and Hollie could hear her silently sobbing in the background.

'Simon got up and gave her a hug there,' Ray informed them. 'There didn't appear to be anything romantic between them. But there was a lot of love and understanding poured into that hug. I made a note of it in my notepad.'

The three of them waited for the speaking to resume on the tape.

'What was it like in the home?' came Ray's recorded voice from 1999.

Moira could be heard sobbing again.

'They threatened us and shouted at us if we didn't behave,' Simon said slowly. 'And they-they—' He became choked.

Hollie was struggling not to become emotional. It looked like Anderson was sharing her struggle.

'That bastard social worker—' Simon stopped dead. 'I'm not giving you names, not yet, just what happened for now. That fucking bastard. He would take us to his office and— When everyone had gone at night, when he was on night duty... he would—'

Through her nausea, Hollie tried to figure out who they might be referring to. It had to be Kenneth Digby. The bastard was dead now, well clear of justice. Her sickness turned to rage and frustration.

'I know it's difficult for you,' Ray's voice gently urged him on the tape. 'But you need to say what happened if I'm going to be able to help you.'

'He raped me,' Simon said, tense and suddenly resolute to get the words out. 'He made me do things that sicken me.'

Hollie's stomach tightened and she thought she was going to throw up. The thought of Moira going through that, never reaching out, dealing with it on her own at such a young age, made her want to scream. Hollie stood up and walked over to the window. Ray was looking down at his feet

'*It was the same with the older girls,*' Moira said softly. '*We dreaded the nights when he was on duty. He'd come up to our rooms with some trumped-up accusation. He'd say we'd been smoking, or spotted kissing at school, some rubbish like that. He'd take us from our rooms and give us some punishment, like scrubbing the floor or cleaning the toilets. This was late at night when we should have been in bed. Then he'd tell us to come to the office so they could write it up in our records. But he wouldn't do that. He would – he'd—*'

Something happened on the tape, and Hollie and Ben looked up at McGregor. It was gruelling to listen to. Hollie wanted desperately to reach out and hold on to Moira. How had her friend managed to carry this with her at university?

'She rushed to the bathroom,' Ray said, his voice breaking. 'She had nothing inside her to throw up, but if you listen to the tape, you'll hear her heaving. She was in a right state. You can see how compelling this would have been at the inquiry.'

'This is explosive,' Hollie replied, trying to steady her voice. 'I wish to God they'd been able to say all this at the time. Did you not play this as part of the inquiry?'

Ray looked wiped out.

'Of course I did,' he said quietly, with seething anger just below the surface of his words. 'But it was deemed inadmissible, as Moira and Simon were no longer able to appear as witnesses. It was even suggested that I was leading them on and had played my part in provoking the hysteria. They used this tape to bring me down.'

'I'm sorry,' Hollie sympathised. Was he leading them on now? He had enough skin in this game to want those men dead. They'd wrecked his life, after all.

'Do they say anything about Carrick and Scott?' Ben Anderson wondered, wiping his cheeks with a tissue he'd drawn from his pocket.

'Wait,' Ray answered. 'It's coming next.'

There was some shuffling on the tape, lots of movement and the sounds of Simon and Ray checking on Moira. Ray got her a glass of water. The pipes made a terrible noise as he ran the cold tap, and Hollie remembered that about her flat.

'*Are you ready to speak again?*'

'*Yes,*' came Moira's voice. '*I want to do this. Carry on. I'm sorry.*'

Oh, Moira, you have nothing to apologise for. Never apologise for what happened to you.

'*Tell me about the trips to Hull Fair,*' Ray coaxed.

'*It happened every year,*' Simon picked up. '*They'd get that odd man round with his minibus. The first time was the worst. We didn't know how it would end up—*'

Hollie clocked that he must be referring to Philip Mortimer.

'*The first time Simon and I went was when we were sixteen. We were so excited. Those men – they seemed so friendly at first. They were from local businesses, and it had been arranged through Ambrose House, so why would we distrust them? They were all sweetness and smiles at the fair. They paid for the rides, bought us hot dogs, candy floss and ice creams and let us go on anything we wanted. We had to meet up for a photograph for the newspaper. I knew something wasn't right when one of them placed his hand on my back on the bumper cars—*'

'*Can you give me a name, Moira? Any names will help—*'

'*Not yet,*' came Simon's reply on the tape, firm and assertive. '*We have to think carefully about this. Those men are dangerous. We'll give you the names last. I need to know we can trust you.*'

'*You can trust me,*' Ray's voice replied, gentle and reassuring.

Moira carried on talking.

'*At the end of the night, we thought we were going home. But they took us to some posh house afterwards. We just got dropped off there with those men. There were other men inside and they were expecting us. They gave us drinks and talked to us like we were grown-ups. It made me feel so uncomfortable when I was sixteen.'*

'What sort of things did they say?'

Hollie could hear how difficult Ray was finding this even through the poor quality of the tape.

'They talked about sex stuff,' Moira continued, sobbing again.

Hollie immediately thought of Lily. Her daughter was a young teenager on the cusp of becoming a woman, with predatory men all around her. She closed her eyes and took a long, deep breath to steady herself. Izzy had navigated it safely, and Lily could do the same. But Moira? She was just a girl at the time.

Hollie wiped her eyes with her hand as the cassette continued to run.

'It started with simple things, like did I like boys and who did I like. Then it got more personal, and they'd ask what sort of things I did with boys. Some of the things they said were disgusting. I didn't even have a boyfriend. And they'd be touching us while they were asking the questions, and it would get more personal. Then they'd—'

'They took us to other rooms and took their turn with us,' Simon interrupted. The emotion was just as evident in his voice, but he seemed more resolved than Moira to say the words. They were so difficult to speak.

Simon's voice was dripping with loathing and hate. If Simon was responsible for Digby's death, she wondered if that was a lesser evil than what those men had done to them.

'I need to know names if I'm going to help you,' Ray urged on the tape, gently. *'If you give me names, we can bring these monsters to justice.'*

Ray leaned over and switched off the cassette recorder.

'Why did you do that?' Hollie asked, glaring at him. She hadn't realised how intently she'd been listening.

'Because this is where I'll forever kick myself,' he replied, his face full of regret.

'Why, what happened?' Ben followed up, intense and focused.

'Listen,' Ray replied, pressing the PLAY button again. There was a silence on the tape.

'They were looking at each other there,' Ray explained, 'wondering if they should give me a name.'

Hollie looked directly at the tape machine, willing them to give the names.

'*We agreed we wouldn't yet,*' came Moira's voice. '*Let's just take one more night to make sure we're doing the right thing—*'

'*I want to punish that bastard Di—*'

Simon's sentence ended abruptly, the speaker now making a swishing noise. Hollie and Ben glared at Ray McGregor.

'What the hell happened?' Hollie challenged. 'He almost said it. You almost got your name.'

Ray sighed, his shoulders slumped, tears forming in his eyes.

'I'll never forgive myself,' he began. 'He didn't mean to say it, but it slipped out in anger. I played and replayed that cassette so many times after we'd recorded it. But when I was transcribing it to shorthand, I'd stopped and started it so many times that the tape snapped. Right on Kenneth Digby's name. The evidence was there, and I screwed it up.'

THIRTY-THREE
1999

Hollie waited for almost two months after *Crime Beaters* aired before reaching out to Elijah. She'd done her research already, by checking out the American Studies department and finding out where to go to locate him. She'd half hoped she might encounter him in the American Studies building, or on campus, as it might have made it easier to start a difficult conversation with him.

She still didn't know what she was going to say. There was no way she expected him to get down on one knee and propose to her, and she was certain that was not something she wanted. She hadn't told anybody yet and had no intention of doing so until she'd got things straight in her head.

But the small bump was there now, she could see it when she looked in the mirror, and the upset stomach – which she'd put down to anxiety – was quite clearly morning sickness. It had taken some hiding from her housemates.

For a moment, she felt a rush of anxiety at the thought of the life growing inside her. She was far too young to look after a baby. What would her parents say? What would everybody else think about her? This was going to mess up her life.

The thoughts crowded in on her and her chest tightened as she considered her options. She could terminate the pregnancy; that way nobody would ever need to know. No, she didn't want that – it was a baby, after all. But how could she keep it? She still felt like a child herself at times, there was no way she could bring up a baby on her own.

She was shaken out of her panic by a thumping knock at the door. It was Humberside Police.

The knock was heavy and distinctive. She was now able to identify when the police were at her door. The house was quiet. Judith and Lucy had diligently gone off for lectures, and Jim was who knew where?

'Hello, Hollie, we've met before. I'm PC Lorraine Perry and this is my colleague, PC Colin Loakes.'

Hollie was wary. She'd trusted these people and some of their colleagues had been less than helpful, even suggesting at times that she might be responsible for what happened to Moira. She wanted them out of the house.

The lazy attempts by the police officers to find Moira had spurred her into action, though, and she'd started to send off for police recruitment brochures. She'd been skipping lectures and was finding it difficult to settle. An idea was forming in her mind.

'We're just here to tell you that the search for Moira is being scaled down now,' Perry continued. 'That doesn't mean it's over, it just means a smaller team will be working on the investigation.'

PC Perry had a look on her face which showed she knew they were letting her down.

'But Moira called *Crime Beaters*. That proves I didn't do anything. If she's still alive, you just have to find her—'

'I'm sorry to tell you, that was a spiteful but convincing hoax. It was checked out thoroughly, but it was somebody wasting police time. These high-profile cases bring out the worst in people.'

'But they said only Moira could have known those things.'

Hollie was almost pleading with PC Perry now.

'I'm sorry, Hollie,' PC Perry replied, attempting to console her. 'Some people discuss police cases on internet message boards. They must have picked up a snippet of information from somewhere.'

Hollie felt completely crushed. They'd been so excited at the prospect of Moira calling into the programme. She, Judith and Lucy had speculated that she'd, perhaps, needed to get away from things for a while and take a break. So long as she was safe, Moira could take whatever time she needed. They'd been relieved at the prospect.

'We always have to consider that Moira doesn't want to be found. Maybe she just decided to move on.'

Hollie wondered if PC Perry knew what nonsense she was speaking. From the look on her face, it seemed like she might be delivering a message from someone more senior. Her words lacked conviction.

'What happens now?' Hollie asked.

'The investigation continues, but with no new information to follow up, there's not much we can do. I'm sorry, Hollie. But if ever any new leads appear, or some new evidence is turned up, it will be followed up properly. This isn't the end of it. We still want to find what happened to Moira.'

It felt like the end to Hollie. This was Humberside Police washing their hands of her. Moira had disappeared into the night, and nobody had a clue where she'd gone.

'She'll still be listed as a missing person, but most of the time – well, she's been gone too long now and there was all that blood on the mallet and the stuffed toy. I'm sorry.'

She was only telling Hollie what she'd surmised already. Yet, hearing the words now, she felt so empty.

As the two officers made their way out of the house, Hollie picked up her coat and put on her shoes. She felt so alone in that moment that she wanted to reach out to Elijah, to feel some human connection.

She locked the door behind her and walked up the path towards the university campus. She didn't know what she expected from Elijah, but it was time to tell him about the pregnancy. At least it was a distraction from Moira, something else to think about. There was no way she was getting rid of the baby. She'd got as far as the abortion clinic once, in a moment of despair and panic, but realised that she couldn't go through with it. But she wished she felt excited about it. Instead, she just felt numb.

Hollie made her way through the campus grounds, heading for the building which housed the American Studies department. She'd even found out Elijah's surname, from a list on one of the noticeboards. It would be so embarrassing not to know his surname when asking for him.

'Hello, I'm trying to get in touch with an American exchange student. He's called Elijah Jones.'

She held out her Student Union card so that the receptionist knew it was just a simple student enquiry.

'He left a folder in the library, and I want to return it to him—'

'That would be a miracle,' the secretary replied, studying Hollie's ID card and then looking up at her. 'Elijah hasn't been here for the past month, so I'm not sure how he'd leave a folder in the library.'

Hollie had been caught in her lie; she felt her face reddening. She held firm – she had to speak to him and let him know what their ill-advised one-night stand had led to.

'Oh, where's he gone? I hope he's not ill.'

'No, it's nothing like that. Poor Elijah had a problem with

his visa. He'd filled in some information incorrectly and it landed him in a spot of trouble.'

'Oh no, where is he now? I need to speak with him.'

Hollie felt an empty sensation deep in her stomach. She couldn't recall a time when she'd felt so alone.

'Elijah's had to go back to the United States. He had to terminate his exchange visit and return home. I'm so sorry.'

THIRTY-FOUR
DS AMBER PATEL

As Amber studied the photographs of Simon and Moira that Ben Anderson had sent over, her stomach knotted. She didn't need to know the context of those photographs, their faces said it all. She'd compared them with the picture of Tori Bellingham that Harry had found by the wheelie bin on the showground. The wallpaper was the same in all of them; somebody had taken these pictures in a single location. Were they sick trophies of some kind? Sometimes Amber couldn't believe the horrific things they had to deal with in their work.

She updated the case file and opened up the other two images on her PC screen. There was little chance of identifying the handwriting from the block capital letters, but there was something about that torn-off logo that was troubling her; she recognised the distinctive colour but couldn't place it out of context.

Amber searched online for a free colour picker to try to figure out what tone of red she was looking at. The colour picker allowed her to determine two precise matches. One was for print use, RGB as she discovered, the other for online use, which she found out was a hexadecimal code.

She looked at what she'd found. The RGB digits were 120, 16, 8 the hex code #781008. It was like looking at coordinates without a compass and she hadn't got a clue if that helped progress anything.

Frustrated with herself, she next turned to the third Polaroid image, the one showing the unknown location. She walked over to the office printing machine to pull out a page of A4, then sat at her desk and started to sketch out how the image had been taken.

First, she drew a circle to indicate the position of the sun. Then, lacking the artistic skills to do otherwise, she represented the person taking the photograph by a stick figure.

The shadow was an unusual shape, and she took some time copying it, trying to figure out what it might be. There was something perched on top, too. At first, due to the faded quality of the image, she thought it was a pigeon.

Staring at it for more than five minutes, something suddenly struck her from left of field; that was no bird, it was just as likely a weathervane, which meant the unusually shaped item immediately below it was probably a clock of some type.

She navigated to her web browser and typed in the words *clock park Hull,* her adrenaline now going crazy that she might be able to locate the place where this photograph had been taken.

'Yes!' she called out loudly, causing several of her colleagues in the office to look up and smile at her. It wasn't the first time DS Patel had made a breakthrough at her desk, and it would not be the last.

DCI Osmond was passing close by and walked over to Amber's desk.

'Have you got something?' he asked, lurking behind her chair and gazing at her PC screen.

Amber could barely contain herself. 'Look, sir, the first thing that came up in the search results.'

She clicked on an image which had appeared to the side of a Tripadvisor article labelled: *East Park Clock and Café*.

'Would you say that's the clock that cast the shadow in the Polaroid?'

Osmond studied the two images, placed side by side on her screens. He was looking at a green and gold, iron Victorian clock and weathervane. Its body was not unlike an old-fashioned streetlamp, but at the top was a boxed shape, with an ornate clock on each of the four faces. A gold-painted weathervane sat on top. Painted on each face, just below the clocks, were the words *East Park*.

Amber swiftly typed in the words *East Park clock Hull*, switched to the image results, then scanned the multitude of pictures there.

'There, that's the view out into the park,' she explained to Osmond. 'There are the trees in the Polaroid. So, where's that arrow pointing?'

She typed in the words *East Park Hull map* into Google and quickly expanded a bird's eye view of the park's layout.

'Fuck!' she exclaimed, immediately covering her mouth. 'I'm so sorry, sir,' she apologised, forgetting who was standing immediately at her rear.

'That's pointing at the small island on the boating lake – look, it lines up directly.'

Osmond was as captivated as Amber now, but as their excitement fired up their minds with activity, they both paused simultaneously as they realised what this might mean.

'Oh my god,' Amber stuttered. 'You don't think this is where—'

'I think it might be,' Osmond agreed.

'Do we tell DI Turner?' Amber asked, craning her neck to look up at him.

'She needs to know,' Osmond replied, sanguine. 'If that's where her friend's body is buried, she'll want to know.'

The two of them looked at the images in silence for a few moments. Somewhere across the office, someone was trying different phone extensions, trying to catch someone at their desk.

'Why have you got that colour palette up on your screen?' Osmond asked at last. 'That's the same colour as the Hull Health Responders logo.'

'What?' Amber asked. 'Are you sure?'

'My wife used to help out there,' he answered, irritated. 'I know that logo when I see it. The number of times those overalls ran into my white work shirts in the washing machine.'

Amber was typing the words into her browser. Sure enough, the Hull Health Responders web page came up and, to the eye, it looked to be the same.

As Amber downloaded the logo and tested it on her colour picker website, DCI Osmond growled across the office, 'Will someone pick up that phone call? This is how we miss vital leads!'

'It's the same.' Amber pointed at the screen. 'Look' – she read out the numbers – 'exactly the same colour.'

'Sorry to interrupt, sir,' came DC Philpot's hesitant voice. 'You need to know this immediately. A uniformed officer just went round to Orsen Scott's house to post himself outside, as you'd requested. Scott's not there, sir. The front door has been left wide open and there are signs of a struggle in the hallway. He appears to have been abducted—'

THIRTY-FIVE

Hollie tensed; it took a moment to absorb the information.

'And there's no body on the premises?' she asked urgently. Orsen Scott should have been assigned protection sooner, and that rankled with her.

'Was his wife there? Is she okay?'

Hollie's mind began to race. Everything was coming to a head now.

'She's out somewhere having drinks with friends in the city. The PC said it was marked on the calendar in the kitchen. They're trying to locate her now—'

'Did any of the neighbours see anything?'

'Yes, we've got a break, boss. A red van, with a partial registration number. It's a hire vehicle, but uniform have placed an alert on it and they're chasing the hire firm for the renter's details. Fortunately, it had a rental sticker on the rear window.'

'Well, I hope they find it faster than they have Simon Rose. Have we got anything on that man yet? Did the neighbours see him entering the house?'

DS Patel's cautious silence at the end of the phone gave her her answer.

'There's one more thing, boss,' Amber continued. 'Do you know anything about the Hull Health Responders?'

'What?' Hollie replied, thrown off balance by the sudden gear change. It rang a bell.

'Is Jenni in the office?' she asked, wracking her brain for where she'd heard those words.

'I'm putting you on speaker, boss,' Amber replied after calling across the office to her colleague.

'Hull Health Responders, who mentioned that to us?' Hollie asked.

Without missing a beat, Jenni had her answer. 'Jane Carrick mentioned them. She said she trained Melanie Digby's son when he joined them. Why?'

Amber released an audible gasp. 'That torn-off slip of paper that you brought back from Ray McGregor's was written on branded Hull Health Responders paper,' she explained excitedly.

'Shit, that means—?' Jennie asked.

'William Digby!' Hollie said at the same time. 'He knew Jane Carrick through his mother and that medical training he did with her. And he's trained to carry out basic medical procedures. He must be helping Simon Rose. But what the hell does he have to do with this case – why would he get involved?'

Another voice joined them from the office end of the call. It was DC Norton, who'd half-heard the conversation from across the office.

'Hull Health Responders provide medical support at Hull Fair,' she interrupted. 'They're there every year assisting St John Ambulance. I was there two nights ago, and they're stationed all over the place.'

'What's their uniform?' Jenni checked.

'Burgundy overalls with a logo on the right lapel,' DC Norton replied, very sure of her answer.

'Shit!'

Both Jenni and Hollie cursed at the same time.

'There was a pair of overalls like that drying in Melanie Digby's house when we called round,' Hollie explained.

'Jenni, Amber, get over to Melanie Digby's house straight away. I want all eyes on William Digby and his movements. Let's bring him in. In fact, call Melanie now before you leave, find out where he is.'

Hollie recalled something else she'd observed while at the house.

'She had a green wheelie bin in the back garden when we visited; see if there's a black one out there, too. If there isn't, see what she says happened to it. He may have used her wheelie bin to move Carrick's body.'

She took a moment – what had she missed?

'DC Norton, contact Hull Health Responders. I want to know if and when William Digby has been on duty this week at the fairground. I also want to know how much medical training these people receive. Would he know enough to be administering lethal doses?'

'You think he might be responsible for the overdoses?' Amber asked aloud.

'I thought it was Jane Carrick,' Hollie replied urgently, her words tumbling out of her mouth. 'But this makes more sense, doesn't it? Except William Digby being involved doesn't add up at all.'

Her mind was in overdrive, thinking how to cover all the angles. Even as she was speaking, Anderson was making calls on hands-free, kicking as many arses as he could to get all eyes open among the uniformed officers for Simon Rose, Orsen Scott, William Digby and the red rental van.

They'd got their first solid lead, but Orsen Scott was out there somewhere and in mortal danger. If Scott died, their links with the past were gone. And what of Simon Rose? If he wasn't their killer, then why had he come back to Hull?

'Okay, we're on the clock, everybody. If our killer has their hands on Orsen Scott, he's in considerable danger right now. Whatever he may or may not have done in the past, we still need to give this our immediate and full attention. DS Anderson and I are heading straight out to look for Digby—' Even as she was saying the words, Anderson held up his hand. 'Got to go,' she said, trying to read Anderson's face.

'You'd best hold your horses for five minutes,' he warned. 'Osmond needs an urgent word with you. He wants you to ring his office directly.'

'I'm so sorry to have to break this news to you.'

On Osmond's advice, Hollie had stepped out of the car so she could take the call in confidence. In her head, she was already speeding up the road on her way to locate and apprehend William Digby as she reluctantly placed the call. And now he was saying what? That he and Amber had figured out where Moira's body might be buried from a faded old Polaroid image.

She couldn't speak; her chest felt like it might implode. She wanted to throw up, but there was nothing there to throw up, as she hadn't eaten in ages.

'Take your time,' Osmond said gently. All she could hear was his breathing cutting across the mouthpiece of his office phone.

With some difficulty, Hollie managed to speak at last. 'Are you sure it's her?'

She knew she was grasping at straws. Moira was the only person who'd gone missing. The Polaroid image of East Park had been included with photographs of Moira and Simon. Whoever was trying to point them in the right direction must have meant for them to figure that out. But how would Simon

Rose have got that information? He'd assured her he didn't know what had happened to Moira.

'I'm getting authorisation to send a team over to the small island in the boating lake. If she's there, we'll find her.'

Hollie tugged at her hair; at that moment she could have torn it all out in frustration.

Osmond paused again at the end of the line and swallowed with some awkwardness.

'Doctor Ruane had a word with me this afternoon. He'd called in with the initial findings of the toxicology report on Gordon Carrick.'

Hollie was still reeling at the possibility that Moira's body might have been hidden in East Park.

'Dr Ruane has confirmed that Gordon Carrick was injected several times with a substance that either disabled him or killed him.'

The DCI left that hanging there while she processed what that meant.

'What was he injected with?' Hollie asked.

'He can't be sure yet,' Osmond continued. 'He needs to run further tests, as the initial results were inconclusive.'

'Does he have any theories?'

'Ruane suspects diamorphine, but as I said, he'll confirm it once the extra tests have been processed.'

Hollie's detective instincts were in full flow now. The sequence of events was not quite clear to her. Had Carrick been murdered in the ghost train ride, as the bloody mallet had indicated? Or, had the diamorphine been used to render him unconscious, so that his body might be easily transported in the wheelie bin that Harry had found? It was possible he was dead on arrival at the ghost train, and then his body mutilated with the mallet afterwards. The diamorphine confused the time line, but it suggested, at least, that this was a well-planned murder, not one carried out in the heat of the moment.

'What's diamorphine used for?' she asked hurriedly.

'Managing pain, according to Doctor Ruane,' Osmond said. 'It's what Harold Shipman used to kill his patients.'

'So it's possible that Carrick was rendered unconscious by the diamorphine, and the physical injuries by the mallet inflicted separately?' she pushed, eager for a confirmation of her theory.

'It would appear so.'

'I need to make a call, sir.'

She didn't wait for Osmond's answer – there was too much happening too fast for pleasantries.

She dialled Amber's phone, which was engaged, so she dialled the desk next to it. Jenni answered.

'Is Amber speaking to Melanie Digby?' she asked, hurried and urgent.

'Yes, boss, she's speaking with her now—'

'Ask her what medication she takes to manage her emphysema, will you?'

There was some mumbling at the other end of the line and then Jenni picked up again.

'Diamorphine,' she replied, as another telephone started ringing insistently somewhere else in the office.

'It's what Harold Shipman used to kill his patients,' Hollie said aloud, sharing Osmond's remark. 'So William Digby must have been using his mum's prescription drugs. She said she was running short—'

DC Norton's voice came over the phone speaker, breathless and direct. The phone had stopped ringing in the background.

'We've got a report of the vehicle that was seen leaving the Scott's house this afternoon,' she began. Hollie could feel the endgame approaching. It was exhilarating to know she might soon have her answers.

'It's been abandoned by The George pub, ma'am, at the junction of Spring Bank West and Walton Street. The engine was still running when it was called in by uniform. He must be on the Hull Fair showground.'

Hollie said to Osmond, 'Call Doctor Ruane, sir; I'm getting over there now.'

THIRTY-SIX

It was dark already and Hollie's breath appeared like a puff of smoke as she leapt out of her car and ran over to the van.

She'd thrown her car up the kerb close to The George pub and she didn't bother shutting the door. Two uniformed Specials were waiting at the side of the vehicle, ready for more senior backup to arrive. Hollie was it.

She'd received several phone updates as she impatiently pushed her way over to the Hull Fair site through the evening traffic. The hire vehicle used to abduct Orsen Scott was registered to a Rudie Voordes from Baambrugge near Amsterdam: Simon Rose's false – or new – identity, they'd assumed. It was being checked out.

Hollie could barely catch her breath. Cases often came like this; nothing to go on, then everything all at once.

It felt like the stage was set for a drama which had been playing out for years. Amber had hurriedly handed her a two-way radio as she was leaving the office, and they were sending as many officers as were available down to the show site. If the van had been abandoned by Hull Fair, this is where William Digby

– Simon Rose – or whoever the hell was behind this, was going to let the situation play out.

Hollie showed her ID to the Specials and took in a quick update. The van doors were locked, and it was sealed off behind the front seats. They'd been nervous about breaking in, but Hollie gave them the nod.

'Get in there now,' she ordered them, 'there might be a man in there!'

As the chastened officers set about breaking into the back, Hollie switched on her radio and selected the channel which Amber had advised using. Hollie pushed the earpiece into her ear and adjusted her hair so it wouldn't be seen as she walked through the showground. Although they were at the edges of the fair, the noise of the rides and the music still made it difficult to speak at normal volume.

The team had arrived already and were spreading through the showground. One by one, they checked in over the radios.

'Melanie Digby confirmed everything,' Amber updated her. 'William is on duty tonight and has been all this week while the fair has been on. And she confirmed that she ran short of diamorphine. She blamed herself, thinking she'd messed it up or had been forgetful. It looks like William might have been dipping into her supplies.'

As the radios crackled, she watched the Specials bashing in the blacked-out back window of the van. Simon Rose wasn't getting his deposit back on that rental.

'Okay, so we're all eyes open,' she picked up, thinking through what had to be done. She was grateful to have DS Anderson out in the field; he'd already taken a lead while she was checking out the van.

'Orsen Scott's life is in danger,' she picked up. 'We're looking for Simon Rose and William Digby; Digby may be dressed in his medic's uniform. No interventions without my say-so, I do not want them spooked.'

They broke off, the crackle of the radios sounding in her ear. The two officers had finally broken into the van and were just opening the rear doors.

Hollie missed a breath as she saw what was inside.

The body of a man, bound with tape, was curled up inside. He was dressed in burgundy overalls.

The interior of the van was too dark to get a good look, so she took her phone out of her pocket and switched on the torch.

'I'll get this—' she said to the two officers, who took the hint and stood back. 'Get an ambulance over here and call it into HQ.'

Hollie gingerly leaned into the van, trying to get a better look at the body, keen to see who it was, but anxious not to disturb any evidence.

She jumped as the body moved. She half-expected it to be Orsen Scott, in spite of the overalls, and her immediate reaction was relief that he was still alive. But as the person in the van turned to face her, their mouth taped up, she realised that she'd never seen this man before.

'Are you William Digby?' she shouted at him, pulling the tape from his mouth. He flinched as it tore off his skin.

'Yes, I'm William Digby,' he replied, subdued and cooperative.

He was dressed in his Hull Health Responders uniform, the perfect cover for a man who wanted to be able to walk anywhere on that fairground site unchallenged.

'William Digby, I'm arresting you on suspicion of the murders of Kenneth Digby and Gordon Carrick, and the abduction of Orsen Scott. I am arresting you to prevent you causing further physical injury to others. You do not have to say anything. But it may harm your defence if you do not mention when questioned something which you later rely on in court. Anything you do say may be given in evidence.'

He looked at her like he was waiting for it.

'Now where is Orsen Scott?' she shouted at him. 'Is he alive?'

'I don't have him,' William replied, confused and dazed. 'Help me with this tape, will you? I can't sit up.'

'You stay like that for now,' Hollie warned him. 'You can do yourself some favours right now by telling me what's going on.' She felt impatient and angry; Orsen Scott was still out there somewhere.

'Simon got him—' Digby began drowsily. Was he on drugs?

'Simon Rose?' Hollie checked. She knew it was a stupid question, but she needed the delay to process it herself.

'Yes,' he answered, subdued.

'But you abducted Orsen from his house, yes?'

Digby gave the sigh of a man who'd realised the game was up.

'I tried to,' he admitted. 'But Simon was one step ahead this time. He was always stronger than me, even when we were kids.'

'You know Simon?' Hollie asked, incredulous that she was still discovering connections which seemed improbable.

'Yes. I got to know some of the kids through my dad's work. But those men abused me, too—'

Hollie stared blankly at him, completely unable to understand how that could be.

'But you're Kenneth Digby's son. He ran the place. Surely he didn't get his own son involved in all that?'

Hollie couldn't link the fragments – the information seemed too scattered to make any sense. She wished she could mute the sounds from the fair, as they were making it difficult to think clearly.

'I thought it was a party,' he replied, cold and detached. 'They didn't know who I was. They did to me what they did to Simon and Moira and all those other kids...' His eyes became distant and detached, as if recalling something which his brain could barely process. 'Carrick and Scott raped me that night, the bastards.'

'And you killed Carrick because of that?' Hollie challenged him.

'He got what he deserved. Who's worse, him or me? He'll never hurt a child again, that's for sure. It was all covered up in that inquiry. And to think I thought my dad was innocent.'

William did not seem like a killer. He was calm and gently spoken, even though she could see his burning anger. This was not the kind of sociopath who usually dominated her work.

'So your father was involved, too?' she asked. 'But how? Surely he'd never let that happen to his own son?' she pressed again.

'I didn't know it at the time. I only found that out recently.'

'How?' Hollie swallowed with difficulty, frantic now to solve this puzzle. She could hear an ambulance siren somewhere along Spring Bank West. She needed to squeeze as much out of him now, off the record, before he was taken in for processing. They had to find Orsen Scott. For all she knew, he might be injured or dead already – every second counted now.

'He asked me to fetch a box of his from the attic a couple of months ago, when Mum kicked him out of the house,' William continued. 'It had been up there for years. He told me not to look; he said it had private documentation in it.'

'And you looked?'

Hollie was hanging on his every word. Every revelation brought her closer to Moira and Carrick's killer.

'I looked,' he answered, as if his mind was trailing back to a particular time and place. 'I found those Polaroids in there and his camera. When I saw those faces... my friends – and that wallpaper – I knew he was involved. They were taken in his office at Ambrose House.'

'It was you who smashed the camera when your father died?'

'Yes, I was furious with him. I made him tell me what he'd done. I threw his camera against the wall, and I lost control of my senses.'

'You killed him, didn't you?' Hollie spoke softly. 'You injected him with his own insulin?'

A single tear ran down Digby's cheek and dripped onto the metal flooring of the van.

'He'd lied to us all those years. He lied to me and Mum. And he helped those men who raped me. I can never forgive him for that. He was procuring teenagers for those bastards. I used a cushion to hold him down so there'd be no bruising, then I rammed those needles into him one by one until he stopped struggling.'

'And Gordon Carrick? It was you who mutilated him?'

He sighed. It was rare to see a killer in the mood for confession, but William Digby seemed almost relieved to be telling his story at last.

'I killed Dad in a fit of anger. I couldn't control myself when I realised what he'd done. A quarter of a century of suppressed rage came flooding out of me. I'd loved him all my life, then, in an instant, he became the most abhorrent thing in my world.' He was sobbing now. 'I figured you'd catch up with me eventually, so I decided to get some justice and kill all three of them – for Moira and for Simon. Gordon Carrick was easy. I invited him to Mum's house and told him what evidence I'd got. Mum was even out with his wife that night, how ironic is that? I killed the fucker with Mum's medicine, then decided to make an example of him by leaving him in the ghost train. I hadn't intended on doing anything else, but when I found that mallet... well, I couldn't contain myself. I'd read about a mallet being found when Moira disappeared. It seemed fitting to smash him up with that.'

'His wounds were shocking,' Hollie replied instinctively. She could see how much this had taken from him. William

Digby was no natural killer. In many ways he was still that defenceless, scared teenage boy. But now he could take his vengeance.

'What he did to me was even worse,' Digby continued through his tears. 'I'd just turned seventeen for Christ's sake. I'd never even had a proper girlfriend. And what he did to me, he did to them, too.'

Digby had given into his tears now, and everything was coming out. If only he'd shared this with the police. It made Hollie want to scream, the number of victims who never spoke out but held in the bile for years instead.

The medics were antsy to get to him now. They'd left the ambulance light flashing, and it was catching her eyes every time it circled around.

'One moment,' Hollie instructed, putting up her hand. 'And make sure this vehicle is swept for evidence,' she called over to the two Specials who were helpfully keeping the public well away.

'I was responsible for what happened to Moira,' Digby continued. 'I realise that now. On her sixteenth birthday, it was me. I didn't know it then, I thought my dad was just pissed with us. But I made him notice her. I'll never forgive myself. How can I forgive myself? It's ruined my entire life, my marriage, my relationships. It had to end like this. It was the only way.'

'So what happened to Moira, William?'

'I don't know. I dropped the photo off at McGregor's house. I thought you could figure it out. I've left everything in my room at Mum's house, by the way.'

'The photos? The evidence?'

'Yes, it's all there. I was going to hand myself in after I finished Orsen Scott. I'm not cut out for this. I know I have to do my time. But it was worth it. I need to tell you that. I don't regret any of it. It's like a huge weight has been lifted off me—'

A sudden crackle came over her radio.

'*DS Patel to all units,*' came her voice.

Hollie turned up the volume to make sure she caught the latest update. Her heart skipped a beat as Amber continued.

'*We've got Simon Rose in our sights. We're closing in on him now.*'

THIRTY-SEVEN

'Where is he?' Hollie asked. 'I've got William Digby here, but Simon has Orsen Scott.'

'Nothing yet, boss,' came DS Patel's voice over the radio. *'Simon Rose is by the ghost train where Carrick's body was found.'*

'Do we have eyes on him still?' Hollie checked. 'Has he got Orsen Scott with him?'

'It was just a uniformed officer calling it into the station; we don't know if Scott is with him.'

Hollie looked over towards the fairground site, taking one of the big wheels as her navigation point.

'Okay, DS Anderson and DS Patel, I'm heading over there now, I'll meet you there. We've got William Digby, but I don't know what Simon's got planned for Orsen Scott. DCs Gordon, Langdon and Norton, stay in your quadrants and keep your eyes peeled. DC Philpot, you're closest to me, come and pick me up by The George pub and make sure uniform don't screw anything up here.'

'Yes, boss,' came Jenni's voice over the comms unit, followed by Philpot and Norton. Philpot must have been close to Walton

Street, as he was there in a minute and took over the scene at the abandoned van.

Hollie recalled the site layout as best she could, navigating via the rides that she'd seen on her previous visit. Screams of delight and enjoyment rang through the air, the thud of amplified music pounded in her ears, and she pushed her way through the crowds, which were reaching peak levels now. It seemed that half the city descended on Walton Street after school and work.

As the crowd became denser around her, and she began to feel more claustrophobic at the assault on her senses, Hollie was transported back almost quarter of a century, back to that night when she'd come to this place with Moira.

Everywhere she looked she pictured her friend, laughing at the stalls, shrieking with joy on the rides, chatting away to her friends. As Hollie looked out for Simon, she began to imagine she was seeing Moira everywhere she looked.

She observed a teenage girl in the distance, probably eighteen or so, but with hair like Moira wore hers. It took her back to that night in 1999, and the panicked feeling of losing her friend engulfed her momentarily, reaching out through the years to torment her once again.

She checked herself. Simon Rose was the target – she had to keep her personal emotions out of it.

At last, a little flustered, she arrived at the ghost train. It was still cordoned off, but some of the police tape had become torn now and people were using the area outside as a space in which to eat their fast food.

'Hello, boss, have you spotted anything?' Amber asked, joining her from the throng as if she'd appeared from nowhere.

'It's so busy, he could come and go in a flash,' Hollie observed. She gave Amber a summary of what had just happened.

'So what the fuck is Simon Rose doing?' Amber asked.

'Where's Anderson?' Hollie changed the subject, anxious not to let Simon Rose slip through her fingers.

'He's over there.' Patel pointed. Hollie couldn't see him in the crowd. She'd have to take her word for it.

As Hollie searched the faces in the crowds, she spotted him: Simon Rose. He was pushing a vendor's cart, and he was wearing a fluorescent vest and a lanyard, no doubt taken from William Digby. Her body tensed and without a word, she rushed off towards him.

Simon had seen her, so abandoned his cart on the far side of the helter-skelter and rushed off between a couple of stalls.

Hollie fixed her gaze on where he'd headed, as she knew that if she lost her mark even for a second, he'd be gone.

This was just like it had been with Moira, her friend disappearing into the night, the sounds of the fairground all around her, assaulting her senses, the lights bright and multi-coloured, and so easy to lose someone in the crowd. She would not lose him, not like she'd lost Moira.

As Hollie stepped between the stalls, her heart racing now, she was in sudden darkness and among the caravans belonging to the show people. Her mind flashed back to that terrible night, and she felt as if she was nineteen all over again.

Her brow was dripping with sweat, despite the cold of the night, and her heart was protesting in her chest, the tension of the predator and the hunted.

The music from the rides became muted as she stepped out of the main thoroughfare, like she'd stepped into another world. She searched the darkness for shadows; the rides threw off light, though it was erratic and inconsistent.

She recalled straining to see Moira's figure, thinking every shadow was her, every silhouette tricking her into imagining she'd seen something that she hadn't and her friend slipping further away with every misstep.

'Simon, it's me, Hollie Turner.'

She'd done this before, calling for Moira.

As a beam of light from one of the nearby rides swept across the darkness, it threw a shadow and she saw where he was hiding, crouched behind a large, white van.

'Simon, let's end this now. Tell me what you've done with Orsen Scott, and we can finish this tonight. I know what William did – you're not our killer. I know you and Moira were about to reveal what was going on at the home.'

Could he hear her? Were her words getting lost in the darkness?

'I think you're here tonight because you want to make an example of those men. But we can do this together, Simon. We can take it through legal channels, we can show the world what's been going on.'

She was inching over to where she'd seen his shadow, but by the time she got within striking distance, he was no longer there. His voice came from some way away, over by a cluster of three smaller caravans. She could hear her colleagues trying to raise her on the radio and she was thankful that they'd opted to use less visible earpieces that night. If she answered them, she'd give her location away.

He called over to her.

'You and I know they'll get to me before it goes that far. These bastards are well-connected, they can close anything down. I'm sorry, DI Turner, but I thought I'd learnt to live with what happened. It turns out I haven't. When I saw that Kenneth Digby had died, I wasn't prepared to let their sordid little secret die with them when they went to their graves.'

Hollie was following his voice, creeping through the shadows, desperate to catch him unawares. She let him speak, buying herself the time to get to him.

'Orsen Scott knows what happened to Moira. Did you know that? The snivelling little shit told me before he passed out. And do you know what he also told me? That an accident would be arranged for me before I ever got to speak out. That's why this has to be done out in the open, DI Turner. The whole city has to see it before they get to me.'

Hollie had sneaked up to the front of the three caravans now and she was edging around the side. She could hear Simon's voice; he was almost in touching distance on the other side of the caravan. As she was about to lunge at him, a bright light swept across the area, thrown out by a nearby ride. She saw her shadow was swept across the grass, a silhouetted warning to Simon of her presence.

'Shit!'

She flew around the side of the caravan, but he'd seen the shadow and had turned to run off already. Hollie tried to grab at him, but she slid in the mud as she made her sharp turn. She hung on to Simon's vest, but as he twisted it slid off his arm. In a matter of seconds, while she was struggling to steady herself from her fall, Simon had slid out his other arm and he was away. She watched as he ran off into the darkness, a dark shadow, determined to slip away into the night.

THIRTY-EIGHT

Hollie felt foolish – her entire right side was caked in mud. It was wet and cold, and she cursed that she'd lost her footing.

She looked into the distance where she'd seen Simon running, but he was well away. Hollie brushed herself down and figured out which direction she needed to head to regroup with her colleagues.

'Sorry, guys,' she updated them over the radios, dejected at her failure. 'I had him, but he got away.'

Hollie heard screaming in the distance. It was the shriek of a crowd, but this stood out in the distant cacophony. These were not cries of joy: they were the sounds of alarm and fear.

She made directly for the source of the sounds, activating her radio again.

'What the hell is going on?'

All she could hear was ambient sound over somebody's open radio channel. At last, Jenni's breathless voice could be heard through her earpiece.

'There's no sign of Orsen Scott, boss. Fuck, he's climbing up the Ferris wheel—'

Jenni's voice crackled away, and DS Anderson's took its place.

'*We've got a situation here, boss. Where are you?*'

'On my way. What's happening?'

Hollie could see the big wheel ahead of her, but she was having some difficulty making her way through the caravans in the darkness. At last, she saw a couple of food stands marking the border of the show site and she stepped out between them. The big wheel was directly in front of her now, about three hundred yards away.

As her eyes adjusted to the brightness around her, she saw that a large crowd was gathering around the towering white Ferris wheel. Phones were being held up to film something – or someone – but she couldn't make out what it was from that distance.

'I'm here now, what side are you on?' she said to any one of her colleagues who might answer.

'*Fun House side, boss.*' It was Harry Gordon's voice. He sounded anxious, like he was out of his depth.

Hollie checked where she was. They were on the opposite side to her, where she'd first spotted Simon Rose in the crowd.

A voice was booming over nearby speakers, but it sounded incongruous, not like the normal patter of the show people adding a thrilling commentary to the rides. This voice was shouting and on edge.

She pushed through the crowd; it was deep and unyielding. She drew out her ID card.

'Police – let me through, please – Humberside Police – I need to come through—'

At last, she made it to where her colleagues were gathered at the side of the Ferris wheel. The structure was immense. DS Patel, DS Anderson, DC Gordon and DC Langdon were there with three beat officers.

'Where is he?' Hollie asked, trying to get a measure of the

situation. They were all looking up, but she still couldn't see why. And that voice kept coming. It appeared to be coming from the Twister ride opposite; it was coming through the speakers there, but nobody was looking that way.

'He's up there, boss,' Anderson pointed, a pained expression on his face.

Hollie glanced up at the carriages which were now motionless where the ride had been paused. She couldn't see anything still.

'Over there, boss. Follow the ladder.'

'Oh, fuck!'

The Ferris wheel was anchored by six massive iron posts forming a prism-like shape which met at the centre point of the massive wheel. Running up each of the posts was a narrow ladder used for maintenance purposes. Climbing up that ladder, and almost at the central hub of the ride, was Simon Rose.

'He's grabbed a radio microphone from the guy operating the Twister ride. It's feeding through the speakers over there. I've got a feeling we're all going to hear what this is about.'

'We need to get that radio mic switched off,' Hollie began. 'God knows what he's going to say up there, we can't let him have a free rein—'

'I'll take care of it, boss,' Harry volunteered. He seemed glad to have something to do.

'Off you go,' Hollie instructed him. 'Officers, make sure the crowd is moved well out of harm's way. I don't want any casualties. Jenni, Simon was pushing a vendor's cart near the helter-skelter – find it and check it out. And get an ambulance here!'

The officers leapt into action.

'How high is that thing?' Hollie asked.

'Fifty metres, boss,' Ben answered. 'They had an article about it in the paper. It's the same height as the Leaning Tower of Pisa. Or the same length as an Olympic swimming pool—'

'Okay, I get the message. Would you die if you fell from that height?'

Anderson looked at her and screwed up his face.

'Let's put it this way, if you didn't die, you'd spend the rest of your life in a wheelchair. Why?'

It dawned on him why she was asking the question.

'There's no way you're going up there, boss—'

'My name is Simon Rose and I need to tell you something very dark about this city—' His voice blared out of the speakers surrounding the adjacent ride.

'Damn, he's using the microphone,' Amber cursed. 'Come on, Harry, get that radio mic unit switched off.'

'I'm going up,' Hollie said. 'I don't think he's the killer. He can help us clear up what was happening at that place. What choice do we have?'

'Let one of the constables do it, Hollie,' Anderson pleaded quietly. 'They're much younger and it's their job to play Spider-Man.'

'No, I know him, and he knows me. God knows what state he's in. He's in a panic, and if he falls, we might never find out what happened to Moira—'

'I think you're too involved, Hollie,' Anderson cautioned.

'You're right, I am too involved. And so is Simon. I'm the only one who'll be able to reason with him. We both want the same thing.'

'Twenty-five years ago, I was brought to this fair by three evil men,' came the amplified voice.

Simon was at the top of the ladder now. He was hanging on with one hand and addressing the gathered crowd using the radio microphone, which he held in the other. He might have been a showman, he was so high up. Hundreds of camera phones were filming it all, the crowd in a nervous state of antici-pation as to what might happen next.

'Bloody hell, Harry, get that fucking microphone switched

off,' Amber cursed. 'I'm going over there to see what's holding him up.'

'You can't go up there, boss. It's too dangerous—' Anderson pleaded.

'You're welcome to do a risk assessment if you need to, Ben. But here's my health and safety input. That man's life is at risk up there and it's likely to get ugly fast with this crowd gathered. I want Simon Rose down safely to tell his story, and I want Orsen Scott and any other bastards that are caught up in this to face justice.'

She turned to make her way to the access platform. Anderson reached out to stop her, then seeing her face, immediately let her go.

'I'll give you a leg up,' he acquiesced.

'Oi, you can't go over there—' the ride operator shouted.

Hollie flashed her ID, and he backed down, moving over to help them.

'That fucker pushed right past me,' he complained. 'Do you want a hard hat and clips?'

'There's no time,' Hollie said. 'I need to speak to him before he does anything crazy.'

Ben and the ride operator helped Hollie onto the bottom of the narrow ladder. From where she was standing it seemed like it was a direct route to heaven, such was the height. It was sloped at an angle, and she thanked her luck it wasn't a straight climb up, as she couldn't have even contemplated that.

She began to make her way up the steps, her feet clanging on metal with every move. Carefully, she placed her hands on the rungs above, making sure her feet were firmly sitting on the rungs below. She went up a short way and looked down. Already it seemed like a ridiculous drop. She felt her legs wobble when she looked up at the height she still had to ascend.

She couldn't look down again. Rung by rung she made her way higher up the narrow ladder. She could sense the anxiety of the crowd below her but knew she had to focus now, or she'd lose her grip and fall to the metal platform below.

She became aware of the people in the Ferris wheel carriages looking down on her from their advantageous height. She caught the glow from their phones as they filmed her every move.

As she got closer to Simon, she shouted up to him, hopeful that he'd hear her, and she wouldn't have to climb any higher. There was protection from the fairground sounds below at that height, but he seemed unaware that she was there.

Simon's voice came over the microphone once again. She could see his lips moving, but his voice was delayed as it was relayed down to the speaker far below them.

'My name is Simon Rose and in 1999, me and my friends were abused at Ambrose House children's home,' his voice boomed.

Even from such a height, Hollie could sense the crowd falling quiet below.

'Kenneth Digby was one of the care workers there,' Simon was breathless from the exertion of the climb. Hollie wished he'd slow; her arms were aching and her legs stinging with soreness.

'Digby abused us when he was on night duty... we were only teenagers... and now Digby is dead.'

The higher Simon climbed, the more erratic the signal became from the radio microphone. As he looked around him, he spotted Hollie in pursuit.

'Get away!' he called over. 'Let me finish this.'

She could barely make out what he was saying.

There was a crackle in Hollie's ear.

'You're doing great, boss. Almost there, hold steady.'

It was Anderson, more on edge than she'd ever heard him.

A second crackle came over the radio.

'*We've got Orsen Scott, boss! Simon Rose had him in that vendor's cart. He's alive! But he's been drugged with something.*'

'It's diamorphine,' Hollie updated them. 'I suspect William Digby was getting ready to kill him when Simon interrupted them. Let the medics know as soon as they get here.'

Hollie stopped climbing for a moment, closed her eyes and paused, centring herself.

'Simon, please don't do this. You've made your point now. End it here—'

'Yeah, and I go to prison anyway, despite being the victim here. What does it take to make yourself heard? This is the only way I get a voice, with hundreds of camera phones on me.'

'*We were taken on trips to Hull Fair... on nights like this... innocent children—*'

Simon appeared to Hollie to be getting frustrated with the sound problems. She could see crowds streaming from all across the fairground to the Ferris wheel. This is how accidents happened, when things got out of hand.

Foolishly, Hollie looked down, sensing movement in her peripheral vision. A huge crowd was gathering all around the Ferris wheel, with hundreds of mobile phones trained on the unfolding events.

A group of men were making their way up the other ladders. They were wearing hard hats and gloves and appeared to be clipping themselves onto the ladders. Either these were police officers, or trained show people, but they'd been spotted by Simon now and he was panicking.

'Who the fuck are these guys?' she snapped over the intercom.

'*They're the maintenance team, they were on site already. They're making for the platform areas to assist you.*' Amber Patel's voice was shrill and anxious.

'Tell them to hang back,' Hollie snapped, looking at the horizontal platforms which ran between the Ferris wheel's pillars. There were access and maintenance points all over the vast structure, but she needed them to give her a wide berth. 'I do not want Simon panicked.'

She looked up once again.

'Oh, for fuck's sake!' she shouted.

Along each of the spokes of the Ferris wheel ran a single maintenance ladder. Simon had moved further up to the centre of the wheel, from where he was now beginning to climb outwards, away from the relative security of the heavy pillars. She could see he was terrified and in a state of frantic panic. What the hell was driving Simon on?

'Respectable men in this city... monsters... our lives a living hell—'

He was trying to edge his way across the Ferris wheel now, no doubt in an attempt to get a stronger signal on the speakers below.

'Men like Gordon Carrick... Orsen Scott... stole our innocence—'

Hollie's head began to spin as she looked up and over into the complex framework of the structure, yet she continued to climb, her eyes closed now, making her ascent by touch. She arrived at the wheel's hub, hardly daring to step away from the ladder and onto the narrow staging area. Across on the ladder, crawling out into nothingness, was Simon Rose.

Hollie didn't think she could join him on the horizontal access. It was one thing climbing along a gently sloped ladder securely fixed to a massive iron pillar. But she simply didn't dare to step out onto that second ladder. It was so open and exposed out there.

'Simon!' she shouted over. He'd grown wild, spurred on by the crowd which had gathered to watch the spectacle, but also increasingly agitated at the microphone behaving so erratically.

'I want everybody to be my witness... someone killing

them... nobody left to answer for these crimes... that ends here today—'

It was eerily calm at that height, even though Hollie was aware of the fairground carrying on below her, thousands of people still completely unaware of the terror being played out above them.

Simon was back on the microphone, his words beginning to cut out now due to the distance he was from the receiver unit.

'Kenneth Digby – abusing kids at Ambrose House – nineties —' came his ranting, interrupted commentary. He was completely breathless now, too, tiring from the climb. *'Orsen Scott and Gordon Carrick used the cover of – children's charity – take those children to sex parties – terrible things—'*

Suddenly, Simon was cut off in mid-sentence. Good, Harry had terminated the radio link.

'Turn the bloody microphone back on!' he shouted over, frantic and losing control. 'Let me say what I've come to say – this is the only way this damn city will ever get to know the truth. They can kill me if they want to, at least the names are out there now—'

There was a sudden clang of metal. Simon had dropped the microphone, and Hollie flinched as she watched how long it took to strike the ground below.

She was so scared, she thought she would pass out. But she had to press on. The men who'd come up the other pillars were close by now, and if she could just talk Simon down, they'd come and get her, and they'd help her down.

Hollie gasped as she reached over to the horizontal ladder and started to crawl along its length. She sensed the atmosphere below her, but she banished all thoughts of this playing out on social media. She had to focus on her sole objective: to get them down safely and secure justice for Moira. She'd abandoned her once, she would not do it again.

Simon had gone as far out as he could go – there was nothing beyond the ladder and nowhere else to move to.

Hollie's head was spinning. Her entire body was convulsing with fear. Only Simon, fuelled by rage and despair, seemed oblivious to the peril of their situation.

Then, in a split second, Simon moved his hand to grab on more firmly, missed the edge of the ladder and keeled over to the side. He reached out to steady himself and managed to keep hold with one hand, but his entire body was now hanging from one rung of the ladder. He contorted his body to try to reach up with his other hand but didn't seem to have the strength.

Hollie, scared out of her wits, edged further along the ladder until she was just above him.

'I can't hang on—' Simon gasped.

'Try and reach my hand,' Hollie called.

'I know what happened,' Simon said, looking up directly into Hollie's eyes. 'I know where she is.'

'Take my hand,' Hollie pleaded, 'let's find her together, Simon. I know you loved her. Let's give her the peace she deserves.'

As she spoke, Hollie watched his hand slipping off the rungs. She closed her eyes tight as she thrust out her hand in a desperate attempt to catch him.

THIRTY-NINE

It was raining heavily as the digging team worked their way across the small island set in the middle of the boating lake. The wild fowl seemed annoyed at their presence like they'd been rudely disturbed in the one place they expected to be clear of humans.

Hollie had never been to East Park before, but it was a wonderful, green oasis hidden on the east side of the city. She recalled having taken Izzy once to the Woodford Centre at its entrance, having secured a lift with a student friend who had both a young child and a car. This was no place now for fond memories of happier times. They were searching for Moira's body. Hollie couldn't have felt bleaker; a feeling of nausea sat heavy in her stomach and her body was tensed, bracing for terrible news at any moment.

It took some coordination to get the small team over to the island, but it had been done as a priority. Her immediate team had insisted on accompanying her, and all five of them were sheltering under a tree while they watched and waited.

Jenni moved her hand up to gently squeeze Hollie's arm, and she left it there, steadying her, a rock for Hollie to cling to as she steeled herself. All Hollie could think of was Moira. She would not rest until they'd checked the entire area.

'You did a great job saving Simon Rose like that, boss,' Jenni said softly. 'Loads of people videoed it from the ground. It took my breath away watching it.'

'I don't want to look at it.' Hollie shuddered. 'It's the most terrifying experience of my life. How those inspection guys managed to talk me down, I'll never know. I was paralysed up there, I honestly thought I was going to fall.'

'You did brilliantly, boss,' Anderson reassured her. 'You're a bloody hero. And Simon Rose owes his life to you.'

Hollie had never been more thankful for his compassion. He'd been at the bottom of the Ferris wheel waiting for her, ready to steady her when her feet finally reached the safety of the ground, with Simon close behind her.

She'd come down to the flashing lights of ambulances and a round of applause from the crowd, who'd now been contained within a proper cordon.

Hollie didn't feel like she deserved that recognition.

One of the search dogs began to bark at a nearby tree. There had been some activity around there while they'd been speaking, and Hollie had tried not to get her hopes up.

'DI Turner!' came a shout.

'Are you all right to do this?' Anderson asked.

'Yes, I want to,' Hollie replied.

The other members of the team held back as she walked over to where the dog was barking. It felt like the longest walk of her life.

A forensics officer was standing over a shallow pit which had carefully been dug out a metre from the tree.

'I think we've found her.' He spoke softly with compassion in his eyes.

Hollie looked down at a rotting skull, its hollow eyes staring at her from the shallow grave. Its side was caved in where it had been struck by a heavy object.

'How soon until we can be certain?' Hollie asked.

'We'll need to run some tests,' the officer replied apologetically.

'What's that in the mud there?' Hollie pointed. They'd missed something when they'd been excavating the area. The officer pushed the soil away to reveal a lucky charm necklace. He used a small twig to hold it up so that Hollie could see it.

'That's the necklace I helped Moira put on the night she met Simon Rose—'

She couldn't speak. Her heart felt like it had stopped. Her mind took her back to Moira's bedsit, ready for a night out, fastening the lucky charm around her friend's neck. She'd always prayed they'd be reunited – but not like this, please, not like this.

'I'm so sorry, Moira,' she whispered as her tears fell. 'I'm sorry I couldn't help you. I'm sorry it's taken so long to find you. You can rest now, we've got them. They can't hurt you anymore.'

EPILOGUE

'I wish to God you'd just trusted me,' Hollie said softly, tugging gently on the handcuffs which bound them together. 'You could have avoided all of this.'

She stared down at the single red rose Simon had placed against the small, marble memorial stone. Hollie had paid for the stone; she wasn't letting her friend have an unmarked grave like her mother. They'd been unable to locate her burial place despite combing through the paper records from the nineties.

Moira Juliet Kennedy

1980–1999

It wasn't much to remember her life by, but what little had been recovered of Moira's body had been cremated and laid to rest at the Priory Woods Cemetery.

'I loved Moira, you know,' Simon said, making no attempt to disguise his distress at seeing her grave. 'I'll never forgive myself for not having the courage to do this sooner. You've read everything I wrote down in that notebook, I take it?'

'Yes,' Hollie replied, deep in thought. 'It's good you made

that cassette recording in 1999 when you sorted yourself out in Europe. Even better that you transferred it over to a digital format. You've got addresses and names in there which weren't even on our radar. I can't believe how deep the abuse ran through the city.'

Hollie thought back to the threat that had been made at the old Rediffusion building. She of all people knew what it was like to be terrified by fear. She couldn't blame Simon; he'd done what he could at the time. And now they had even more evidence to suggest that her predecessor, DCI Bryan MacKenzie, was caught up in the cover-up.

Orsen Scott was still alive – thanks to Simon intervening with William Digby. And Digby's haul of evidence from his father's collection was more than enough to secure a conviction. Kenneth Digby had collected trophies; even after his death he'd left enough of a trace to condemn them all.

'Was the cassette where we named them all in Kenneth Digby's box of treasures?' Simon asked, bitter and resentful. 'I dropped that on the ground on that last night by Stepney station. I always figured the bastard found it.'

Hollie looked down at her feet, gently shaking her head. A tear ran down her cheek, splashing on Moira's headstone.

'Yes, and I've listened to it. We thought you'd dropped it off at Ray McGregor's, but it turns out it was William Digby who did it. He wanted to give Ray the scoop he was denied all those years ago. We had to convert it to a digital file and get it cleaned up. It's powerful stuff. If only you'd got it to Ray McGregor in 1999, before Digby stopped you—'

She choked up. It still wouldn't have saved Moira. She was dead before they'd even managed to summon the police, her body magicked away in the back of an ice cream van, a returned favour by some other Hull criminal. Orsen Scott was playing ball. He knew it was his only slim chance of not ending his life in prison. She steadied herself, then looked at him.

'Where have you been hiding all these years, Simon? There was no trace of you.'

'I hitched a ride in a lorry over to Amsterdam. As soon as I was on open roads, it was easy. I got casual work, saved up some money and bought myself a new identity. I'm an accountant now, would you believe it? Rudie Voordes, small business accountant. I wrote everything in that notebook as soon as I arrived. Every name, address, date I could think of. I did it while it was still clear in my mind. But I didn't dare step out of the shadows until I saw that Kenneth Digby was dead. That's when I reached out to his wife.'

'What happened back in 1999, Simon?' Hollie pushed. She needed to understand this. 'They suspected you because you'd been staying at Moira's house, and you disappeared at the same time as she did. They even suspected me of hurting her, because there were signs of a cup being thrown against the wall.'

Simon smiled, as if remembering something in the past.

'I tried to convince Moira not to go with you to Hull Fair,' he explained. 'I threw the cup to be dramatic. She wasn't listening to my warnings, so I did it to show her how serious I was. But she just ignored me anyway. She wanted to spend a last night with you and the girls, Hollie. She knew everything would change once we gave Ray McGregor those names the following day. But we never made it that far.'

Hollie had been forcing back the tears, but hearing those words, she gave up and let them flow. They were partly tears of relief, of knowing that her friends were looking out for her right until the end. Simon stayed silent, seeing she needed a moment.

'What's the bail hostel like?' Hollie asked at last, wiping her eyes and moving onto less emotive ground.

Simon snorted. 'They're called Approved Premises these days. I think it's to make them sound better than they are. Bearing in mind I've spent time living on the streets, I'd almost describe it as luxurious,' he replied, sneering.

'Well, you've only yourself to blame—'

He interrupted her before she could finish her sentence. 'You know as well as I do that you'd have hauled me in, and you'd have been distracted for a couple of days while you checked out my story. Orsen Scott would have been dead by then. I couldn't risk it; one of those men had to face justice. I didn't know who was killing them, but I had to get there before Billy did.'

Hollie looked at him.

'You called him Billy? He goes by William these days.'

'You know, Billy was in love with Moira, too,' Simon continued. 'She had that effect on us. I think he resented me for it.'

'Everybody loved Moira, you know that.' Hollie's voice faltered. 'You were her friend. You know what she was like.'

Hollie couldn't control her emotions anymore and she let out a small snort as her tears broke through and she began to sob.

It tormented Hollie that she was unable to reach back and hold her friend and tell her how many people had cared deeply for Moira during her short life. Amber had made contact with her former support worker in New Zealand, and they'd reminisced about the Moira they both knew in a long Zoom call. The support worker had also helped to fill in some details of Moira's last movements in those final days.

Hollie stooped down to place her own flowers at the base of the stone, stretching out her free hand and carefully laying them next to Simon's rose.

'Goodbye, Moira. I'm pleased we could do right by you in the end. I'm sorry we took so long.'

She returned to her standing position and turned towards the waiting police car.

'I'll speak up in support of you when your case comes up,' she promised, her voice steady and firm now. 'I hope you'll be spared custodial time. We couldn't have tied this up without you.'

Simon stopped in front of the vehicle as the uniformed police officer released Hollie from the handcuffs.

'So, this is why you became a cop in the first place – to somehow repay Moira for letting her down?' He searched Hollie's face like he was seeking some consolation there.

She paused, thinking back to those difficult, empty days after her friend's disappearance.

'I think about Moira every day,' she began slowly. 'Every bad guy I lock up is for Moira. Every one of those bastards I take off the streets is one small way I can repay her for letting her down when she needed me most. And I'll never stop repaying that debt – never. Not until I take my dying breath, or they retire me.'

A LETTER FROM THE AUTHOR

Thank you very much for reading *Her Final Secret*. If you enjoyed the book and would like to join other readers in keeping in touch, stay in the loop with Paul J. Teague's new releases by clicking on the link.

www.stormpublishing.co/paul-j-teague

Writing *Her Final Secret* was an excellent opportunity for me to incorporate Hull Fair into a plot; you can't really set a series in Hull without dedicating at least some pages to the city's biggest annual attraction.

Hull Fair has been based in the city for more than seven hundred years. It attracts over half a million attendees annually and it is the biggest fair in Europe.

I attended Hull Fair in 1997, when I was working for BBC Radio Humberside as a presenter. My first child had just been born at Castle Hill Hospital, and my in-laws were visiting from Scotland. We'd been to see my wife and new baby in the hospital during visiting hours and had a free evening ahead of us. It seemed rude not to show them the fair while it was in town.

I don't recall much about that night, other than playing a game of bingo and winning a child's plastic mobile toy, the sort of thing babies play with before they can walk. It seemed a practical item to select from the prizes on offer, bearing in mind the recent change in my domestic situation.

All three of my children played with and loved that toy. And, interestingly, my wife's stepmum knew the chap who was stationed at the bingo stall. Like most show people, he was a traveller and knew her from the shows in Ayrshire, where she lived.

From memory, that's the only time I attended the Hull Fair, though I will have reported on it many times on the radio. My wife and I paid a visit on a research trip while I was in the middle of writing this book. Candy floss was consumed, and fun was had, but it was all in the name of literary accuracy, of course.

It's a well-organised operation, as you'd expect, and we were delighted that we could catch a shuttle bus from where we were staying, close to North Ferriby and the Humber Bridge Park, both previous locations used in this series of books. In fact, being so close to the Humber Bridge Park allowed me to double-check how many CCTV cameras are located there, an important detail in my first DI Hollie Turner trilogy. I hope whoever is on the other end of those cameras didn't spot us driving around and taking photos of the cameras – it must have looked very suspicious. It won't have been the first time somebody's asked me what I'm up to when researching books!

Hull Fair was packed, but it was great to be back, it's such a fabulous event. I took a ride on a ghost train, just to remind myself of the details, and had my fortune read by a palm reader, just for fun. The things I do for these books :-)

Now, I have an admission to make: I love going to palmists. It's a while since I've been. The last time I had a reading was in Blackpool, a couple of years ago. That was also for book research, by the way, and was for my *Don't Tell Meg* trilogy which has a series of scenes set in the seaside town.

There's something about palmistry that fascinates me. I'm one of those people who's not a believer, but neither would I dream of dismissing it. There's something about it that draws me in. The same goes for spiritualism. I feature a spiritualist called Steven Terry in my *Don't Tell Meg* trilogy, and I liked him so much, that he makes regular appearances in my *Morecambe Bay* series.

My characters are always sceptical of Steven, but he usually comes up with something terrifying or useful to the investigation. So I remain open-minded and fascinated by these topics – and Steven Terry may well make an appearance in a future DI Hollie Turner story if the plot line calls for a touch of the supernatural.

I was keen for this story to move on some of the threads that were introduced in Book 1. For instance, we have DI MacKenzie, the man who Hollie replaced in her new role with Humberside Police. It occurred to me while writing this book that, had he served with Humberside Police for all his career, Bryan MacKenzie might well have been a PC at the same time as Hollie was a student in the city. On a big case like that involving Moira, it's not much of a fictional leap that they might have encountered each other, even though at the time, it wouldn't register with Hollie.

So, now we know MacKenzie was up to no good when he was a younger policeman and there are hints of what he might have been involved in that resulted in his gruesome death. Hollie and Anderson are now caught up in a shared secret, and this will carry over into future stories, as we get closer to finding out who killed him and why.

This also seemed a great opportunity to introduce Izzy's dad and fill in a bit of back story, as that particular plot line was first encountered in Book 1 of the series. Elijah almost became embroiled in the disappearance of Moira when I was planning out the story, but I decided to give Hollie a break, and just allow him to disappear into the ether without getting caught up in a crime along the way. Elijah is a good guy, but Hollie has to make a difficult decision about whether to let him know what happened after their one-time encounter. In the end, she toughs it out and goes it alone with her baby.

I took a couple of trips down memory lane with this story, and it was handy that it's set in 1999, my final year working at BBC Radio Humberside before moving to Cumbria in 2000.

I've given two statements to the police in my life, neither of them for anything significant I'm delighted to add. The first was regarding a stolen car radio, where my vehicle was fingerprinted and I went to Lancaster police station to give, what was then, a handwritten statement, much as Hollie gives in this book. Hollie's observations about the vandalised table reflect my own thoughts at the time. These were pre-journalism days for me, and I'd expected it all to be – dare I say it – a bit posher than that. I also recall very clearly having my statement read back to me and thinking that I'd have rather written it myself as it was what I'd said, but not my choice of words.

The second time I gave a statement was in more recent times, when the property next to ours had been the target of an overnight theft of items from the garden. This time the police officer typed my statement into a portable machine while the statement was taken down in my home. We weren't quite at the voice recorder stage by that time, but the technology was changing already.

Jacksons stores were all over the place when I lived in Hull – they were a local convenience shop founded in 1891. They were great shops and stocked everything. They were bought out by Sainsbury's in 2004 and their distinctive blue/green shopfronts are now a dim and distant memory.

My wife used to work at the University of Humberside – which no longer exists – and she spent many a happy lunch break at the Good Fellowship Inn – which, I'm told, had a superb carvery – and the Old Grey Mare, which used to serve her favourite steak baguette. Those establishments are just along the road from Hollie's fictional student house.

I used to attend the comedy club at The Turnpike, on the junction of Beverley Road and Cottingham Road, but that has long since been demolished and replaced with a Lidl. Writing books is a great way of keeping these locations alive.

It's worth mentioning that although I use a lot of real-life locations in this series, I do glide in and out of fiction, and these books shouldn't be considered as a local history guide – they just capture the spirit and essence of the city.

Ray McGregor is loosely based on a Hull journalistic legend, a gentleman who is, alas, no longer with us.

This newspaper reporter was hugely respected in Hull, and I had the privilege of working alongside him when I worked at BBC Radio Humberside, after he'd moved over to radio.

He was an old-fashioned journalist, not the sort of lighter-weight reporter I was, and it was quite intimidating to be in his presence in the newsroom. He would jot down news stories in shorthand and read them out live in news bulletins from his scrawled notes.

It was one of my proudest days at BBC Radio Humberside when he told me what great interviews I had done on the radio one day; compliments were hard won from a reporter with his expertise and experience.

Ray McGregor's tenacity, integrity and commitment to journalism are all drawn from observing this reporter at work; I'm so pleased I got to work alongside him, if only for a short time. I must stress that Ray's storyline is completely fictional and not at all based on anything we were ever involved in reporting as journalists in Hull.

The theme of this book is a difficult one, but we're all too familiar with reading about true-life stories like this online or in the papers. My story is completely made up, no part of it is based on real-life people, situations or locations, but it does draw on the too-frequent and tragic stories I had to introduce during my radio presenting career.

Let's finish on a bright note and a trade secret. When I have Hollie visiting characters in their homes, I search out properties on Rightmove which suit the kind of property type and decor I'm looking for. It helps me to picture the lives and tastes of my characters. It's also a great way of snooping on some fabulous Hull properties!

If you'd like to hear about future releases, please connect with me on social media. You'll find me on Twitter at and Facebook.

Or sign up to my personal email newsletter on the link here.

www.paulteague.net/storm5

I'd be grateful if you would leave a review if you enjoyed the fifth book in this DI Hollie Turner series, as this helps other readers to discover my books.

With best wishes, Paul Teague

facebook.com/paulteagueauthor
x.com/PaulTeagueUK

Printed in Dunstable, United Kingdom